Trusting for Tomorrow

Dear Morgan,
You've been through
so many changes
yourself —
may this book
encourage your heart!

Jenit Mi

IS. 30:21

A NOVEL

Jennifer Arrington

Pleasant Word
A Division of WinePress Group

Cover Photograph by Eric Gevaert—Fotolia.com.

Cover design assistance by Danica Papali.

Pleasant Word (a division of WinePress Publishing, PO Box 428, Enumclaw, WA 98022) functions only as book publisher. As such, the ultimate design, content, editorial accuracy, and views expressed or implied in this work are those of the author.

The author of this book has waived the publisher's suggested editing and proof reading services. As such, the author is responsible for any errors found in this finished product.

Unless otherwise noted, all Scriptures are taken from the *King James Version* of the Bible.

ISBN 13: 978-1-4141-1300-5
ISBN 10: 1-4141-1300-5
Library of Congress Catalog Card Number: 2008907822

Acknowledgments

I WOULD LIKE to first thank my loving, encouraging, and optimistic husband, Albrey, for all his proof reading, computer assistance, criticisms, and generosity. Although a self-professed hater of romance novels, he read mine with a fine-toothed comb, and was unrelenting in his opinions. When I was ready to shelve the project as a mere happy memory, he would not allow it, but instead brought me into contact with James Snyder, a local author, who gave me valuable advice and guidance. When the children's naptimes were no longer a sufficient space of writing time, he took them out for large chunks of time so that I could have the peace and quiet necessary to complete *Trusting for Tomorrow*. Thank you.

Next, I would like to thank Terri Walker, my editor, who took *Trusting for Tomorrow* from a skeletal story to a fleshed-out complete product. Thank you so much for all your work, suggestions, input, *and* for all the commas!

Thank you, James Snyder, for answering my many questions regarding the publishing industry, and for inspiring me to continue.

Then to the many proofreaders who lent their criticisms and corrections: Dot Moorman (my dear mother), Debbie Guerrant, Jennifer Lloyd, Aly Carver, and Christine Moats. Each one of you gave me valuable input and advice. Thank you.

To my own girls, whose daily antics gave me fresh material for my writing, thank you for your smiles, laughter, love, and sweet kisses.

And to the One who makes all things possible:

"To God be all the glory!"

Prologue

SOME THINGS WERE never supposed to happen.

Critical condition – that's what they had said. *Critical condition* – she needed to come immediately. She managed to reverse out of their driveway, managed to jerk the vehicle into drive, and floor the accelerator. The car leapt forward as she grabbed the steering wheel, straightening the van's crooked course.

"Please God, don't let him die. Please God, don't let him die…" Katherine could hear herself mumbling over and over, willing Leyton to live, willing God to alter the inevitable course of the accident. Maybe if she didn't stop, maybe if she kept repeating the words, they would become reality.

"Please God, don't let him die."

She missed her first stop sign, and pulled out onto the main road. An oncoming car blasted its horn angrily, disappearing into the darkness, causing her to depress the brakes with such force her chest hit the steering wheel.

"Got to wear a seat belt," she yanked the strap over her shoulder and shakily tried to connect the clasp, "got to calm down, got to breathe." Obeying her own audible commands, she took a shallow, trembling breath, and gingerly depressed the accelerator once more.

"Please God, don't let him die. Please God, don't let—" her mantra halted; there was a roadblock ahead. Flashing lights pierced the night sky, briefly illuminating pieces of the scene before her: shards of wreckage, a jack-knifed truck, a mangled smaller vehicle, the backs of EMS workers, clusters of bystanders, a waiting ambulance. Chafing at the delay, she rubbed her sweating palms on the cloth seat. A police officer was diverting traffic. As she inched closer, pieces of the awful sight came together to make a complete picture. Then her eyes fastened onto the smaller vehicle. It was a jeep, a blue jeep.

"Nobody could have survived that..." She was still mumbling aloud, as if she needed to hear herself talk in order to keep functioning. Then, understanding hit, squelching her ability to breathe. Her foot jammed the brakes, the seatbelt tightened across her chest. She sat frozen as the mangled blue jeep provided irrefutable evidence. Thousands of potential scenarios bombarded her mind, all ending in one dreadful conclusion.

This was Leyton's accident.

A police officer was waving his arms, cars were honking impatiently at her noncompliance.

The police officer was knocking on the window.

"Ma'am?"

She fumbled with levers, trying to open the window.

"Ma'am, are you OK?"

She glanced sideways and then back to the wreck. "My husband," she managed, "That's—" she gestured vaguely toward the jeep.

The police officer followed her gaze, and seemed to understand. "You wait here," he assured her, "I'll get some help." He jogged off to a group of uniformed men, pointing back at her. A woman was shaking her head negatively, the officer kept gesturing.

Prologue

They weren't going to help her, not quickly enough. Suddenly her mind and body, consumed by the single goal of making it to Leyton's side, began to function. In one swift motion, she swung her van around the roadblock. Cars behind her gratefully followed. Someone from behind yelled something unintelligibly.

Driving now with a single-minded determination, she mumbled to herself steadily, "I can get there, I can make it, I can get there, I can make it." It was as if the words kept her in focus, preventing the prior scene from overwhelming her consciousness and robbing her of the ability to drive.

Minutes later, she pulled into the emergency area at St. Mary's hospital. Yanking the keys from the ignition, she struggled from the car and slammed the door.

"Ma'am, you can't park there!" A security guard was coming towards her.

She threw her keys in his direction, "I have to make it," she pleaded apologetically, then turned and ran into the waiting area. She didn't look back, afraid if she did, he would force her to park elsewhere, and waste more precious time.

Inside she pushed her way to the front desk, trying to get somebody to help her. Finally, a nurse in rumpled scrubs pointed the way, and she ran, barging through the double doors. Five pairs of eyes bored briefly into her, angry at the intrusion. Katherine ignored them, and barely listened as a nurse quietly explained his condition, focusing instead on the face of the patient they were working on. It was Leyton—Leyton, her life's love, her young husband, and the father of their baby girls. His blond hair was matted to his head, his lips pale and still. Sounds penetrated from all directions as she stepped slowly toward the bed. Someone tried to take her by the arm and lead her out, but she shook them off.

Leyton was looking at her, his eyes speaking to her, telling her he loved her. Time and space had no meaning, the cacophony and urgent commands of the emergency team faded into the background. It was as if she and Leyton were the only ones there. She was afraid to move, afraid she would break the connection. His eyes were telling her more, and she stared back, unblinking, imploring him to stay with her.

Then his look changed, and she watched in horror, as his eyes seemed to glaze over. A machine blared out, high pitched and constant, piercing her consciousness. She turned toward it, staring at the flat green line etching its way across the grey screen. She glanced wide-eyed around her, confused by the cessation of activity, and turned back toward the screen, listening to it's piercing finality, listening to it signal the end of what should have been a lifetime of loving.

Someone clicked the machine off, and reality became suspended in disbelief. She sank to the floor, unable to withstand the weight that seemed to crush from all sides. She was aware of someone imploring her to come with them, but she couldn't respond, couldn't comprehend the devastation of all her hopes and future dreams...

Without Leyton there could be no more bright tomorrows, there would be no more love. Somehow, she would have to make her way alone, find the strength for her children, find the wisdom for decisions, and face life without someone to love. Some way she must exist without his laughter, his encouragement, and his reassuring presence. Someday she would fully understand the true impact of his death, but never, never again would she place herself so completely in the care of another. Never again would she allow herself to trust in the continuity of life, when now she knew the agony of life's fragility. And never again could she possibly know the joy of true love.

Chapter 1

A SINGLE SWELL came ashore, lapping quietly. Everything was grey, void of color—the line between sea and sky indiscernible so Katherine could not make out where one ended and the other began.

The air was still, the breeze gentle, and the ocean quiet, as if all waited in anticipation for what was to come…waited for that first glow of sunlight to infuse the world with color.

A solitary cloud hanging suspended above the horizon began to glow palest pink, brightening as the radiance extended along its edges.

Now the water reflected the cloud – the rippling grey broken by one pink shimmering mirror image. A boat passed through its light.

The breeze increased, as the round orange top of the sun, now partially visible through a previously unapparent cloud, made its appearance. A bird flew by, silhouetted against the changing sky. The sun, like a giant glowing unfinished puzzle disappeared completely behind the cloud, brightening it. Then, as if gaining energy, the sun exited, all parts of the puzzle complete, now strong enough to cast a golden path across the sea to where Katherine and the girls sat, as if beckoning them to walk down its pathway of promises. She imagined this was what the pathway to heaven must be. The beauty pierced her soul and her heart lifted in gratitude to the Master Designer of it all.

Katherine pictured another sunrise long ago when the angel said, "*He is not here, he is risen…*" That was the beginning of all hope for humanity, when life conquered death.

She remembered the time after Leyton's death where not even the beauty of a sunrise or the knowledge of the resurrection could penetrate her soul. Back then, it was as if everything had died, even her ability to rejoice in beauty before her. She had felt grey, unresponsive to the light around her, merely going through the motions of life for the sake of her children.

However, the words of the Psalmist, "*the entrance of thy words giveth light,*" had proven true. Daily and even hourly prayer and Bible reading had allowed God's love to infuse the gray in her soul with light. Now the sunrise held multiple messages for her and as she sat with her sleepy-eyed girls cuddled against her, she whispered in their ears that the beauty before them was a gift from God; that even though there was sorrow in life, God was there, constant, understanding, and unchanging. He truly would never leave them nor forsake them.

"Look, girls," she whispered quietly. "Remember it was grey? The light from the sun is pushing all the grey away. You can see colors again, because the sun has provided light." Eight-year-old Amber nodded, seeming to understand.

"Mommy?" Alyssa had raised her head to look into the face of her mother.

"Yes, my darling." Katherine waited, wondering what childish perspective her youngest might add after seeing her first sunrise.

"Can we eat breakfast now?"

Chapter 1

Katherine smiled, perhaps five-year-old Alyssa was too young to appreciate what she had just seen and heard. Hunger ruled, and besides, the girls knew they would return to the beach after breakfast. It was finally summer vacation, and Katherine had promised the girls unlimited beach days. Today was Day One and the last thing on their lips at bedtime the night before was the reminder of her promise to take them to the beach. Knowing her girls and their habit for waking before dawn, she had packed for the day the night before, so when they awoke early the next morning she had hurried them into the car to beat the sunrise. Katherine had thought watching the sunrise with her girls would be a poignant way to start their summer vacation. And, with summer finally here, she wanted every part of it to be a picture book in their memory banks that happiness was possible, even without their Daddy.

Those final days of the school year had been exhausting, but the anticipation of relaxing with her children all summer long had kept her going. Grades, parent conferences, exams, report cards, closing ceremonies, end-of-year records…it had all seemed interminable, until one afternoon she had checked off the last item on her end-of-year teacher list, and realized she was finally able to leave.

She had walked her keys down the strangely quiet hallway that led to the school's office. Hallways that once echoed with vibrant motion, children's voices, and the sounds of slamming lockers, now only heard the quiet swish of her soft-soled sandals. The silence was welcome, and she allowed the stillness to wash over her. As she smiled her final goodbyes and waved at her few remaining coworkers, she realized for the first time in three years she was actually free of the heavy sorrow that had accompanied her ever since Leyton's death. She knew it would return, but the reprieve was an unexpected blessing and added to the anticipation of the days ahead. Now, she was elated to have seen

3

the sunrise with her girls. Now, it truly felt like summertime had begun.

They drove south along the beach, heading for their favorite Jupiter breakfast place, the Olde Lighthouse Restaurant. Situated within view of Jupiter's stoic landmark, it provided a 24-hour menu of southern favorites, historic pictures, and local flavor.

Walking inside and choosing their seats hurriedly, the girls knew exactly what to order when the waitress approached their table: grits, eggs, and biscuits with plenty of butter and jelly. Katherine added orange juices to the ensemble, hoping to infuse some vitamins into their breakfast and then coffee and oatmeal for herself.

The girls ate with gusto, hungry from their early morning adventure and anxious to return to a morning of beach activities. Katherine watched them, amused at their energy and ability to eat, talk, and wave their arms for emphasis, without spilling a drop of anything. Why they couldn't accomplish such a feat at home was a mystery to her, but for today she'd just enjoy the scene.

"I guess we might not need the sandwiches I packed for the beach," she commented during a lull in their conversation.

"Not me, Mommy," eight-year-old Amber smiled, "I'll be hungry faster than you can believe."

"Me too," mimicked Alyssa. Katherine wanted that to be so, Alyssa was far too thin for Katherine's liking.

Finishing up, Amber proudly counted out the tip to leave on the table while Katherine took their receipt up to the cash register to pay. Then, walking back out into the humid air, Katherine breathed deeply.

"Can you smell the air girls?" she asked. They were so close to the ocean, she could detect the salt in the air.

"I can smell cars." That was Alyssa.

"I can smell sausages." That came from Amber. Katherine let it go; children were too literal.

Chapter 1

Loading back into the car and heading once again for the beach, the girls strained to see if the early morning swell had developed. They were not disappointed.

"Look, Mommy, real waves!" Amber cried in surprise as the ocean came into view once again.

"Man, we are going to get 'washing-machined'." The response was full of childish foreboding.

Katherine grinned inwardly at her girls' definition of getting trapped inside a crashing wave. She knew from experience the description was appropriate. Easing her car into a parking space along East Ocean Drive, her heart surged at the sight before her. The sun, having traveled high into the sky by now, sparkled off the ocean and a glassy swell broke on the shore, spraying white foam into the air. Vast, unbridled beauty, that was the ocean, and after all these years, it still took her breath away.

Katherine put the car in park, gathering her auburn hair into a haphazard ponytail in anticipation of the heat, and then climbed out quickly to keep an eye on the girls who had already clambered out and were chaotically grabbing their gear. Unloading and carrying the endless paraphernalia that always accompanied such a trip took time. With bags, beach chairs, an umbrella, and a cooler, Katherine knew she must look humorous negotiating the boardwalk steps down onto the beach. Her girls, pulling their boogie boards behind them, while hanging onto buckets of beach toys, made an even more amusing sight. Step, slide, plop went the board after them; step, slide, yank (the board often hung up on the stairs), teeter precariously, then grab the railing. Katherine wondered how they made it down the wooden slatted stairs without any serious injuries.

Next came the sand. Walking through hot dry sand with crimped toes hanging onto flip-flops was always a challenge, but their feet were too tender from months of shoe-wearing school days to go barefoot. By the end of the summer, they might be able to manage the sand without shoes, but for now, shoes were a necessity. Amber had managed to walk ahead, gesturing where they needed to settle, but Katherine shook her head and pointed further back from the water. The incoming tide necessitated a safer distance. Eventually, after a few deliberations, they plunked down at the perfect spot.

Amber was first in, squealing and laughing. Alyssa, slightly more timid, was next. They shrieked from the waves, "Hurry, Mommy! Hurry! We're waiting for you!" Laughing, Katherine ran to join them. There was once a time when a long walk and then a quiet read was her typical day at the beach, but those days were over. Now participating in the antics of childhood was the norm. She always joked with her friends that having children allowed you to act like a child again, and no one even seemed to care. That would surely change as her children reached their teen years, but for now she would enjoy childhood right along with them.

Amber ran back to get the boogie boards they called their 'surfboards', and announced it was time to see who could 'surf' the furthest. The contest was on. Quite soon, other children had joined in, and Katherine realized she could go sit on shore and watch for a while. This was the first summer both girls could swim, so she no longer had to be directly next to them in the water. Walking toward her towel, she noticed other families congregating in their own little spots along the beach. Toddlers ran aimlessly, mothers called frantically. Some children were building sandcastles, and one group was even burying an unlucky sibling in sand up to his ears.

Sitting down, she watched as a man and his boys dumped almost as much beach gear as theirs onto the sand nearby. The boys were talking and gesturing excitedly, begging whom Katherine assumed must be their father to hurry up and come in the water with them. He was laughing, telling them to give him a minute, and then with a loud, "Let's go!" he led them,

Chapter 1

whooping to join the foray of racing surfers. An unbidden pang hit her chest.

No, she thought sternly, *today is not a day for sadness; just enjoy yourself. At least a father is able to take the time to be with his children…good for him! Concentrate on what you have, not on what you've lost.*

Her mini sermon to herself over, she squared her shoulders, smiled briefly toward them and turned back to watch her girls.

"Look how far I went, Mommy," Alyssa proclaimed loudly. Katherine responded enthusiastically, grateful to see her more apprehensive child playing so vigorously. She couldn't help but compare Alyssa to Amber. Strong, vivacious Amber embraced her little life with an infectious enthusiasm. Alyssa, however, was her antithesis. Katherine often worried if Alyssa's reticence was truly a personality trait or the result of physical frailty. *Failure to thrive,* they had said when she was a baby. *She needs more rest* – even though she slept more than any child her age. *Anemic,* so Alyssa now took her daily chewable vitamin with iron. Weren't children supposed to be filled with boundless energy? Alyssa's own grandmother was more energetic! Despite all this, Alyssa's yearly physicals never raised any significant red flags. Yet, Katherine still wondered at her petite frame and *weak constitution* – as that energetic grandmother was apt to say.

Mentally shaking herself, Katherine forcefully pushed the worries away. This was summer; she was supposed to be enjoying her children, enjoying her life. She had recently read during her devotional time the *"heart of the children rejoice"* when they see the joy of their parents. She was the parent; she needed to evidence that joy for her girls. Resolved to continue paying extra attention to Alyssa's health and to ensure the summer was full of rest, healthy food and outdoor fun, she focused again on the swimming children, laughing as the father, who had joined in with his boys, was tumbled onto the sand.

He looked up, saw her laughing, and yelled back, "Hey, you're not supposed to laugh at strangers." She shrugged and laughed more, embarrassed he had noticed, yet pleased by the pleasant exchange.

There were at least ten would-be 'surfers' out there now, all bobbing around, struggling to maneuver themselves into the perfect wave-catching position. It was unusual for there to be waves in the summer. Most of the time, it was almost completely calm, and perfect for snorkeling. Katherine could see the true surfers farther down the beach, straddling their boards, waiting for the next set of waves to come in. There was even a lone, desperate kite boarder trying in vain to grab some power from the slight breeze blowing offshore. He looked out of place, his kite bright and wavering against the blinding haze of a summer sky. Katherine loved to bring the girls during the wintertime to watch the kite boarders catch air and defy the senses by remaining suspended while their kite held them aloft.

Just then, Amber came running from the water. Watching her daughter walk purposefully with her blonde ponytail swinging pointedly from side to side, Katherine thought for the thousandth time how much Amber looked like Leyton. She had his blonde hair, his strong build, and his energy and desire to be part of anything active. Alyssa, on the other hand looked more like Katherine. Her auburn hair, albeit stringy and trying its best to grow longer, was a stark contrast next to Amber's blonde looks and flashing brown eyes. Alyssa's beautiful green eyes, were often shadowed by heavy lids, and dark circles. To Katherine's dismay, nosy people often asked if the girls had different mothers. Katherine used to laugh and say no, that Amber was a carbon copy of her Daddy, but even now, that was hard to do. Mentioning Leyton at all was a reminder to all of them he wasn't just at work and would be home later, he would never be home again.

Chapter 1

Amber was now directly in front of Katherine, poised and ready to deliver her accusation: "Mommy, that boy ran into me and hurt my back!" She had a real sense of justice, of how the world was supposed to run, and if someone or something didn't follow that plan, she became highly offended.

To Katherine's surprise, the boy came right up to Amber, apologizing profusely. "I'm sorry, I really didn't mean it! I couldn't see you." He was as skinny as most active boys his age were, and just slightly taller than Amber.

Katherine could see he was near tears when his father walked over echoing his son's apologies. "I'm sorry, Jack just didn't see her." It was amazing how much father and son looked alike. Both had the same strong features and startling blue eyes. Their brown hair, wet and streaked with sand, evidenced how rough they had been playing. The man had shielded his face from the sun in order to see Katherine clearer, and Katherine noticed the many laugh lines surrounding his eyes.

Amber had calmed down, her sense of justice mollified. "I'm fine now," she said, "come on, let's go and build a sandcastle."

"No, a FORT!" the boy responded and off they ran leaving the father standing awkwardly next to Katherine.

"Well *that* was easy," Katherine smiled tentatively at the man.

"For once," he leaned over and held out his hand. "Hi, Michael Manning."

"Katherine," she replied taking his offered hand. She liked how it felt, strong and friendly. Surprised at the thought, she watched as he smiled and then was off to help the fort builders. Quite soon, Alyssa and what was obviously Michael's other boy had all joined in. Katherine watched, unsure, attempting to gauge the situation. She probably shouldn't allow her girls to build sand castles with a strange man. But, he was with his children and Katherine sensed he was a good father who was just there enjoying his boys. Surely, it couldn't hurt for her girls to join in. Besides, it was the law of the beach. People with dogs became instant friends with other people who had dogs in tow. People with children established an instant camaraderie with others with children. Then, no matter how much you enjoyed the company, you went your separate ways at the end of the day and never saw each other again. That was how it was, and so she sat back and for the third time, told herself to relax. She had a beach chair, and she was going to use it!

As she watched the girls, her mind began to wander back over other beach days. She remembered Leyton's laughing eyes; the way he would swing the girls around in high arcs over the waves; how she would scream at him that they were going too far out, to be more careful; his habit of digging deep holes for the girls and waiting for the waves to make it into a swimming pool; how he would wink and then tell her to take some time for herself, so she could disappear on her coveted beach walks.

She had such beautiful memories; she just had to be careful to keep them in check so as not to make her overly nostalgic. Too much nostalgia would weigh her down with sadness. She constantly reminded herself to be thankful for those memories, to let them have a positive effect on the present in which she now had to live alone.

The tide was coming in, and finally the inevitable wave crashed over the fort. Alyssa and the younger boy started wailing.

Amber laughed and yelled, "We have a swimming pool!"

Wow, thought Katherine, *she remembers too.*

Jack yelled, "Let's help the wave!" and took a running leap, landing on what was left of their efforts. At this, the younger kids wailed even louder, but soon they too had joined in on the destruction and their wails turned to laughter. Finally, exhausted, they collapsed into the makeshift pool as Katherine walked over to survey the damage.

Chapter 1

"That was quite a wave," she said. "I wish I could have taken a picture of your hard work before it hit."

"That's OK, Mommy," came Amber's quick reply, "my friend and I had more fun jumping on it than we did building it." Katherine and Michael caught each other's eye at the use of the word "friend." Katherine was surprised. Amber usually didn't warm up to other children so quickly.

"I'm hungry, Mommy," Alyssa spoke up. Katherine smiled—they would eat those sandwiches after all. It was amazing the effect the sunshine and salty air had on the children's appetites. On beach days, she frequently would find herself making two lunches. She called it her children's four-meals-a-day meal plan: breakfast, early lunch, late lunch, dinner. Trying to ward off a full-fledged meal with a snack was useless, they just kept asking for more and more until at the end of the snack they had, in fact, consumed a meal's worth of food. All the meal preparation found her running out of recipe ideas, so today she had hastily slapped three peanut-butter-and-honey sandwiches together, and thrown in three washed apples. She knew they would eat another meal when they got home, she could be more creative when everything didn't have to be packaged, stored, and cooled but could rather be consumed on the spot.

"Hey," continued Amber, "I have a good idea. We can share the lunch we made with our friends." Katherine glanced anxiously towards Michael as he blurted out that they had plenty of their own food. Nonetheless, the children ran back to their respective beach piles and pulled out all the food to share, dumping it onto one centralized location. Katherine raised her eyebrows in surprise at the amount of food the boys were contributing.

"That's quite a stash," she commented. He must have an organized wife. She glanced sideways at his ring finger, noticing it was void of a ring and switched her assumption to a well-paid nanny.

Michael, following her eyes, and wondering at her thoughts quickly explained. "We just arrived a few days ago and Grandma has been spoiling us mightily. My skinny boys may actually fill out a bit this summer." He came over to sit nearby. "I hope you don't mind the invasion," he added apologetically.

"You were appropriately invited by my daughter," she responded, trying her best to remain slightly aloof.

"Just so her mother doesn't mind."

"No, it's fine." Then, feeling she was sounding stilted she added, "Thanks for helping the kids build a castle. I could tell they were having a great time."

"We all were. It was my pleasure!" He paused for a while, surveying the children. "By the way," he continued when his younger boy came over, "this is Simon, my other son. Your girls introduced themselves while we were building." Simon was another clone of his father.

"It's nice to meet you, Simon," Katherine smiled genuinely. Being friendly to children came easily.

Simon responded by pointing dramatically to his mouth, indicating it was full of food.

Michael, sensing Katherine's reticence at sharing lunch with a stranger kept the conversation light. Once most of the food had disappeared, Michael looked at his watch and exclaimed it was time to go right away. "We're in hot water, guys, we're late. We've got to leave *now*." Amidst protests and quick goodbyes, they were gone. Appropriately, a cloud covered the sun, and suddenly it seemed the day had lost its zest.

They were so genuinely nice, Katherine thought wistfully. *Pity in today's world it isn't safe to open up to strangers.*

Katherine swam again with the girls, but the cloud cover continued to roll in threatening a summer storm, so they too headed home.

During the drive home, Amber spoke up from the back seat. "Mommy, can we ask Jack over to play sometime?"

Chapter 1

"We could, but we don't have his phone number."

"Oh *no*, what are we going to *do*?" Amber managed, spoken with as much drama as any child could muster.

"Well, maybe we'll run into them again sometime." Katherine kept her response calm, knowing that matching drama with drama would only work her eldest up further.

"OK, we will have to go back to the same spot at the same time tomorrow just so they can find us."

Smiling at her daughter's eight-year-old logic and thankful the conversation was over, Katherine agreed.

Chapter 2

THAT BEAUTIFUL FIRST day at the beach had been followed by tropical storm-like conditions, ruining any attempts to return to their favorite spot and Amber's dream of meeting up with her new friends. After days of rain, however, Sunday was clear and sunny.

Katherine was having an unusual Sunday morning with Amber, who had decided their number one priority was to go to the beach and find Jack and Simon.

"But Mom," she argued, "what if they're there this morning and we're at church?"

Katherine looked down at her, exasperated. "Amber, you love Sunday School and we're not going to miss it. If the weather is still nice, we can go after church. Besides, we probably wouldn't run into them again anyway. That often happens with people you play with at the beach. Besides, they could have just been here on vacation, honey. Jack's Dad said they were with their grandparents. They may have even gone home by now."

"But Mom, what if they just moved here or something," she objected, "we should have asked for their phone number. They were the funnest boys I've ever played with and now—," she paused, ramping up to a full-fledged eruption, "—now we're never going to see them again!"

"Amber, control yourself," Katherine responded, now fully exasperated. "We don't give our phone number out to strangers and you know that."

"But Mom, they weren't regular strangers, they were *nice* strangers."

"Yes, honey, they were nice. But it's time to put them out of your mind, and get ready for church." When Amber opened her mouth, ready to try a different tack, Katherine added hastily, "Besides, they may be going to a church themselves this morning and wouldn't be at the beach anyway." That seemed to pacify Amber, for the moment, and Katherine breathed a sigh of relief. Sometimes she felt like her daughter was an attorney-in-training. When she got something on her mind, she would not let it go until she had argued it from every possible angle. Katherine would eventually become aggravated from repeating herself, and then later she would feel frustrated with her inability as a mother to squelch the arguments before they started. Thankfully, today it seemed her adult logic had temporarily won over her eight-year-olds persistence.

Leyton would have known how to handle Amber's argumentative side, Katherine thought. *He would have made a great attorney himself. If only he were here, we could figure out a way to let her use her logic positively instead of as a way to make the world run the way she wants.* Katherine sighed ruefully, thinking that this was one more thing to add to her endless 'should-be-doing-already' list.

Katherine turned her attention back to the task at hand. She had chosen a knee length pressed cotton A-line skirt with a fitted jade capped-sleeve top. The outfit accentuated her slim waist, and she gave herself a brief smile as she slipped on some white low-heeled sandals. Clasping small gold hoop earrings, an early gift from Leyton, in her ears, she walked from her room to collect the girls.

Once in the car, the morning's tirade over going to the beach seemed all but forgotten as Amber explained to Alyssa that in her Sunday School class, the quietest listener got to collect the offering. Katherine listened appreciatively then raised her eyebrows in surprise as Amber went on to add that she would watch to see who put in the largest amount of money. "Josh usually has the most," she explained matter-of-factly to her captive younger sister. "His parents are really rich, so they give him more money. I think my teacher is glad because now she can buy more Sunday School clothes."

Katherine was horrified. What had they been teaching them in Sunday School anyway? "Amber," she interrupted gently from the front. "Your teachers don't use the money, the church uses the money and—"

"Look at the turtle in the road!" Alyssa screamed, "don't hit him, Mommy." All discussions of the value of offering over, Katherine swerved expertly, avoiding the stationary reptile and sighed inwardly. She would have to remember to speak to Amber's teacher about letting another child collect the offering. Then, she would have to make sure they spent some of their Bible Time during the upcoming week talking about money and giving to God's work.

Turning into the church parking lot, Katherine prayed quietly for the wisdom she needed to raise her girls alone. She sometimes felt like that was her most common prayer, but she had claimed the promise of James 1:5: "*If any of you lack wisdom, let him ask of God, that giveth to all men liberally, and upbraideth not; and it shall be given him.*"

After delivering Alyssa and Amber to their respective classes, she sat down gratefully in the peaceful sanctuary and felt some of the morning's tension ease from her shoulders. She loved

Sunday, a chance for some quiet, a chance to pause and reflect on the past week and to refocus for the week ahead…

Before she could fully relax, however, she was startled by Amber's high-pitched voice breaking her reverie. "Mommy, Mommy, look! Jack's here! I just can't believe it! Jack's really here at church!" Amber was indeed dragging Jack by the arm as if he were a prize to be shown to everyone. Katherine turned more sharply, only to see a slightly embarrassed Michael following close behind. He caught her eye and shrugged his shoulders smiling.

By then Amber and Jack were standing directly in front of her. "Can you *believe* it, Mommy? You were right when you said they probably wouldn't be at the beach today because they came to *our* church! And I didn't know God answered prayers *that* fast because I just prayed in the car that they would come here and how could they have gotten ready in such a short time?" Then sucking in a hurried breath, she looked at Jack, "But how did you know to come *here*?" Without waiting for a response, Amber looked back at Katherine, "Now Mommy we need to get their phone number before they leave and we never see them again, OK?" She grabbed a pen and tithe envelope from the back of the pew and pushed them toward Jack. "You can write your number there because people we see at church aren't regular strangers." She was glancing sideways at Katherine for confirmation when Michael, now directly behind Jack, struggling to contain his amusement, assured her that he would give Katherine their phone number.

He leaned over the children and gripped Katherine's hand saying, "If you didn't remember us right off I'm sure you do now!"

Katherine smiled, a little bewildered, and just shook her head. "Oh we remember you; Amber hasn't stopped berating me for not getting Jack's phone number since the minute we left the beach."

"Well then, we're glad we picked this church to visit." He paused, looking down in fresh amusement at his grinning son and the animated Amber. "Should I take them to their class now?"

"Oh *no!*" Amber responded enthusiastically. "I've been going to this church since I was born so I know the way, and I can make *sure* Jack doesn't get lost." She was nodding her head and rolling her eyes for emphasis.

Katherine stood up hurriedly, "We're proud of you for knowing the way, Amber, but I'll just go along with you." Then she turned to the amused Michael. "I'll be right back. You're welcome to sit here if you would like," she added in an attempt to make him feel welcome. Michael thanked her, relieved. He had wanted to ask, but didn't want to seem forward.

By the time Katherine returned, the service was about to begin. She quietly slipped back into her seat, very aware that Michael was right next to her, seeming larger than life, and slightly intimidating in his Sunday dress. He wore a deep blue-collared shirt that made his eyes even bluer than they had seemed at the beach. Taking in his neatly combed thick brown hair and the faint scent of his aftershave, she could feel a blush of self-consciousness warming her cheeks and hoped in vain that he wouldn't notice.

"Mission accomplished?" he winked with amusement. There were those eyes again.

"I hope so," she whispered back. She felt flustered and awkward, unable to turn her head to meet his gaze.

"Well," he said in a hushed tone, "my boys have been telling me for days to find the fun girls from the beach. This will be a great lesson for them—when you put God first good things can happen to you!"

Katherine could feel her cheeks getting even warmer, and barely managed to nod her head in agreement. She knew people around her were straining their ears to hear everything that was being said. Various people had been trying for months now to set her up with random eligible men, but she had always refused. She knew they were probably dying of curiosity as to who this good-looking man sitting next to her was. Her mind searched frantically for an easy explanation to the questions that would be there, when Michael, eyeing her wedding rings for the first time, whispered anxiously, "I'm sorry, I should have asked if we needed to save room for your husband."

Her rings! She always wore her rings. She clasped her hands tighter together and said, "Oh no, he won't be here, I mean, I wear this to remember him, I mean he, well, he's..." She trailed off as unbidden tears filled her eyes. She wanted to run, but knew that would make an even bigger scene. Her face, now a deep red, she glanced helplessly up at him.

"Hey," he said quietly, understanding, "it's OK. Please don't try to explain. I should have been more considerate. I'm so sorry." He fumbled in his Bible and pulled out a picture of the children sitting in their fort at the beach. "Here," he said trying to smooth things over, "I can make another copy of this. Would you like it?" Then without missing a beat, he explained how their latest toy was their own "photo workshop" at home. Jack was apparently really into it. He rambled on and Katherine thanked him inwardly knowing he was doing it to allow her time to regain her composure.

Katherine couldn't concentrate on anything the pastor said during the entire service. She couldn't believe that a random man she had met at the beach was actually sitting here in church with her. It seemed bizarre. Plus, she was finding it difficult to understand the conflicting emotions that had seemingly come out of nowhere. Michael wasn't the first man who had paid her some attention since Leyton had died. However, there had never been any response on her part. She had assumed that part of her – the ability to be attracted to and interested in a man – had died with Leyton. Leyton had been everything she had

Chapter 2

ever wanted or needed. His blonde good looks, athleticism, and the depth in his loving brown eyes had captured her as a teenage girl and stayed with her all their years together. They had shared such a good marriage that she had counted it enough, and had long since decided she would remain single the rest of her life. With her children, her teaching, her church, and her extended family nearby, she felt that was sufficient. Besides, she liked the predictability of her life and shuddered at the thought of getting emotionally involved with another man. She had finally found an even keel, and did not want to upset the careful emotional balance she had reached after the months of mourning and adjustment. So, not only was she surprised by her response, she was also irritated with herself.

Jarred from her thoughts by the sound of piano music, she realized that the service was over. It was time to rush off and collect Alyssa and Amber. Two well-meaning women were already trailing after her, trying to ask her who her date was. Amber was pulling at her arm asking if Jack could come and play, and she was aware of Michael walking off to one side, eyeing her with concern. Once they had collected Alyssa and Simon, Michael spoke up.

"Would you mind if I gave you my phone number so if Jack and Amber want to get together and play we could arrange it?" Before Katherine could respond, Amber was jumping up and down saying, "Yes, and you could even come and eat lunch with us today!" Katherine looked down at her daughter and then up at Michael, but before she could reply, he smiled at Amber and explained that they had other plans, but would hopefully see each other again soon. Amber slumped in disappointment, and Jack said, "What plans?" Katherine breathed a sigh of relief, and Michael said, "Here's our number" as he hastily scrawled something on the back of a business card. Handing her the card, he grinned, taking a step backward, and then calling to his boys headed towards their car.

When they were finally in their own car headed home, Katherine glanced down at his card. He was a pediatrician. The address was Michigan. They must be here on vacation.

I would hate to be married to a pediatrician, she thought, *all those neurotic first time moms calling at all times of the day and night. I remember how I was. I wanted my own personal pediatrician when the girls were babies.*

Chapter 3

WEDNESDAY MORNING BROUGHT with it another beautiful South Florida day. The girls had spent Monday snorkeling around Peanut Island collecting various treasures, and Tuesday fishing in the Loxahatchee River with some friends. Amber, however, had not forgotten her desire to see Jack, so finally on Wednesday morning, after noting that the day would be perfect for another beach trip, Katherine gave up and dialed the number written on the back of Michael's business card.

Here goes, she thought, taking a deep breath, *no turning back now*. Nervously, she began turning the card over and over, her fingers flipping it until a wrinkled crease formed down the center.

His deep "Hello!" startled her, and for a while, she couldn't think of what to say. She was horrified to find herself acting worse than a giddy teenager

"Hi," she finally managed, "its Katherine."

"Katherine!" Michael answered. His pleasure was unmistakable. He had been about to hang up; calls with initial silence usually meant a sales call. "I'm so relieved you called—Jack has been driving me crazy about finding out where Amber is so they can play."

Katherine laughed, "I can empathize."

"Thanks, I appreciate it!" Michael paused, debating; wanting to ask if they would accompany them on a day trip, but unsure as to how to go about it.

"So, have you had a good week so far?" Katherine asked, anxious to say anything that would fill in the glaring silence. She knew her voice sounded high and fake, and she wished with all of her being that she had never called. She began folding the card and unfolding it.

"Who, us?" Michael was obviously feeling self-conscious too. "Oh, yes," he recovered, "we're really enjoying ourselves. In fact," his voice took on some bravado, "we were planning on driving up to Stuart to try out a place called 'Bathtub Beach.' It apparently has protected swimming for the children. Have you been there?"

"Not in a while, but it is a very nice beach for children. I just never think of it since it's a bit of a drive."

"Well," he drew the word out, giving it a deep drum roll quality, "would you ladies like to join us?"

"Oh, sure, I mean, I'm sure the girls would love that." The business card was so creased it was now barely legible. Katherine placed it next to the answering machine, smoothing it with her fingertips. She sighed inwardly, why couldn't she talk right? Of course, *she* would enjoy herself too!

"Would you like to commute together?" He wondered if she really wanted to go or was just being polite.

"Oh, um...sure."

The line fell silent once again until Michael finally prompted, "OK," there was that same deep drawn out sound, "then you have to tell me where you live so we can stop by and pick you up."

"Oh, yes, of course."

Come on, Katherine, get your brain in gear, she thought desperately. She hastily gave the directions, and they set up a time to meet and then hung up. When she put down the phone, she was not surprised to find her heart pounding and her palms sweaty. She would definitely have to gain some composure before she ruined a potentially fun day.

She glanced down at her wedding rings and debated whether to take them off for the day. After all, the purpose was to discourage unwanted suitors, and since she would be with a man, that would send its own message. Plus, if she kept them on, people would think *they* were married. Her mind went back and forth making it difficult to concentrate as she went to get the girls ready for the day.

Amber was ecstatic, and Alyssa seemed excited too. Katherine, for her part, was in a dilemma over which bathing suit to wear. She finally settled on the one she had worn when she first met Michael, thinking that the sameness would make it less of an issue. She wasn't ready to be putting on attractive bathing suits for a man. She did, however, choose a sundress to wear over the bathing suit instead of her usual formless cover-up. Funny that she should care so much, but for some inexplicable reason she wanted to feel feminine. She went to the beach all the time, and never gave much of a thought to her appearance, and now, here she was, wanting to look nice, *and* still in a quandary over her rings. In the preparation to get all their gear together, however, she forgot about the rings until she heard a knock at the door. Amber ran to get it and let Jack in. Katherine, in a moment of decision, quickly slipped the rings off, grabbed their bags, and went to the door to meet them.

"Hi," Michael said. "You look nice."

"Thank you." A feeling of pleasure washed over her. How nice to get a sincere compliment. She was glad she had worn the dress.

"Why are you wearing your favorite dress to the beach, Mommy?" Amber called out loudly as she lugged the overloaded snorkel gear towards their car. Katherine felt her cheeks color and chose to ignore her daughter. The last thing she wanted was for Michael to think she had dressed especially for him. Now, all she needed was for Amber to ask her where her rings were. Children, unfortunately, noticed everything.

After rearranging Alyssa and Simon's booster seats, they were all in Michael's SUV and ready to go. The mood in the vehicle was festive with Katherine finding the situation somewhat surreal. She couldn't remember the last time she had ridden in a car with a man that wasn't a family member. Strange as she felt, it also felt comfortable, like *they* were a family, and today was just one of many family outings. She glanced over at Michael and caught his eye. He smiled appreciatively before turning his attention to the road and she did her best to redirect her thoughts, focusing on Jack and Amber talking excitedly, and Alyssa and Simon comparing booster seats.

"Mine has two cup holders that come out like this...see?" Alyssa explained to Simon.

"Wow," he replied, "I'm going to have to ask my Dad to buy me one of those."

Hearing them, Michael glanced over at Katherine. "Great," he joked, "they've been in the car together for two minutes, and already our booster seat isn't good enough."

"Oh, I'm sure he'll like many other items we have too," Katherine warned, glad to have something benign to talk about. "I *know* you don't have lens defogger for your masks, frogs painted on your fins, or towels with alligators on them!"

"No, we don't." He feigned dejection. "Here I thought we were well prepared. What was I to expect going to the beach with a true Floridian?" Then a pause: "Are you a true Floridian?"

"I feel like I am," Katherine answered, staring out the window at the empty spaces along I-95. That was another reason why she liked Jupiter; there were still open spaces, even if you did have to drive along the highway to find them. South of them, it was solid concrete jungle all the way to Miami. She liked living where she could find undeveloped land. In fact, Jupiter had recently acquired some in-town land as part of their open space program, for which she was glad. "I've lived here since I was fifteen," she continued. "My Dad was transferred out of state after I graduated from high school, but I never left. The ocean is in my blood. If I can help it, I'll always live here." She was about to add more, but caught herself. She didn't want to spend the day talking about herself, because she knew it would end up becoming a discussion of the last three difficult years, and she didn't want to turn a play day into something serious and sad.

They were now riding next to farmland, where spaces between rows of perfectly planted trees were visible, each only for an instant. Staring out the window was easier than looking over towards Michael. She found herself intensely aware of his looks, his deep voice, and those smiling eyes. She didn't want to seem rude, though, so she attempted a new line of conversation. "I noticed you have Michigan on your business card, are you vacationing here for the summer?"

"No, I'm actually setting up practice down here with an old med school friend. My parents live here, and with my wife gone, I thought it would be good for all of us to be close to my parents. There was nobody left in Michigan anymore, no reason to stay."

Katherine wanted to ask what "gone" implied but didn't have the nerve. Once again, silence settled around them.

"So, do you work outside the home?" Michael asked to fill in the now awkward silence.

"Yes," Katherine gratefully replied. I'm a teacher at the same school the girls attend."

"A teacher? What do you teach?"

"Junior high math."

"Junior high? Isn't that supposed to be the worst age to teach, and aren't your children a bit young to be attending the same school where you teach?"

Katherine laughed. "First of all, it is a challenging age, but I actually enjoy figuring out ways to get difficult students to respond to me. It's kind of a mental game, and if I really get to know them, and what makes them tick, I can usually figure out what works."

"Sounds exhausting."

"Other things are more exhausting. You're a single parent, right?" When Michael nodded, Katherine continued. "Exhausting is never getting a break—day in and day out. School starts at eight and gets out at three. Plus, there are weekends and holidays. Even though my students wear me out, I get a break from them."

"That's why we moved down here. Like I said, my parents live here, and I'm looking forward to having them give me a break here and there."

It was Katherine's turn to nod in understanding. "Secondly, the girls aren't too young to be at the school where I teach because it's a private school – K4 – 12. It's a wonderful place, great environment for the girls. Plus, teacher's children receive a large tuition break," Katherine winked conspiratorially.

"Ah. You know, you don't exactly seem like a math person."

Katherine chuckled. "That's because I'm not. I'm a history and English person. After… well, after I had to go back to work I didn't think I could handle the workload that teaching English, in particular, carries with it."

"I think some math teachers might take exception to that."

Katherine shrugged, "All the math teachers I ever worked with were always the first to leave in the afternoon. Anyway, I got emergency certified in math and found that although there were less essays to grade, teaching – or should I say teaching well—is a time-consuming profession no matter what subject you teach. But, I've stuck with it. I love my students, I love being at the same school as my own children, and I love the school where I work."

"Sounds like I need to find out about this place! Where is it?" While Katherine responded to Michael's questions, she could hear the children in the background chatting happily and that made her feel so good. They were truly having a great start to their summer. Enjoyment simply felt good. After Leyton died, she had felt like every day for the rest of her life would be an effort. Simply getting up in the morning was a feat to be accomplished. Then, the never ending cycle of caring for the girls, handling their questions and needs, and working again for the first time in over five years, had made her feel like she was a machine. *Keep going, keep going, keep going,* had been her constant mantra, when all she had really wanted to do was crawl into a small dark space and hide from reality. The life insurance policy she had received after Leyton's death had more than paid off the house, and she had put away the remainder for the girls' future college tuition. In addition, there had been an insurance settlement from the accident and her father-in-law was helping her manage it. However, it wasn't a bottomless source of money and the need to work and earn a steady, although modest income to pay for day-to-day living seemed paramount to Katherine. Moreover, she knew if she didn't get out and work, she would simply shrivel up inside of herself. So, she worked, and the money she earned was what they lived on.

At first, the sheer exhaustion of doing everything for their family, plus having a full time job had almost been too much for her. However, at least that way she had been able to sleep at night without any effort. At least that way there had been no room for the black loneliness to consume her. Now, three years later, here she was with her children, simply enjoying a day! It seemed that in itself, was a miracle.

When they arrived at the beach, it was all they could do to keep the children contained while they unloaded all their beach gear. "It's like hanging onto wild horses," Michael laughed.

"I know," Katherine agreed, "always ten steps behind them, that's me!"

They managed to keep the children with them as they navigated through the parked cars, and walked the path that led to the beach, but once the gear had been dumped on the sand the children ran pell-mell into the water. Katherine laughed and looked helplessly at Michael. "I guess we don't get out enough," she shrugged. "We've only been to the beach just about every sunny day since summer started." Katherine closed her eyes and inhaled deeply, she loved the smell of the salty air.

"Yeah, you really need to do more," Michael joked. "Now if you were a *good* Mom, you would camp on the beach."

Opening her eyes, Katherine surveyed their paraphernalia piled around them, "Looks like with all this stuff we could camp."

"Yes, and I guarantee we've forgotten at least five critical items that are absolutely going to prevent someone from having as good a time as possible." Michael's lighthearted laugh sent a tingle down her spine right to her toes. She dug them down into the hot sand to quell the strange sensation.

"I know," she agreed, wondering at the feeling. "I have to get after my girls for that. I find myself constantly telling them to use and enjoy what they have, and forget about that highly necessary absent item." Before Michael could agree, Simon ran up complaining that they hadn't brought his beach shoes and his feet were hurting on the shells.

Michael laughed, "Well today your feet will just get a little bit tougher, Son. And, if we forget your beach shoes twenty more times your feet might get as tough as mine."

Chapter 3

"But Dad..."

The whine was quickly interrupted as Michael interjected, "grab your mask and you and I can get a head start on snorkeling." The necessary beach shoes were quickly forgotten as Simon dug around frantically for his mask and snorkel. Michael turned and winked at Katherine as if to say, "What a pro I am," and then asked if she would join them. She nodded assent, collecting the girls' equipment too, knowing they would also want to snorkel.

Soon they were all snorkeling along the worm rocks that bounded the 'bathtub' portion of the beach. Katherine instructed the children – and the rather surprised Michael – not to touch the rock. "Living worms are constantly adding to this reef and we don't want to ruin that," she explained. At Michael's look of disbelief and the choruses of "Yuk!" "Ugh!" "Worms?!" she continued, "The worms are called *Sabellariid* worms and they use sand to make these tube houses." The children leaned in closer to get a better look at the rocks.

"You never know what you're going to learn from a math teacher," Michael quipped.

"Why can't we see the worms now, Mommy?" Amber asked staring at the seemingly 'dead' exposed rock with a look of morbid fascination.

"Well, it's low tide right now so the rocks are sticking up out of the water. The worms would dry out, so they cap the end of their house-tubes. That holds in sea water, and also keeps us from seeing them."

"Cool," came the eight-year-old response, as the other children lost interest and plunged into the water.

The water was reasonably clear, and the children squealed through their snorkels, sounding like misplaced seals as they pointed out the iridescent outlines of blue angel fish, a cigar-shaped blue head wrasse, and even a rainbow parrotfish.

Suddenly, the squeals grew louder as Amber and Jack, who were leading the way, came to an abrupt halt, standing up and gesturing wildly. Everyone else piled into them, looking towards where they were pointing.

"Mom!" Amber dramatized, "Look! It's got to be the biggest barracuda ever!"

"Did you see its teeth?" Jack added.

Katherine went back under water to look, and sure enough, there lay a three-foot barracuda, teeth showing, sinister and still.

"Poor guy is probably as scared as you are!" she said, standing up again.

"Are you sure it's safe?" Michael intoned. "That thing has a mouthful of teeth."

"Oh, don't worry," she smiled, enjoying his discomfort, "they're *piscivores*. That means they eat fish."

"Glad to know I'm snorkeling with a marine biologist," Michael grumbled, taking Simon's arm and swimming gingerly past the offending fish.

Laughing to herself, Katherine held onto Alyssa's small hand pulling her alongside, reveling in the sheer enjoyment of pleasurable togetherness with her children and their new friends. It was truly a treat for a mother's senses, and she was so thankful for this summer in particular. She felt like it was finally easy to enjoy her children without the gnawing pain of loss eating away at her. She was so grateful, and watching the children swirl around her in their eagerness to be the first to see the next fish or brightest shell, she allowed the happiness of the moment to saturate her mind and fill her heart.

Reaching shore, having snorkeled the full arc of rocks, they all tumbled onto the sand, the boys dumping out the treasures they had collected in their pockets. Talking excitedly, they compared their finds, discussing who would get to take home what, when suddenly a ghost crab bolted past. The movement caught Jack's eye, and at his holler, the treasures were quickly forgotten and the chase was on. The crab gracefully disappeared into a nearby hole in the sand, and the children immediately began scanning the beach for a new possibility.

Jack, however, was trying to dig the original crab out of its hiding place, his eventual success tempered instantly by a howl of protest. Alyssa and Amber looked on in fascination as the crab hung tenaciously to Jack's finger, while he jumped and shook his arm frantically, trying to get the crab to release its grip. It was probably at that moment that Amber and Alyssa both decided that boys were definitely a lot of fun to be around. The crab finally let go, and Jack ran crying towards his father. Michael, trying to hide his amusement asked, "Did you think that crab wasn't going to put up a fight?"

"No-o-o-o," came the tearful response.

The other children quickly ran up to see Jack's wound, and suddenly embarrassed, he stopped crying and pulled his hand away from his father's grasp.

"It doesn't hurt, I wasn't really crying."

"Yes, you were," Simon accused.

"No, I wasn't," Jack countered, glancing anxiously at Amber and Alyssa.

"I think he was just yelling for us to see what happened," Katherine tried.

"Oh yes, that's what I was doing," Jack agreed hurriedly.

"It sure was huge," said Alyssa, still wide-eyed.

"Nope, you were crying," insisted Simon, "I should know."

Michael, knowing the 'wound' was fine, hurriedly suggested—to a chorus of "Yeahs"—that they build a fort since the tide was coming in. Katherine could hear Simon muttering under his breath that he knew when Jack was crying, and that Jack just didn't want everyone to know it.

Katherine, amused by the entire interchange, sat down gratefully on her chair to watch the fort building. It felt so good just to sit. This little beach was a true gem. She needed to make the effort to come here more often, it really wasn't such a bad drive, and the children were really enjoying the diversity of critters swimming and running around. Looking out at the calm pool of water and the ocean that stretched out past the natural rock barrier, she let out a long, contented sigh. The breeze coming off the ocean teased at the loose hair surrounding her face that had escaped from her ponytail. She tipped her chin up and closed her eyes, enjoying the sensation. If Michael came on many more beach trips, she might actually use her chair more than she had anticipated. What a pleasure to sit and watch her children playing happily in the company of these new friends and being able to relax at the same time.

Once the fort was built, and Michael had taken all the appropriate pictures, he walked over to where Katherine was sitting. "Hey," he teased, "you're looking way too relaxed."

"Guilty as charged" she smiled back. "Have a seat and maybe nobody will need either of us for awhile."

"I'd be glad to," he answered, opening a chair he had brought and sitting down next to her. Katherine suddenly felt tongue-tied, very aware of his closeness. It was already getting easy to banter around and be natural when four children surrounded them, but these brief snatches without interference made her feel self-conscious and a bit stilted. She felt like she was suddenly incapable of decent adult conversation— probably the result of being surrounded by children constantly. Her brain was not on an adult wavelength anymore.

They sat in silence, Katherine searching around frantically in her mind for something to say that was normal and casual, when Michael spoke.

"So, Katherine-of-the-Sea, do you have a last name?"

"Oh yes," she said, copying his bantering tone, "that would be *Dr.* Katherine Douglas, PhD in marine biology, particular area of interest: reef worms of South Florida."

"Pleased to meet you, Dr. Katherine Douglas," he dipped his head slightly in acknowledgement. "Do you always use this title?"

"Only when I want to impress people like you," her voice was mischievous. She looked over at him and laughed, "Are you impressed yet?"

"Absolutely." He paused, a grin on his face. "Let's see...I already know that Amber is eight, since she and Jack seem to think that being the same age is an unbelievable accomplishment!" They both smiled at that. "But, how old is Alyssa?"

"She's five. Just made it into kindergarten by a few days and feels very important to be in 'real school' now. How old is Simon?"

"He's almost to the day a year younger than Jack."

"Wow, you had a busy time of it. That's like having two babies at once. What great practice for a pediatrician!"

Michael nodded slowly. "Yeah, I wonder now how I managed. I guess caring for two babies back to back like that did indeed impact my decision to go into pediatrics. There I was studying medicine, and yet I felt so helpless as to how to care for my own children and how to interpret their needs." He grew quiet, lost in his own thoughts. A gull cried from somewhere nearby, and then somewhere in the distance came a reply.

Katherine, listening and nodding, wondered briefly at his pronoun usage.

They sat in silence again, enjoying the scene of playing, laughing children before them. "So," Michael spoke again, reaching over and briefly touching her arm, "how difficult would it be for you to get a babysitter so that I could take you to dinner one evening?"

Katherine caught her breath at the shock of the intensity of feelings his touch had caused. "Well," she began, then stopped and looked out towards the horizon. How could she tell him that she would love to, but didn't want to "start" anything. She didn't want to use the cliché "just friends" yet she wanted to prevent the easy-going companionship from developing into something serious overnight. She knew that despite her resolutions to remain single, with this man there was already such a strong attraction, it would be hard to remember what those resolutions even were.

"Hey," Michael interrupted her softly, "tell me what you're thinking at least....just give it to me honestly and I won't mind, I promise."

"OK," she looked up, hesitated, then took a deep breath and went on. "I would love to go out with you but I don't want any 'labels' attached. You know," she continued upon seeing the quizzical look in his eyes, "labels like 'boyfriend', 'girlfriend', 'dating', 'seriously dating'. I can't handle the labels, it's hard to explain, but for now this easy-going camaraderie is all I want. Am I making sense?" She raised one eyebrow in a quizzical way and looked over at him.

He was quiet for so long that she added hurriedly, "I'm sorry for sounding stupid, I just don't go out anymore, but you're different from others who have asked. I thought I needed to be up front." *Great*, she thought, *I should have saved this line of conversation for our fourth date. Now he thinks I'm an idiot. All he wanted was to take me out to dinner. He did ask me to tell him what I was thinking, though....*

"No, no!" He took her hand and squeezed it. "Your honesty is refreshing. What you're trying to say is that instead of black tie and roses you would prefer jeans and daisies. We can do that. Just tell me you'll go out with me and I'll be happy."

"Yes, that would be nice," she smiled, liking his description. He still had her hand, and she was unsure how to end the pleasurable moment when Alyssa came up screaming, "My tummy hurts. It hurts so badly. Mommy, I'm going to be sick!"

Katherine jumped up, calling to Amber to stay nearby Michael. She put her arms around her and started running, half carrying her, half running. "Let's run to the bathroom, honey, and see if we can fix it."

Michael had jumped up too. "I'll get the others rounded up," he called after her. Before they made it to the restrooms, though, Alyssa was ill all over the sand.

"It's OK, honey, it's OK. You'll be OK," Katherine repeated over and over as Alyssa's little body seemed to convulse with each retching sound.

Alyssa looked around at the nearby beachgoers and cried, "Every one is watching me Mommy, make them go away!" They had indeed attracted some attention, but a helpful lifeguard was getting everyone to stand back.

He handed Katherine some paper towels so she could wipe Alyssa's face off. "Did you snorkel today? Sometimes if you swallow too much salt water this happens. One time when I was a kid…" He kept talking until Alyssa had calmed down and was cleaned up.

"Thank you," Katherine smiled, "you're so kind."

"That's my job," he smiled back. "Here, young lady, here is a really cool piece of coral I found that you can show your brothers and sisters. Take care of yourself, and next time you go snorkeling don't swallow half the ocean!"

Katherine turned to see Michael and the children plodding through the sand with the entire collection of beach gear haphazardly dangling from their hands and shoulders. When they reached them, he leaned down and said, "Here, lets carry you, and then we'll get a good look at you in the car." Katherine watched as he picked her up and started toward the parking lot. She could hear him asking her questions, and Alyssa responding through her sniffles. Tears welled up and she swallowed hard. Alyssa barely remembered Leyton, and it was bittersweet to see her in Michael's arms.

Katherine took a deep breath. "Thank you God," she whispered. Then gathering the bags Michael had dropped, she followed after them. When they reached the car, he was just standing up.

"She looks fine to me, probably swallowed too much saltwater like the lifeguard said."

"I hope so," Katherine responded. Somehow it seemed with Alyssa that things were never quite right. She was always the child getting sick from too much candy, or in this case, too much salt water. Other children ate candy and swallowed salt water, yet continued on as normal. Nagging memories of other times surfaced, suddenly relevant now that yet another incident had occurred. Michael, wondering at Katherine's obvious concern, reached over and squeezed her shoulder, "Hey, I'm sure she's going to be just fine. If she doesn't bounce back, or if she continues to get sick, you should get her checked out by her doctor. Or," he winked, "I know of an excellent doctor that could be of further help."

Thank you," Katherine answered, smiling at his innuendo and hoping Alyssa was indeed 'fine', "I'll be sure to only go to the beach with pediatricians and nice lifeguards from now on."

Alyssa fell asleep on the way home. Whenever she had one of these "spells", she was so weak that all she could do was sleep. There had to be a root cause for this. Children didn't become ill for no reason. Something was wrong with her child, and as much as she wanted to believe it was truly nothing to worry about, her gut feeling told her otherwise.

Amber, Jack, and Simon, exhausted from their day outdoors were all quiet. Katherine tried to put her worries over Alyssa aside in order to enjoy the peaceful drive home. It felt luxurious to just sit in the passenger seat and relax after a beautiful day on the beach. How many times after a day trip had Katherine felt exhausted driving home while her girls slept in the back? Then, when they got home and she really needed a nap herself, the girls would be awake and refreshed, ready to go again, and a nap would be a mere tantalizing impossibility. This was so much better, having someone to share the childhood chores with. Katherine sat up a little straighter, not wanting her thoughts to take her any further.

Minutes later, as they pulled into her driveway, Katherine looked gratefully across at Michael. "Thank you for a wonderful day."

"No, thank *you*," he said, then added, "And don't forget to let me know when we can go out, just the two of us."

Katherine smile in response, enjoying the feeling of warmth spreading through her.

Chapter 4

MICHAEL SAT ON the patio at the condo they were renting. He had managed to acquire a month-by-month lease, which was perfect for their situation. Although he enjoyed the resort-style amenities the development provided, he was anxious to move into a house where his boys could be their rambunctious selves without disturbing the neighbors.

The boys were asleep, and he savored the peace. He sat alone in the dark, a habit acquired over the years since Morgan had died. Leaning back, he stared unseeingly into the night, the Florida sounds enveloping him. He could hear what sounded like marbles being clicked together (perhaps a tree frog?), the short sharp up-and-down whistle-blow of crickets, the infrequent call of a nearby owl, the rustling of what he hoped was a lizard. He wondered briefly if Katherine could identify night sounds as easily as she could identify worm rocks. He'd have to ask her some time, some time when they could sit outside alone in the quiet...

No labels...what was she actually afraid of? Part of him wanted to tease her and arrive for their date with a box of shipping labels, but the rest of him knew that she might think he was making fun of her feelings. He leaned his head back, staring at palm fronds silhouetted against the moonlit sky. Here he was essentially starting over – a new state, new medical practice, and…Katherine.

He pictured her sitting at the beach, lecturing them on reef worms and barracudas, smiling that warm appealing smile. He had a feeling that despite her uncomplicated appearance and girlish playfulness, she was a woman of great depth. What would someone like Katherine think of Morgan? He sighed deeply.

Morgan.

They had been two ambitious first year medical students at the University of Virginia School of Medicine. Both had that self-assured, cocky attitude that often comes with realizing goals and heading toward an ambitious, yet attainable future. Morgan's background lacked the security of Michael's, and she was desperate to prove herself independent, successful, and unbeatable in a world that had been so unstable for her as a child. Her father had left her mother when Morgan was young, and although her mother worked hard, she had always kept Morgan at arms length, almost as if Morgan was the cause of all her hardships. For Morgan, there were no kiddy gymnastics, no swimming lessons, no music classes, and none of the special after school programs that her peers enjoyed. She discovered early on, however, that she was generally smarter than those peers were, and found out quickly that she could gain adult attention by doing well academically. Consequently, by high school, she was a teacher's favorite, the star of her school's academic team, and was enrolled in as many of the Advanced Placement courses that were available to her. By her junior year, she was already receiving scholarship letters from schools around the country; and by the time she graduated, she had enough college credit to enter the University of Virginia as a sophomore on a complete scholarship. During her valedictorian speech at her high school graduation, she did not thank her mother who hadn't even taken off work to come, but instead, her teachers and her school for providing her with the opportunities to be somebody and go somewhere. Her best friend's mother included her in the graduation party for their own daughter, and later, staring out into the blackness of a Virginia night, Morgan had quietly whispered to herself, "There, I did it. I didn't need a father, or encouragement from Mom, just hard work. I have proven to everyone that I have what it takes. Now nothing will stop me. The future is *mine!*"

With that attitude, she completed her undergraduate work in three years, and was accepted into the University of Virginia School of Medicine at age twenty. She was the youngest first-year med student in her class, and she was determined to be the best. She had a few friends, but never allowed people to come between herself and her clearly defined goals.

That first year of medical school was probably the happiest in her life. She was on track to realize her greatest dream – being a successful physician and proving to the world that she could be independent and succeed without help from family. In fact, as she later admitted to Michael, she often thought smugly how everyone else in her class was there because of dependence on family for one reason or another.

For the first time in her life, she was beginning to enjoy a male friendship with Michael, her anatomy lab partner. She couldn't help but like his quick mind and ability to relax and have a bit of fun in the middle of all the work that they constantly confronted. Besides, spending countless hours a week hunched over the same cadaver – that Michael had dubbed "Nero" – was bound to allow them to get to know each other well. They became fiercely competitive, and were constantly comparing test grades, lab abilities, schedules, and anything else that they could think of as fair game.

They never officially started going out, but they both found themselves spending more and more time together. Being in the same class and having the same priorities made this a natural progression. They would often study together late into the night at Morgan's place and Michael would frequently end up sleeping on her couch instead of heading home.

Michael shifted in the patio lounger as he shook his head regretfully. He should have never allowed that to happen. He knew now how that seemingly insignificant compromise was the beginning of a series of events that had changed both of their lives forever.

He remembered the night clearly. They had studied, and talked, and sat together. Everything had seemed so right, but when Michael awakened the next morning, he knew that everything was not right. He had been raised to believe that contrary to the media and the culture of the day, the only right time for a physical relationship with someone was within the bounds of marriage. He felt deep concern that Morgan would be angry, but her good judgment was also clouded with the excitement of a first love.

To his relief, things seemed to return to normal. They continued to study together and spend all their time together, but were careful to maintain a physical distance. However, things were far from normal.

The night before their first final, prior to summer break, Morgan found herself inordinately tired and not as mentally sharp as usual. She was also extremely cranky and crossly told Michael to go home and study on his own, that she needed to get some sleep. Michael chalked it up to exam-time stress and went home. The next morning sitting down for the final, he was surprised to see Morgan's chair empty. Deeply concerned, he asked to excuse himself so he could call her. The proctor wouldn't hear of allowing him to leave as the papers were already being passed out. Morgan finally walked in thirty minutes late, flustered, nervous, and with dark circles under her eyes. Michael, doing his best to concentrate, was finally answering questions somewhat competently, when he saw Morgan get up and run from the room. A second proctor followed her, returning with her a few minutes later and so it continued throughout the entire three hours.

Morgan failed that final, and although she had sufficiently stellar grades to pull off a pass for the year in the course, she was devastated. She blamed Michael for distracting her and kept to herself throughout the rest of finals week. He was deeply worried, besides the fact that he missed her terribly. Finally, the day of the last exam, he caught her in the hallway and told her they needed to talk.

"About what?" she answered dully.

"About why you have been acting so strangely," he answered exasperated.

Suddenly she was angry. "Sure we can talk," she blurted out. "Let's talk about how *I failed* a final; how I probably barely passed the rest of them, and that thanks to *you* I'm *pregnant* and about to become the youngest med school dropout in UVA history."

Michael was stunned. He stood there dumbly trying to formulate a response. Morgan stared at him with contempt, and when no words were forthcoming turned her back and walked angrily away.

When the reality of the situation hit, Michael chased after her. "Morgan! Don't leave. Just wait!" He grabbed her arm to turn her toward him, and then gripped both her shoulders. "It's a good thing, right? A baby is a good thing. It's a human being, a little person, someone we can love. We can make it all work. We made the baby together; we can find a solution together. Right?"

Morgan snorted sarcastically. "That's why I fell for you. You're too idealistic, you see the world as a rosy wonderful place, and it's not. *I* should know."

"Come on Morgan," he pleaded, "let's just go somewhere where we can talk and figure this out. Please?"

She finally acquiesced. They spent the rest of the evening going over their options. That night Michael placed the call to his parents to tell them he was marrying Morgan, the girl who he had referred to before as simply his study partner. His parents were understandably shocked and distraught, but despite all their pleading, Michael had been resolute.

Thankfully, both Morgan and Michael were recipients of a combination of scholarships and loans that covered both their tuition and living expenses. In addition, during the brief summer, they stayed in town and worked in research labs at the University, which provided a small stipend. By living frugally, they were able to save most of their stipends while continuing to live on their budget allowed for living expenses. Added to that, Michael moonlighted on nights and weekends as a waiter. It was exhausting and a strain, but being married and part of a little family had brought out a softer side to Morgan that Michael was enjoying.

Reality set in when the new school year started and Morgan found she couldn't push herself to the limits she had before. "I'm just a lazy, dumb, pregnant woman," she would complain as she struggled to study each night. Michael found that he was doing even better than before, however, and Morgan resented this. She had always been everyone's star pupil and it now seemed that she was often dismissed as a candidate for anything other than a family doctor. An underlying bitterness began to form.

Jack Robert Manning was born conveniently during Winter Break. When Michael's mother came to see her first grandchild, she voiced her fears to her husband that Morgan did not seem too enamored with her baby. He dismissed her fears, unable to see the obvious himself. Michael, picking up the slack, became a combination of Mr. Mom and Super Dad, feeding, caring for, and getting up through the nights with little Jack.

When the spring semester started, life became even more difficult. Morgan still barely acknowledged Jack who had yet to sleep well at night. Thus, Michael was not getting much sleep at night himself. When he dropped off two-week-old Jack at the sitters that first day, he thought his heart would break – break for Jack who was being left in a strange place, and for Morgan who just didn't seem to care. He had a hard time concentrating, and his grades were plummeting. Morgan however was doing fine once again, thrilled to see that her brain was once again sharp. This improved her spirits and as spring approached, she finally became more interested in Jack and the mood around the tiny apartment improved considerably.

During spring break, they took their first trip as a family to visit Michael's parents who had just moved to South Florida from Michigan. The plan was to visit for a few nights, leave Jack with the grandparents, and then go on to the Florida Keys for a couple of nights alone. Their time in the Keys, in effect, became their honeymoon, and Michael, for the first time began to think that their marriage had hope. They snorkeled together off Molasses Reef, rented a kayak and explored mangrove islands, and simply basked in the sun alongside the hotel pool. Above all, they talked and talked about their plans and goals, with 3rd year just around the corner. After an idyllic three days, they packed up, heading back to collect their baby, their faces aglow with hope and anticipation of the future. Driving north on US 1 toward Miami, with the wind blowing through the car, Morgan reached over, took Michael's hand and told him she loved him. Michael stopped the car, got out, and wrapped his arms around her. It was the first and only time she ever said those words.

Finals came again, and once more Morgan found herself struggling with fatigue and nausea. This time, however, she realized instantly, and with horror, what the cause was. She was pregnant again and she was livid. That night, a home pregnancy test confirmed what she knew, and she met Michael at the front door tight-lipped and angrier than he had ever seen her. She threatened to either abort the baby or kill herself.

Finally, Michael, unable to bear her wrath any longer, picked up Jack and walked out. He walked and walked and walked. He remembered vividly looking up at the sky and asking God – if God could really hear him – to help him sort out the mess he was in, to send someone to help him and to show him how to help Morgan.

Coming home, he walked in and said to Morgan quietly, "I told you once before. We did this together and we will make it work together."

This pregnancy, so close to the first one, took its toll on Morgan. By her fifth month, she was put on bed rest, unable to attend lectures or rotations. She seemed to have slipped into a deep depression, and Michael tried in vain to push her to get help. "I know what's wrong with me," she would say bitterly. "I'm sitting on a couch, getting lazy and stupid waiting for another baby while I should be in my 3rd year. I'll never finish now." Michael would assure her that delaying a year with her track record wasn't going to affect anything, but she did not believe him. "The funny thing," she added bitterly one night, "I barely even *like* children." With this attitude Michael did his best to keep their bubbly, pudgy, smiley little Jack out of her way. He would pick him up from daycare and walk him home through a park, wanting to make up for the time that they had both been stuck indoors. There was often an elderly woman in the park, and they would smile and exchange pleasantries. Her name was Mrs. Wilson and she would ramble on about her grandchildren while always managing to find an interesting little treasure for Jack to hold or have. One day it would be a special "banging stick", another day a large smooth rock, sometimes a snack from her purse, or a cup to fill with treasures. Needless to say, Jack loved running into Mrs. Wilson, and Michael enjoyed the diversion himself, especially since going home was not a pleasurable event.

Chapter 4

Simon Andrew Manning was born just three days shy of Jack's first birthday. Morgan refused to hold him. Michael had her evaluated by a physician, and begged him to do something, but nobody seemed to take her condition very seriously. *It will pass*, they all assured him. The *"baby blues"*, as they referred to it, was apparently quite common.

Mercifully, baby Simon slept well from the beginning. Once again, Michael was doing everything. When the spring semester started, Morgan became even more difficult. She couldn't start back until the fall, and the waste of time ate at her constantly. Finally, worried that she was truly a danger to herself and their children, Michael scheduled an appointment for her with a psychologist. On the day of the appointment, he planned to come home for lunch and then take her himself. He wasn't sure what excuse he would give her, but he knew if he told her ahead of time she would refuse to go. He was hoping that there was medication for her, that it was perhaps a case of post-partum depression, and that in light of the recent findings in that area they would do something about it.

The night before the scheduled appointment, Michael arrived home exhausted with both boys. He had been too tired for their usual romp in the park. But, when he came in and was confronted by Morgan shrieking about how dare he schedule a psychiatric appointment for her without her knowledge, he turned and left once again. Simon was wailing and Jack was whining "Eat, eat, eat." Michael felt he was at the end of all solutions. Tears were rolling down his own cheeks as he turned into the park. As usual, Mrs. Wilson was there and hearing the noise, she walked over and gently picked up the inconsolable baby.

"There, there," she soothed, and glancing at Michael asked for a bottle. Mechanically Michael leaned forward and dug the last clean water bottle and formula packet out of the diaper bag. Mrs. Wilson deftly mixed it up, talking in consoling tones to Simon. Once he was sucking gratefully on the bottle, she turned her attention to Jack. "Let's see what snacks I have here in my bag, little guy." Jack walked over and peered in while she rummaged around and finally handed him some pretzels. He clambered up clumsily next to her and sat swinging his chubby legs while he ate.

Finally, she looked over at Michael. His head was in his hands, and the tears were coming down in full force now. This little act of kindness by someone he didn't really know had broken the stoic do-it-all and handle-it-all mentality that had driven him thus far. Mrs. Wilson waited patiently until he was done.

Eventually, he wiped his face and looked up ashamedly. "I am so sorry," he mumbled.

"For what, young man?! I just got to feed a baby, and sit next to sweet Jack. What a wonderful feeling for an old woman like me! Besides, everyone needs a release." She hesitated then added, "Is there someone I can call for you or something you would like to talk about?"

Before Michael could think twice, he was telling her about Morgan, how bad she was, how he feared for her life, and how desperate he was to have a real family, despite the challenges that faced them. Mrs. Wilson listened while Simon, now content, slept on her shoulder and Jack played with a stick in the nearby playground sand.

"Michael," she said gently, "I have a Friend who can help you through all of your difficulties. He knows all, sees all, and understands all. Best of all, He loves you more than you could ever imagine."

Michael looked at her quizzically.

"God." She paused, and then went on. "The Bible says that we can 'cast our every care upon Him because He cares for us.' We don't have the solutions, but God does. All we have to do is ask."

"But," Michael said embarrassed, "isn't it a bit wrong to only decide you want God when you have a problem?"

"Well, sometimes problems come into our lives so that we will see our need of Him."

Michael shook his head. "I don't know; I would need to think about that. But maybe for now you could pray for me."

"Better than that, I'll have a few close friends pray for you, in confidence of course. Plus, you could bring the boys to our church on Sunday. Put them in the nursery and sit in a wonderful service where the preacher makes the Bible seem real and relevant to whatever you are going through." She dug in her purse again and handed him a pamphlet with the church address and times written on the back. Michael reached over and accepted it from her.

"That bag of yours is full of goodies," Michael smiled. "You wouldn't happen to have a sixteen-ounce steak in there would you?"

"Glad to see you're feeling a little better," she smiled back. She gently laid Simon back in the stroller and patted Michael on the shoulder. "Thank you for allowing me to be useful this evening. I'll be praying for you."

"Thank you," Michael responded.

As he walked home, with the boys bundled into the double stroller and the cold evening air nipping at his face, he mused how ironic it was that many months before he had asked God to send someone to help him and how Mrs. Wilson had been there just when he needed it most. As he zipped Jack's coat up higher, and pulled the little cap down over his reddening ears, he thought over what Mrs. Wilson had said. Maybe he would take the boys to her church on Sunday; if anything, it would be a change of routine for them. Picking up the pace in the approaching darkness, he tucked Simon's blanket more securely around him. The trees still had their winter bare, and the temperature was plummeting with the setting sun. He broke into a slow jog, not wanting to rattle the rickety stroller too much, but anxious to get his boys out of the air.

Feeling somewhat optimistic, he let himself and boys into the apartment, surprised that the door was unlocked. He walked into the bedroom expecting to see Morgan hunched under the covers, but the bed was empty. Walking around, he called her name joined in by Jack's "Ma-ma, Ma-ma?" With a feeling of mounting dread, he went about the usual task of getting Jack fed and ready for bed. Simon was thankfully still asleep. He debated whether to change him and transfer him to his crib, but instead wheeled him into the bedroom and closed the door. Every time Michael heard a noise he looked up, hoping it was Morgan. She hadn't taken her bike, hadn't left a note, and hadn't taken her wallet or bus pass. Once Jack was in bed, he walked around the tiny apartment unsure what to do next.

An hour passed, and the dread deepened. He started calling a few of their classmates, although he was sure that Morgan would not have gone to see them. She had cut herself off from everyone once she had had to drop out at the beginning of third year. He even tried the medical library, asking them to page Morgan Manning, but to no avail.

By 10 P.M., he was beside himself. Taking a deep breath, he called the police station. The officer on duty wasn't very helpful. Women had a right to go somewhere without asking their husband's permission. He hung up the phone frustrated, and after waiting for almost fifteen minutes called back. He was met by a similar response. Not to be deterred however, he waited another fifteen minutes and called again and then again. Each time, he reiterated that she was a mother of a tiny baby, that she was struggling with depression, and that she was probably walking around in the cold somewhere. Finally, in an effort to placate him, an officer asked some curt questions and said he'd put out an all points bulletin on Morgan.

Chapter 4

Setting the phone down, Michael lay back on the couch, spent, intending to only close his eyes for a few moments. What seemed like seconds later, he was awakened by banging on the front door. To his horror, he realized that he had fallen asleep and it was now 2 A.M. Dazed and confused, he stumbled to the door. Trying to focus, he saw two officers staring back at him.

"Michael Manning?" one asked.

"Yes?"

They came inside and stood awkwardly in the tiny space by the doorway.

"My wife...?"

More silence. Then, one of them spoke. They needed him to come down to the morgue and make an ID. Dread settled upon him like a physical force. He felt incapable of movement, much less speech. The officers prompted him gently, asking him if there were children under his care, telling him to call someone to come and stay there. It would only take an hour at the most. He didn't remember how it happened, but there was Justin, a classmate, in the apartment. He didn't know who had arranged that, didn't remember them leading him to the patrol car. He only remembered looking out of the backseat window and wondering if the sluggish nightmare in which he was trapped would end soon. He remembered the bright lights of the hospital hurting his eyes and the loud 'ding' of the elevator doors as they opened. He remembered the cold of the morgue and the still figure draped beneath a white sheet. He remembered gasping at the sad familiar face that was now so cold and still. He remembered being gently led out to a sitting area to answer questions. He remembered being back in the apartment and Justin sitting on the couch. He remembered someone giving him a pill and telling him to get some sleep. That was all.

He didn't know how he survived the next few days, only that people seemed to come out of everywhere to help him. His parents were there the next morning. People he barely knew brought food, watched the babies, and prompted him into arranging for the funeral, which was held at Mrs. Wilson's church. The pastor of the church, although he had never previously met Michael, treated him like a son, leading him through the proceedings with love and concern.

Two weeks after what seemed a lifetime of events, his mom was still with him, and they were sitting in the cramped living room discussing the next few months.

"Go back to class, Michael," his mother said gently.

"I just don't know if I can face it all. Besides I am now impossibly behind, I don't even know if they'll let me back."

"Go tomorrow morning. Go to your classes and rotations as if you have missed nothing. Then, go and speak with each professor or person in charge, asking them what you need to do to continue with the semester. I am staying here at least until the semester is over. Now do this, because you can."

Michael finally acquiesced and somehow managed to finish out the semester. His classmates seemed to rally around him and he developed a strong friendship with Justin, who had been at his house the night of Morgan's death. On Sundays, they would all attend Mrs. Wilson's church together. Many times during the services, he would feel a tugging at his heart, a call to action. He was unsure, though. Christians seemed weak, to blame everything on God, to be unscientific. He didn't know if he was ready to "jump camps." However, one Sunday morning as he sat in church, he realized that regardless of what anyone thought - believers or non-believers - according to the Bible, he would one day have to face God. He knew deep down that the Bible had to be true, that there was something so compelling, yet so simple, that seemed to draw him and make him realize that he needed God desperately. In addition, he felt immense guilt over Morgan's death and felt like he had not done nearly enough to prevent it.

Chapter 4

That morning the preacher was preaching from Matthew 11:28, *"Come unto me, all ye that labor and are heavy laden, and I will give you rest."* Michael closed his eyes and let the words sink into his soul. Oh, he was heavy laden; laden with guilt over Morgan's death, laden with the responsibility of two babies and the difficulty of maintaining his studies, laden with the insurmountable task of somehow making everything 'right' again. He felt like no matter how hard he tried, he wasn't good enough, that people must point at him and wonder, that it was as if the sickening guilt he felt would never go away no matter what he did. Hearing pages turning, he realized that people were turning in their Bibles to another text. He listened, agreeing inwardly that the verse pretty much summed up what he was about. The verse was Isaiah 64:6, *"...and all our righteousnesses are as filthy rags..."* All the good he had tried to do, and all the work he had done to right the initial mistake of getting Morgan pregnant had culminated in disaster.

I'm pretty much a pile of filthy rags myself, he thought despondently. *Maybe I should leave; I didn't come to church to feel worse about myself.* However, the preacher was reading another verse now, one that caused Michael's spirit to leap with hope. It was I John 1:9, *"If we confess our sins, he is faithful and just to forgive us our sins and to cleanse us from all unrighteousness."*

OK, Michael thought. *I can do that, I can tell God about all my sins, but why would He forgive me? I've done nothing to deserve forgiveness.* Then, almost as if he was having a dialogue directly with the preacher, the answer came in the next verse that he was reading: *"Not by works of righteousness which we have done but by His own mercy He saved us..."*

"You see," the preacher explained, "we don't deserve to be forgiven, God in his mercy has saved us. God calls us to place our faith in Jesus Christ. Listen to John 3:16, most of you can quote it, but listen to it like you are listening for the first time. *'For God so loved the world...'* That means God so loved you," he said looking up at the congregation. "Let's continue: *'For God so loved the world, that He gave his only begotten Son, that whosoever believeth in Him, should not perish but have everlasting life.'*" The preacher looked up again. "God has given us a gift—Jesus Christ, God's Son—but it's up to us to receive that gift. If you take His gift, you are in essence saying that yes, you believe that you have sin; yes, you believe He paid the price for that sin when He died on the cross; and yes, you want Him to forgive you of your sin. It's so simple, if you want the 'rest', the peace in your heart that we read about in Matthew 11, if you are 'heavy laden' with too many burdens to bear, Jesus will take them from you, but it's up to you. It's a personal decision; nobody can do it for you." The preacher kept talking, but suddenly Michael knew what he had to do. He knew that this was what he wanted; what he so desperately needed. With trembling knees, he stood up and walked straight to the preacher. The pastor, sensitive to what was happening, quit preaching and took Michael by the arm leading him out a side door where they could talk in private. Michael was dimly aware that the song leader was leading the people in an impromptu hymn, and part of him was mortified that he had interrupted the service that way. Nonetheless, the preacher was hugging him and telling him that if he wanted, he could pray right there and receive Jesus Christ. He would be free from all the sin and guilt he was carrying. Gratefully Michael bowed his head and prayed haltingly aloud: "Dear God, please take away my sin, I have messed up so badly. I need you so much. Thank you for your gift to me..."

When he was finished, the preacher hugged him again. "Welcome to the family of God, Michael," he said enthusiastically. "You are now God's child. You are forgiven, because the Bible says if we *'confess our sins He is faithful and just to forgive us our sins'*. Do you realize that?"

Michael nodded, a slow smile spreading on his face. "I can tell!" he responded. "That sick feeling in the pit of my stomach is gone." Then concern crossed his features once again. "But what about Morgan, what if her death really was my fault? I mean, murderers can't just murder and then confess it to God and go on, they still have to pay for their crime."

"True," the preacher said slowly. "God's forgiveness is for any sin. Some of those sins, even though forgiven by God, would still carry a penalty imposed by man. However, Morgan was hit by a car. That means you are not a murderer. And, according to other reports and your own testimony, you did everything humanly possible to help her, and it did not work. So, that means that you were not even an accomplice."

Michael nodded, slowly processing what the preacher had just said. "Thank you," he said simply.

Then with a light heart, and a look of hope in his eyes, he went to collect his boys from the childcare area. Driving home that afternoon, he reveled in his newfound joy and freedom from guilt, knowing now for the first time that the promises in the Bible were meant for him!

Michael shifted again in the patio chair outside, his thoughts now back in the present. He wondered what Katherine would think of his story. He felt secure in the fact that he had done what he could for Morgan given their circumstances and he hoped that Katherine would see that. He stood up and stretched, thinking back over his fourth year, his residency in pediatrics, the many moves that had brought him and the boys to this opportunity here. He was so thankful to be near his parents, in a practice with his good friend, Justin, who had remained a close friend even after medical school was over and their residencies had taken them in different direction. God had been so good to him. He had surely lifted him from the clay and set his feet on a rock (Psalms 40:2). Turning off the lights, he walked into the boys' room to check on them.

Michael reached down and smoothed back Jack's brown hair, so like his own. In a way, it was a blessing that the boys looked so much like him; it dissuaded strangers from making comments about a mother the boys would never know. As he moved to gently cover Simon with the kicked-off blankets, he wondered if once they found a house he could make it feel like a real home for the boys. Their lives had always had a transient feel, and he wanted that to change. Simon rolled over just then and opened his eyes, grinned at his Dad, and then closed his eyes again. Michael smiled, a tenderness filling his soul. These boys were his boys, and as was his habit, he quietly prayed for them, thanking God for their blessings, and praying for guidance in this latest transition, a transition which was hopefully their last for a long time.

Walking from their room, his thoughts returned to Morgan. The police report had ruled her death as a suicide. She had apparently stepped in front of a car that had hit her before the driver even saw her. There had been an investigation into the driver's culpability, but Michael had not pressed charges. He knew that in the frame of mind Morgan had been in, she had probably been oblivious to the oncoming traffic. He was grateful that even if she had intended to end her life that night, his boys would never have to face that, because nobody would ever really know. He had tried to get in contact with Morgan's mother, but she had never even responded. Thankfully, the boys didn't seem to realize yet that there could be grandparents on their mother's side. To them it seemed logical that without a mother you couldn't have other grandparents. One day, when they were older, he would tell them the whole story. He whispered a prayer for their continued protection, both physically and mentally, and turned gratefully towards his own bedroom. He fell asleep

Chapter 4

with a picture of Katherine's silky auburn hair, smiling green eyes, and joyful laughter filling his mind.

Chapter 5

A FEW DAYS later Michael, anxious and nervous regarding the outcome, called Katherine to see if she would consider having dinner with him. He had wanted to call her the day after their trip to Bathtub Beach, but had been afraid it would be too soon. Given what she had said about dating, he didn't want to scare her away. He was thus relieved when she agreed readily to go out the following evening. She apparently had already arranged for her girls to spend the evening with their grandparents so she could have a night to herself; however, she confided in him that some adult company sounded enjoyable. Whether relegated to 'adult company' only or not, he was still immensely relieved as he hung up the phone.

He looked over at his boys, pleased. "Seems like I have a date, fellas," he said jovially.

Simon ignored him but Jack looked up with a half sneer. "Just so she doesn't wear smelly perfume and then try to kiss me…"

"When did that happen?" Michael laughed.

"You know, that realtor lady who came over was like that."

"But that wasn't a date, she was just arranging for us to go and look at houses!"

"Oh Dad," Jack rolled his eyes in that know-it-all-mock-grown-up way that only children can do, "*you* know what I mean."

"No Jack, actually I don't," Michael was now really amused.

"You know," Jack said standing on his tip toes and teetering around the room. "Oooooo, I just love this condo …Ooooooo, you're a *doctor* …Oooooo, what adorable little boys you have," Jack mimicked, flitting around, gesturing wildly with his hands.

Simon was now paying attention too, and decided to add his own rendition. "Ooooooo yes, and I just love the name 'Jake'." Simon then stopped the theatrics as suddenly as he had started, "Why do you think she can't remember that Jack's name is Jack, anyway?"

"Yeah," Jack chimed in, "maybe something's wrong with her *brain*."

Michael was now rolling with laughter. "Well you two," he said, "tomorrow when we look at houses all day with her we'll all remind her that Jack's name is Jack, OK?"

The boys instantly fell to the floor in horror as if they had been shot. Michael watched in amusement as they writhed in agony crying "All day?" "Do we have to?" "Please can Grandma watch us or Amber's mom?"

Michael shook his head, "No, Grandma is watching you tomorrow night so I can take Amber and Alyssa's mom out to eat. So, you're going with me tomorrow. You can help me decide which house we should live in."

This new bit of information was all it took for the boys, who were surprisingly interested in the fact that he was taking Katherine out, to forget to continue complaining.

"Cool, Dad," Jack said, "I like Amber's mom. Maybe next time you take her out, all us kids can go too."

"Ooooooo," Simon instantly jumped in with a singsong voice, "Amber and Jack sitting in a tree..."

He didn't get any further because Jack had tackled him to the living room floor. Michael left the room shaking his head in amusement, glad that they were glad he was going to take Katherine out the next evening.

The next day turned out to be extremely frustrating. After spending an entire day looking at houses with the boys in tow, Michael realized what a big mistake that had been. His second mistake had been picking a realtor who constantly dropped hints that she was single. Pity he hadn't picked up on her overtures as fast as his boys had. Besides, none of the houses had "clicked" with him. Between the 1970's orange and green linoleum of one—had people honestly never heard of updating?—and the permeating animal smell of another—"Why does this house *stink* so bad?" was Simon's instant query—Michael had decided he would be forced to look in a higher price range. Maybe it was all part of the realtor's ploy to get him to do just that, but since he didn't have the time nor inclination to update or sterilize a house, he would agree to look at more expensive homes. Granted, he could probably afford it, but with the prices already over double what he was used to, he had hoped to find something more reasonable. He had thus far managed to live below his means in order to have extra money for only the best nanny and for all the expenses that came with running his life on very little spare time. Now that his parents were close by, he could forgo the nanny, and settle for a once-a-week housekeeper. But, even those were hard to come by and expensive. Maybe he would just go it on his own for a while, and see how he did. The whole house-buying dilemma was definitely starting to weigh heavy on his mind.

He wondered what it was about buying a house that defied logic. Here you were, about to enter into the most expensive purchase of your life, and you were relying on gut feeling? He felt at a loss. Maybe the missing ingredient was having a woman's opinion, that is, a woman other than the realtor. He wondered briefly if Katherine would help him out, but then just as quickly dismissed the idea. If she didn't like labels, then looking at houses with a single man would probably spell disaster for her.

Florida was so different from anywhere he had lived before. With all of the gated communities that came with their association rules and inflated homeowners' fees, and with the plethora of private schools from which he still had to choose, he felt as if he was experiencing some strange form of culture shock. He was going to have to pick Katherine's brain about the area at least a little tonight. She would have no need to fear any romantic overtones with the amount of questions he had for her.

He dropped the boys off at his parent's house early enough to give him time to swing by and purchase some daisies and still head home to get cleaned up. He could sense his Mom had wanted to barrage him with questions, but he didn't give her an opportunity. He left her waving from the porch, the questions written all over her face. If Katherine didn't like labels, then he would not elaborate other than a simple 'dinner with a friend' was truly all this evening was going to be.

Adding more gel to his unruly hair, he sighed as he surveyed the result. The Florida humidity had wreaked havoc on his usually well-groomed appearance. He should have had the barber trim his hair shorter, or at least sell him the cement version of the gel he was using. The thought made him grimace. It had been years since he had given a second thought to his appearance, and now he was worried about his *hair*? He cocked his head, looking at his reflection quizzically and wondering what Katherine had done to him. Never mind that he had already changed his shirt three times, finally settling on a Tommy Bahama-style shirt his office staff had purchased for him in Michigan as a going away present. They had laughingly told him that Florida men wore them all the time and he had joked back that true Florida men could wear whatever they wanted and still look the part.

Putting in his contacts, he wondered if she wore them too.

Let's see, he mused, *I have blue eyes, she has green. That would mean our children would have...* He caught himself again. He had better reign in his thoughts; otherwise, a certain unattached, auburn-haired, slightly freckled, smiling woman would be running away from him as fast as she could. The imaginary scene made him shake his head again as he glanced at his watch, grabbed his wallet and keys, and headed out the door.

Driving toward Katherine's, he felt some of the tension from the day began to ease. It was another beautiful evening. The late afternoon sun cast its muted glow on the few clouds that colored the graying sky with pale pinks, purples, and yellows. Crossing over the Intracoastal Waterway, he noticed the crystal clear water of a rising high tide and a flock of pelicans gliding inches above the calm surface as if flying in cadence to some unheard melody. The ever-present palm trees lining the road waved majestically as if in tune and he thought again, how much he loved Florida. He was here to stay. No more winters, no more snow to contend with. No more bundling his boys in so many clothes that they could scarcely bend over, much less be squeezed into confining car seats.

A horn blaring behind him startled him out of his reverie.

Walking up to Katherine's door with the daisies in hand, he felt suddenly self-conscious. He had gone on very few dates in the years since Morgan's death. At first, he had just not wanted to date, feeling like he had failed his wife, and he was unwilling to try a relationship with anyone again. He had eventually worked through those feelings of insufficiency, and the fear of failure that had plagued him, but it was still a few years before he had attempted to date anyone. After that, he had been too busy building his practice and being a single Dad to have the time to look for the right person. Katherine had just happened along so naturally, nothing had been forced.

She opened the door before he could knock.

"Hi," she smiled shyly and then even bigger when she saw the daisies. "They're perfect," she said. "Come on in while I put them in water." He followed her in, taking in her simple sundress and sandals and that gorgeous sleek auburn hair. The dress's halter top and aqua blue color set off her slim figure and contrasted sharply with the richness of her hair. He could barely detect the faint scent of flowers, and wondered if it came from her perfume or the potted plants that accented her doorway and entryway.

He wanted to tell her how beautiful she looked but replaced it instead with the mundane. "This is a nice house, how long have you lived here?"

"Three years. I really love the house. It's been a haven for me and a great neighborhood for the girls."

"I've looked at houses all day, and it seems that once you get in that mode, you can't keep from thinking about it."

She gave him an interested look. "Well, I guess that really wasn't the case for us. Leyton—that's...my husband," she stumbled awkwardly and then recovered, "he basically found the house we're in, and sort of had to convince me that it was the right one for us."

"You didn't like it at first?" Michael asked surprised.

"Oh no, I liked it. It was just..." Katherine paused realizing she didn't want to go there tonight, "How about we save that story for another night?" She knew she sounded forced, and tried to soften her refusal to answer by adding: "But, if I could give you any house hunting advice, I'd be willing. I've lived in the area since I was a junior in high school, so I might be able to be some sort of help!"

That was just the lead in Michael was hoping for. "Well," he breathed deeply thinking– *here goes* – "would you be opposed to looking at houses with me?"

"Tonight?" she asked surprised.

Michael laughed, embarrassed, shaking his head. "Oh no, no, no! Tonight I'm taking you out to dinner! Just maybe in the next few days I could show you some listings my realtor passes on to me, and you could give me the heads-up on the neighborhoods or maybe even come along to see the ones you think – or I think – would be most desirable."

"Well...I guess I could do that. At least I could definitely give my input on the neighborhoods."

Michael breathed a sigh of relief at the same time berating himself for bringing the housing issue up before they had even left her house. There was an uncomfortable pause as they stood looking at one another. Finally, Michael dipped his head in embarrassment, "I'll just go ahead and admit up front that I'm not exactly suave and practiced with the whole 'date' concept."

"That's OK," Katherine smiled back, "because neither am I!"

"Good!" Then holding out his arm for her to take, he said in a more relaxed tone, "Let's get this show on the road and have a good time regardless."

The evening turned out to be by far the most enjoyable that Katherine had spent with a man since Leyton's death. Throughout the evening, she would catch herself, surprised at what a good time she was having. Michael was so relaxing, so easy to talk to, so unassuming, and so openly appreciative of her company that it put her at ease. It all seemed too good to be true, but she decided to enjoy the evening for what it was. She knew that once he found out how opposed she was to the idea of a serious relationship with anyone, he would find someone else to take out, but for tonight, she put those thoughts from her mind.

They talked about their backgrounds, and realized that at one point during their childhood they had lived within thirty minutes of each other in Berrien County, Michigan.

"Well, what do you know?" Michael said, looking at her appreciatively. "I can't believe I would have missed an auburn-haired little girl with big, green eyes and a pretty smile."

"Well then, I'm sure our paths never crossed." Katherine quipped back. "Let's see…did you ever go to the state fair?"

"Oh, yes, we sure did! I even entered a pig one year!"

"A pig?" Katherine asked incredulously. "You don't seem like the farming type."

"I'm not. But I had a good friend whose family lived on a farm so one year I joined the 4-H club, and they allowed me to adopt one of their pigs. It became my project that year. Our 4-H club even went by the name of 'Pigs R Us'!"

"You're kidding!"

"Nope, it's the truth. My poor mother wasn't too excited about the whole thing, but my Dad thought it was a great diversion. In fact, I think my mom wanted to burn my Pigs R Us T-shirt. It was too much for her. You know, I won some sort of award too, so if you had come to the livestock section on the awards night you could have even applauded for me!"

"Oh," laughed Katherine. "I don't think my parents even allowed me near the farm section—too many smells for them to handle!"

They laughed and talked on, comparing notes the way people do when they find out at one time they lived in the same area.

"So where did you go to junior high?" Michael asked next.

Chapter 5

"Oh, we never stayed anywhere more than two years, so junior high was in a whole new place."

"Really? Why did you move so much?"

"My father's job. Each move brought a nicer house and more spending money, so it kept my Mom happy. Plus, she said it kept her from getting bored. I, on the other hand, hated to move and promised myself that one day when I had children, they would never have to change schools unless it was absolutely unavoidable. So far I've been able to do that for them!"

"Yes, but people who've lived a lot of places are more interesting." Michael countered.

"Well, I'll take that as a compliment, but I think it makes children feel insecure. It did me, but thankfully it also taught me how to make friends quickly."

"So, you think I shouldn't have uprooted my boys to move down here?"

"Oh no! I didn't mean that at all." Katherine said with consternation. "Plus, you moved here to give them more stability, right? Didn't you say that one of your primary reasons for moving was to be closer your parents?"

"Yes, that's true. And, hopefully this new venture works out, and we're here to stay. I promised myself after this last winter in Michigan that it was my last. Who knows, maybe within a few years my boys will be as beach-savvy as your girls are. They haven't been too happy about being shown up by some little girls!"

Katherine laughed. "My girls act like they were born for the water. Leyton used to joke that all they were missing were some gills. He had Amber snorkeling by the time she was three."

"So how long has...uh... Leyton been gone?" he asked, feeling ill at ease saying the name.

Katherine hesitated. It was a legitimate question, so she tried to respond evenly. "Three years. Alyssa was just two, Amber was five..." Her voice trailed off, thinking of that awful time, of Alyssa asking for her Daddy, Daddy, Daddy; of Amber's constant pleas to be held and to play with her 'Da-ee'; of the impossibility of caring for them, and helping them understand while she herself could barely get through a day. She visibly shuddered.

Michael, watching the range of emotions sweep across her face, wanted to kick himself for asking the question. He reached over and placed his hand over hers, "I'm sorry for bringing that up tonight. I didn't mean to be so insensitive."

"No, it's a normal question," she shrugged self-consciously, "How long has your wife been gone?" she said, using his previous terminology and eager to get the focus off herself.

He released her hand and leaned back, watching her steadily. "Seven years…Simon was just six weeks old."

Katherine's eyes widened in surprised – no wonder he had spoken of taking care of babies as if he had done it alone. He *had* done it alone!

"So you could say that I've had a little longer than you to get used to the fact," he continued. "The cliché is right, you know, time does heal. But, there will always be the lingering 'what if.' *That* never goes away; at least it hasn't for me."

Katherine nodded, empathy filling her heart, wishing she could just reach out and hug him and ease some of the pain that they had both suffered. Thankfully, though, their food arrived just then, providing a much-needed diversion. Thinking it wise, Michael changed the subject and they talked until the food was cold. Michael couldn't believe how refreshing it felt to spend uninterrupted time with her. There was so much to say and Katherine was an engaging person. Finally, after the waiter had been back to their table three times to ask if something was wrong with their meals, they decided they had better eat.

"It's so nice to have an adult conversation and not be interrupted." Katherine said.

"Except by the waiter," Michael put in.

Chapter 5

"Well, some time I'll make you a meal at my house and then there will be no pesky waiter to interrupt our conversation. That is, provided the children aren't around! You know," she continued, "during the school year when I teach I'm so tired of talking by the time the day is over that I'm not much in the mood for any kind of conversation. But in the summer I have to caution myself from having much too involved conversations with total strangers who really could care less about hearing what I have to say!"

Michael laughed. "Let's see, they say that women have 30,000 words a day that they like to use. Probably when you're teaching you use them all up before the day is over, but in the summer you're ending each day with an excess."

"Oh yeah?" she responded. "And how many words do they say men like to use a day?"

"I think 15,000," Michael answered and then added with a wink: "If you ever feel like you have an excess of words left in the evening, you could always call me up. I'll listen!"

"How kind you are," Katherine responded with a laugh. "Do you charge for this service?"

"Mmmmmm...for you? Free!" He even went on to elaborate that he had many free cell phone minutes left at the end of the month that were simply going to waste.

After they ate, they walked along the sidewalk looking in the store windows, commenting on what they were seeing. When they came to a bookstore, Katherine exclaimed without thinking, "Oh, let's go in and get a coffee and read!"

"Am I *that* boring?" Michael asked in mock disappointment.

Katherine caught herself, embarrassed fully. "Oh no! It's just...well, I always see people doing that, and, I wonder what it's like to have so much free time..." She turned away from the door, inwardly thinking that she'd made him feel badly, only to walk right into him. He caught his breath, enjoying the brief

71

moment of closeness, then steered her back around and led her into the store.

"Now come on, if that's what you would like to do, then that's what we're going to do! Besides," he added, "I like their coffee, and you look pretty when you're embarrassed." He glanced sideways at her, appreciating how her flushed cheeks made her eyes seem even greener.

Katherine averted her eyes, now thoroughly flustered. "We can go, you know, it was just an offhand suggestion," she attempted lamely.

He laughed, "Oh no, this is a great idea. Plus, you can truly find out a lot about a person by the type of books they enjoy."

"Is that so?" Katherine managed, trying to act nonchalant as she maneuvered them towards the car mechanics section. "Now let's see..." she feigned interest, perusing the books and then broke out laughing at the look of surprise on Michael's face. And so it went for the rest of the evening. They ended up staying until the store closed, and as Michael walked her to her door that night, he commented that it was the most enjoyable trip to a bookstore he had probably ever had.

"I hope you mean that," Katherine looked worried.

He took her arm again and gently turned her towards him. Then looking in her eyes he added seriously, "I mean it."

Chapter 6

KATHERINE AWOKE SLOWLY the next morning and then snuggled down dreamily into the covers. The down comforter and pillows felt luxurious against her skin and she buried herself deeper into their softness. Added to the knowledge that there were no children to wake up with in order to meet their early morning demands, was the overriding picture of a grinning Michael. The combination was blissful, and Katherine drifted back to sleep thinking that for a single parent it didn't take much to feel like a million dollars. She awoke again to the ringing phone, and realized with a start that it was nine o'clock already. Trying desperately to clear the sleep out of her voice, she unsuccessfully managed a scratchy hello.

"Katherine?" A pause and then a teasing note. "Were you still asleep?"

"Mmmmmm...maybe." she confessed. "I meant to get up earlier, but the peace was just too...um...peaceful?"

Michael laughed. "Do you still want to go with us this morning?"

"Oh sure, it won't take me long to get ready."

"Let me bring you breakfast and that will make up for waking you. You do eat breakfast—don't you?"

"Uh…Ye-es," she said mimicking the sarcastic sing-songy replies of her junior high students.

"O-K," Michael responded in kind. "I'll be by in about thirty minutes. Is that enough time?"

"Sure, it only takes me ten minutes to put my teeth in, and then I'm good to go." Katherine couldn't believe she just said that, what had gotten in to her this morning?

"Please tell me you're kidding," Michael pleaded.

"Well, I guess I could be mean and lie, but yes, I am kidding, and yes, I'll be ready in thirty minutes."

With that, they said goodbye, and Katherine jumped out of bed with an anticipation of the morning ahead that further surprised her. She grimaced at her own attempt at humor, and thought that she had better get herself in check or Michael and his realtor would think she was a true moron.

With a quick decision to put her hair in a ponytail, and to wear a comfortable pair of capris and white T-shirt with sandals, she was ready ahead of time. When Michael saw her a little later, he wanted to comment on how appealing she looked, but stopped himself, unsure if she would take that as inappropriate. Katherine noted the look of appreciation in his eyes, though, and it made her flush. She wasn't used to this kind of attention, and it was definitely going to her head. For the second time that morning, she cautioned herself to remain in check.

They stood at her kitchen counter, and quickly delved into the bag of warm bagels and cream cheese and 'doctored' their coffees companionably. Katherine looked up at Michael with a mischievous grin. "I know this may let on that I never do anything, but this is *so* much fun!"

"I couldn't agree more! I think it's from the sheer absence of responsibility that usually weighs on us single parents. I'm really enjoying having some built-in babysitters so close by. I should have moved years ago. Besides, I don't usually get to spend my free time with someone as enjoyable as you!"

Katherine flushed again. She turned slightly away to hide the goofy grin that she knew was visible, and was saved by the ringing of his cell phone. It was the realtor telling him where to meet her.

Driving to the first house, Michael handed Katherine a stack of MLS sheets he had brought along. "The top four are the houses we are able to look at today. I sort of put the rest of them in order of preference, and thought you might like to make sure that I didn't put the best house at the bottom of the stack."

Katherine was so absorbed in studying the sheets when they pulled up at the first house, that she was surprised to see a perfectly coiffed, expensively dressed woman standing on the curb. A pair of high-heeled sandals and matching purse set off her business suit, cut close to her curvy figure with the skirt short enough to show off well-toned legs. Katherine was further taking aback by the gushy greeting and peck on the cheek that the woman gave Michael at his car door. "Oh, and you brought your—?" the realtor said, waiting for Michael to fill in the blank.

"—good friend Katherine." Michael completed, looking over and smiling at Katherine. "Katherine, this is Melissa." Katherine reached over Michael, at once aware of his closeness along with the overpowering smell of Melissa's perfume, and shook her hand somewhat clumsily. Climbing out of the car she suddenly felt extremely dowdy with her pulled-back hair, and now-wrinkled capris.

Michael must have chosen the most perfect looking realtor in the area, she thought grumpily, walking hurriedly to catch up to the pair who were almost at the front door of the house. It seemed as if the day had turned sour, and she felt like a spare part. The realtor had Michael completely engaged and was expounding on the virtues of the house while Katherine was looking around in consternation. She glanced down at the MLS sheet, appalled at the price they were asking.

"So what do you think, Katie?" The realtor asked looking at her as if she were an afterthought.

"Katherine," Katherine said simply.

"Pardon?"

"My name is Katherine," Katherine said quietly and firmly.

"Oh!" She gave a musically practiced laugh.

Katherine just looked at her blandly, and the realtor turned away to find Michael, never waiting for the answer to her original question. Katherine wished she could pull Michael aside and tell him that this was not the house he wanted. Once they got in the car, she would give the list of negatives that were running through her head. The house, sitting on a busy corner, would absorb all the passing headlights as people turned down the street at night. This would definitely disturb them, especially whoever slept in the front bedroom. The sloped driveway provided little playing space and a pool took up the entire backyard to the point that there was no room for any greenery. And that was just the outside...

When they finally did get to the car, Michael seemed in high spirits. "So what did you think?" he asked in anticipation.

Katherine, surprised by his enthusiasm, wondered at the houses he had looked at on previous days. Before she could answer, however, her cell phone rang. It was her mother-in-law calling to say that Alyssa had just gotten sick and was laying on the couch crying, asking for her Mom. Katherine listened, her heart sinking, "I'll be right there, Jean," she assured her, "tell Alyssa I'll be there within five minutes."

Ending the call, she looked over at Michael apologetically. "I'm sure you gathered –Alyssa is sick and I should be with her." When Michael nodded, she continued, "Would you mind just dropping me off at my in-laws before we go to the next appointment?"

"No problem," then, as an afterthought, "I'm sorry she's not feeling well again."

As Katherine gave directions, Michael waved to the realtor to tell her that he would meet her a little late at the next location.

Arriving at her in-laws, Katherine gathered her purse and the now-cold coffee and half-eaten bagel. Funny how a promising day could turn so awful so quickly.

"I'll be glad to go over those MLS sheets with you later," she offered lamely. "And, I do think that last house was quite overpriced," she added shrugging.

"Oh," Michael responded surprised and then as Katherine climbed out he added, "I hope Alyssa is fine. I'll call you later, OK?"

Sure she's fine, Katherine wanted to say, *just like all the other times.*

"'Bye," she managed out loud, and closing the car door, rushed up the front walk wondering what kind of a low-key pediatrician Michael must be to not even ask what was wrong with Alyssa. Maybe the glare from Melissa, super realtor, had clouded his brain, but who would blame him? She was the complete package—everything Katherine wasn't: sophisticated, polished, professional, coy…

Hurrying inside, Katherine was met by a sobbing Alyssa. Sitting down and cradling Alyssa's head, Katherine was given the play by play from her upset mother-in-law. "She started the morning off quietly, and refused to eat any breakfast. Then she threw up all over the kitchen floor, and started complaining that her head hurt. I put her on the couch with an ice pack, but she hasn't stopped crying since. That's why I went ahead and called you. I really don't like that this happens so often to her.

You should really have her checked out for this, well whatever this is, Katherine."

Katherine's heart sank, she and Jean were such good friends, but her tone right now almost seemed accusatory. Surely Jean didn't think she was neglecting Alyssa? Unbidden words rose to the surface and Katherine closed her mouth, taking a deep breath to keep herself from responding defensively. Finally, after a second deep breath she managed calmly, "I actually have had her seen for this, but nothing came of it. You know children and their stomachs, I may as well call and say she has a mosquito bite. Her pediatrician is not concerned about her at all."

"Well, maybe you should consider switching pediatricians."

Katherine stared thoughtfully into space as she smoothed Alyssa's hair from her forehead. She knew what was coming next.

"Why haven't you asked Michael to take a look at her?"

Katherine shrugged. "I'm just not sure it's a good idea. Plus, he hasn't exactly offered any advice; he is the one who dropped me off today, so he knew she was sick again, and he didn't say anything."

"Oh?" There was a pause, Jean clearly wanted to ask why they had been together, but then changed her mind and returned to the subject at hand. "Maybe he's waiting for you to ask," she offered. She stood, walking into the kitchen, returning shortly with a fresh ice pack. She made soothing sounds as she removed the now-melted ice pack from Alyssa's head and replaced it with the new one.

Maybe he's too enamored with his realtor to waste his time, Katherine thought, appreciating Jean's loving care of Alyssa. She wished Jean would drop the Michael angle. She really did not want to talk about him especially after remembering their enjoyable time the night before in stark contrast with the ruined morning.

Chapter 6

"You know, I've started keeping a log of what she eats in the hope that I'll see some sort of a pattern, but so far there is no pattern that I can tell." There! Katherine hoped that would get her mother-in-law on a new track. "Did you guys eat anything unusual last night?"

"Well, we did go across the street for a birthday party, and have cake and ice cream and –"

"—and cookies and chocolates filled with gooey stuff!" completed Amber bouncing into the room. "Mom, you should have been there, Dylan had the coolest birthday cake you have ever seen and his own *mother* made it!"

Katherine couldn't help laughing—obviously her own homemade cakes didn't rank very high. She turned in confusion towards Jean. "Who's Dylan?"

"Oh, a new family moved in across the street, and they asked us over for birthday cake since their boy has no little friends in town yet. It worked out wonderfully that Amber and Alyssa were here. Dylan is only three, but I think his parents were glad to have children over, no matter what their age!"

"Well, maybe Alyssa ate too much junk last night. In fact, that would be the second birthday party in a row that has made Alyssa sick. It just doesn't make sense, because she eats cake and ice cream and junk at home, and it doesn't necessarily make her sick."

"Yes," Jean agreed, "but children do overload at a party. I'm sorry, I should have watched her more closely."

"Oh no! Amber is fine, and knowing her she probably managed to eat twice as much as Alyssa did. Isn't that right Amber?" Katherine asked playfully, looking fondly at her older daughter.

Amber just shrugged with a mischievous grin on her face. Katherine looked down at the now sleeping Alyssa and sighed. At least her arrival had calmed her daughter enough for sleep to take over. She knew from experience that Alyssa would be sick for the rest of the day. She needed to get her home and figure out what to do next.

Later that afternoon, she sat down with the food log she had been keeping on Alyssa and wrote down this latest episode. Reading over the entries, she realized that it did seem that large amounts of cake and cookies were to blame in many of the instances. She looked over at her daughter who was sound asleep once more, this time in front of the TV. Maybe there was a way to cut sugar out of her diet without making it a big deal. Birthday parties, and there were plenty of them, would be the hard part, but she could do something at home to start with, especially since it was summertime and she had greater control over what Alyssa ate. She went online and looked up sugar-free recipes but gave up after awhile, deciding instead to visit the health food store nearby and get help from a real live person instead of wandering aimlessly in cyberspace, getting confused by the plethora of vitamin and health food companies peddling their wares. In the middle of her searching, Michael called, but she let the machine pick it up. She was too tired to talk to him right then, and she didn't want to feign cheerfulness, nor hear about his outing with the perfect woman either.

When Alyssa finally woke up that afternoon, Katherine dragged the girls to their local health food store. Meandering around, she eventually found what she was looking for—a sugar-free cookbook. Thumbing through it, she found a few key recipes, and then walked around slowly looking for some of the ingredients. An employee, noticing her confusion, came over and offered help. "Oh this is a great book!" she gushed. "Are you guys going sugar-free?"

"We're going to try it," Katherine ventured cautiously.

"But I like sugar, Mom!" Amber protested.

Katherine shushed her and turned her attention back to the salesperson. "Could you tell me what's the difference between this fructose stuff listed here," she said, pointing to an ingredient listed in the book, "versus regular table sugar?"

"Um, fructose is easier to digest for some people, but if you're diabetic, it's still going to raise blood sugar like regular sugar. It depends why you are going sugar-free."

"Well, I guess it's just a test. I think that my youngest gets sick from regular sugar. I saw that sometimes you can replace regular sugar with fructose, and I was wondering if that would do the trick."

"Yes, it will do the trick if her body is just not digesting regular sugar. Fructose is a simple sugar, a monosaccharide, so our digestive system doesn't have to use any digestive enzymes to break it down. Table sugar, or sucrose, is a little more complex, it's called a disaccharide, so our bodies use an enzyme to break it down. Sometimes people are missing that enzyme, and then regular sugar makes them sick."

"Wow," Katherine said slowly, trying to absorb what she was hearing. Science had never been her forte, and she was feeling increasingly overwhelmed, especially since she wasn't even sure if she was on the right track.

Sensing her hesitation, the salesperson went on. "Why not buy a bag of fructose and when your recipes call for sugar, use the fructose instead and see how your little girl does? It's not that big of a deal. Of course, you would have to avoid store-bought sweets while you're doing your test. But, I bet within a week or so you would know if you were on the right track."

Katherine nodded gratefully. Feeling more positive, she purchased the recipe book and the fructose and took the girls home, grateful that she was at least taking some sort of action.

Later that night she finally sat down to return Michael's call. She was still feeling irritable over how the morning had gone, and over his apparent disinterest in Alyssa's health. She schooled herself for a further letdown as she dialed his number. Consequently, she was surprised when he answered the phone, obviously glad to hear from her, and immediately asked how Alyssa was.

"She's doing better. She slept all day," Katherine answered, grateful that he did seem concerned.

"And she was throwing up again this morning?"

"Yes, and complaining that her head hurt."

"You know, some children have really sensitive stomachs. Nonetheless, you may want to have your pediatrician look at her again. Ask him to run some tests he hasn't run before."

"OK," Katherine responded doubtfully. Then after hesitating a bit she told him about her current plan to cut sugar from Alyssa's diet.

His response was less than enthusiastic. "You can try what you want to try," he cautioned, "it certainly can't hurt. But, please don't go wasting a lot of money based on the advice of a health food store worker who benefits from you spending your money there."

"I only bought a book and a two-dollar bag of fructose," she answered defensively.

"That's fine," he responded quickly noting the defensive tone to her voice. "Like I said, it certainly can't hurt, I'm just saying be careful about spending a lot of money in those places."

Katherine did not want to argue with him, so she changed the subject and asked how the rest of the houses looked.

"They were OK, I actually liked the one we saw together the most, but you said you thought it was way overpriced."

"Maybe I'm wrong; I haven't even given the housing market the slightest consideration since we bought this house over three years ago."

"Yeah, Melissa mentioned that could be the reason."

And I'm sure she said a lot more too, Katherine thought. Why did he even want her help anyway?

"I still would like you to go and look at a few more houses with me," he went on, as if reading her mind.

"I'm not sure I'll be a real help, based on the little bit I saw today," Katherine responded hurriedly.

"I'm not looking for help with pricing or generic things that realtors know," he tried to explain. "I just want an opinion from someone who doesn't have a monetary interest in the whole process."

Great, thought Katherine. *I don't have the clothes to even begin to compete with Melissa, and he wants me to keep going with them.*

"Melissa is very good, but she's just a bit much, if you know what I mean, and I want someone along that can inject some common sense into the equation."

Was he reading her mind?

"Oh – ah - sure. Me and my common sense will tag along next time too." The response came out more sarcastic than she had intended.

"Katherine?" He was confused by her tone. Women could be so complicated sometimes.

"Yes?"

"Hey, if you really don't want to come along next time that's fine."

"No, it's not that at all," she backpedaled hurriedly. "Sorry for my tone, I'm just a bit worn out from this whole Alyssa thing. Just let me know ahead of time when you want to look at more homes and I'll gladly go along."

Michael breathed a sigh of relief and they talked more about Alyssa before he asked if she would go out with him again. Katherine was stumped. This morning he had barely looked at her once Melissa was in the picture, and he had hardly shown any concern for Alyssa, yet he still wanted to go out with her? She didn't know how to reply.

"Katherine, are you there?" he asked anxiously.

"Yes."

"Didn't you enjoy yourself last night?" He sounded sad and vulnerable and her heart twisted.

"Yes, yes I did!" *Just the day after that was miserable*, she thought wryly. She felt badly, hating that she had led him to believe their perfect evening had been anything but just that.

"I know we didn't have the best time this morning—" he started.

The man *was* reading her mind!

"—but maybe we could go out again and have a repeat of the good time we had last night. I thoroughly enjoyed myself."

"Sure," Katherine said, still uncertain. She wondered why he didn't want to take out his unencumbered, time-to-do-her-toenails realtor, but thought she had said enough dumb things for one day.

They ended their conversation with Michael promising that he'd be in touch soon, and Katherine hung up the phone feeling befuddled.

It was definitely time to quit spending so much time with him. Things were already starting to feel complicated.

Chapter 7

DESPITE HER RESOLVE to the contrary, Katherine once again found herself sitting across from Michael at a restaurant near the water the following Thursday evening. They had even looked at houses again, only this time, all the children were in tow. Katherine had offered to watch them instead of coming along, but Michael was adamant that he wanted her there. His realtor had not done a good job at hiding her disappointment over all of the added company, but despite everything, they had seen a house that seemed quite promising. In fact, they were scheduled to look at it the following day for the second time.

"So, it's your favorite house so far?" Michael asked for the umpteenth time.

"Yes, Michael," she smiled in response. "I think it's perfect for you and the boys, plenty of room and plenty of yard space along with the pool, and it's a great neighborhood."

"Close to your house," he added with a wink.

"Amber will be happy about that."

"So will Michael," he shot back and then added, "*I* like it because if I ever do get married, there would be plenty of room for a wife and a few children!" He was watching her steadily for a reaction.

Katherine's heart flip-flopped at the thought, and even as she could feel the flush beginning to warm her face she quipped, "Just so your new wife doesn't mind that you have a female friend living nearby with two little girls."

He shook his head in mock dismay. "Oh, I'd just have to tell her that was how it was going to be and if she had a problem with it, than she shouldn't marry me!"

Katherine knew her face was beet red by now.

"Why are you blushing?" Michael asked innocently.

"It's warm in here," she countered looking away, and wondering how he could affect her so easily. After all, he was just a friend.

Feeling severely uncomfortable under his direct gaze, she hastily changed the subject. "You know my fructose plan for Alyssa is working so far!"

"Really?" His lack of enthusiasm for the subject change was clear.

"Yes, Alyssa has gone a week without any headaches or throwing up sessions."

"Hmmmm, I wonder why it's working?"

"Maybe her body wasn't digesting the sugar, like the health food lady suggested."

"I suppose so," he said uncertainly, and was relieved to see that their food was arriving.

He felt like Alyssa was possibly experiencing some sort of stress, but he knew to say that now would probably ruin their evening.

After they ate, they took a walk along the beach; stopping to sit on some chairs set out for hotel guests.

"You know, if we brought our own cushions, these would be really comfortable," he quipped.

Chapter 7

"The point is to make them uncomfortable for free loaders like us!" Katherine laughed back. "We could go and find a bench somewhere, but I just love the view here." She breathed in the fresh ocean air. There was always a different scent at the ocean in the evenings, with the wind blowing steadily off the darkening water. She loved how the water reflected the colors of the changing sky as the sun set. It was truly her favorite time to be at the beach, and she gave a sigh of contentment.

"You always see the most beautiful sky when you don't have your camera with you," she said softly, in awe of the view before them. Pelicans flew by in formation and she turned her head to follow their path. The Jupiter Inlet lay beyond them, busy as ever with boats returning from day trips while others were leaving for nighttime fishing. She had a school friend whose husband would fish half the night, come home, sleep a few hours, and then get up for work the next morning. She wondered if his boat was among the boats roaring out of the inlet. She loved to watch them as they left the inlet, changing from idle speed to full throttle, like children set free after a day of school. Leyton had never been a fisherman, he had enjoyed golf in his spare time. She had never understood the love of golf, but watching those boats charging out into the open ocean as the sun was setting, made her understand the draw of fishing.

"Or you see sea turtles hatch for the very first time," Michael added. Katherine looked back at him quickly, trying to pick up the thread of conversation.

"You've seen sea turtles hatch already?"

"The boys didn't tell you? It was amazing. I brought them out early one morning, and I was walking along trying to keep up with them when Simon let out a loud 'whoop!' Jack and I ran over to see what he was pointing at. It was a sea turtle the size of –" he reached out and took her hand, turning it over and traced the outside of her palm. Then, keeping her hand in his, he continued, "While we were watching that turtle, suddenly

Jack hollered, pointing close by. Sure enough, there was another one, and before we knew it, they were all around us, literally boiling out of the sand. I think we counted twenty-three. The boys were ecstatic. It was by far the most incredible sight—no offense to your worm rocks, mind you—we had ever seen at the ocean. We actually got in the water and swam out with one of them. The baby turtle swam surprisingly quickly and finally we had to turn back."

Katherine was watching his animated face and enjoying the feel of her hand in his. He stopped talking, and looked down at their hands smiling inwardly. Then his thoughts turned serious and he made an inward decision. Now was the time to tell her his story, before they got any closer. He squeezed her hand gently and said quietly, "Let's go find that comfortable bench you mentioned earlier, I need to tell you about Morgan."

Katherine looked at him in surprise. She had a feeling she knew who Morgan was and what was coming, but the abrupt change in topics surprised her. They walked the entire way in silence, still holding hands. When they reached the bench, they sat down and he squeezed her hand again before releasing it. Then, placing both his elbows on his knees and clasping his hands together in front of him he looked out towards the ocean. "I need to tell you about Morgan," he said again.

Katherine sat quietly while he launched into his story. When he came to the part about Morgan having no interest in Jack, she felt tears prick her eyes. By the time he had told her about Morgan's death, they were both crying. Katherine just sat there, wiping the tears from her eyes, not wanting to interrupt him, or break his train of thought. When he told her how he had accepted Jesus into his life, and gained freedom from the torment of his guilt, she smiled through her tears, understanding. Finally, he was silent. She waited to make sure he was finished and then knelt directly in front of him. She took both his hands and said softly, "Michael you are the most wonderful man that I've met

Chapter 7

since Leyton died. I just want you to know that." He looked up at her with relief in his eyes and then pulled her gently to a standing position and took her in his arms and trembling, drew her to him.

"Thank you, Katherine. Thank you, thank you, thank you." He whispered into her hair. He had been so afraid that she would have been shocked by his story. Instead, she was standing there telling him he was wonderful. The relief he felt was immeasurable. Finally, he stepped back, wiped his hand across his eyes, and said, "Whew! I usually don't make it a habit of baring my soul…"

"Well I'm honored you felt free to do so with me."

They stood there close, until Michael, feeling the need for some comic relief stepped back and said, "Hey, do you think we can make it to that ice cream place nearby before it closes?"

Katherine laughed in return.

"It depends how fast you're willing to run!" she called as she dashed off down the beach towards the parking lot. Michael had no problem catching up with her, and they arrived at his car gasping for air, laughing, with sand all over their feet.

Chapter 8

WITH SUMMER WINDING down. Alyssa was continuing to do well on her sucrose-free diet, and Katherine was grateful that the solution had seemingly been so relatively simple. Michael had long since started working, and the boys were with their grandparents while he was at work. Once a week Katherine would either have the boys over, or they would all pile into her car for a beach trip. Those were fun-filled days.

She was getting to know Michael's parents a little each time she saw them. They were friendly, enjoyable people, and she was grateful for another positive influence in her life. Since Leyton's death, she could become so easily discouraged that she tried to surround herself with positive, uplifting people. She was grateful that God seemed to be placing the right people in her life—people that encouraged and strengthened her. Eventually she hoped that she would be able to help those who were suffering as well, but for now she found herself avoiding negative, needy people.

Afternoon thunderclouds filled the sky as they headed home after a long day of swimming, snorkeling, and exploring along

Blowing Rocks Preserve on Jupiter Island. Michael had asked Katherine to drop the boys off at his parent's house that evening. Katherine glanced at them in her rearview mirror.

Saturated with sun and sand, satisfied and subdued, she thought, grinning at her own alliteration. There were still vestiges of an English major in her brain somewhere!

The children had run along the base of the rocks before the tide came in, screaming as the encroaching waves threatened their safety. Eventually she had called them all to play away from the rocks, but not before they had discovered caves, crabs, and imaginary treasures.

Thank you, Lord. Thank you for these children, for the chance to enjoy them and revel in Your creation. Thank you for the privilege of watching the wonders of the ocean through the eyes of my girls and two mischievous little boys. Thank you for providing the perfect friends for my girls, for the boost they provide to my lonely little family. Thank you for the health and freedom to spend an entire day playing in a setting so beautiful...thank you...

While unloading the boys, Mrs. Manning suggested that Katherine leave the girls as well, and treat herself to an impromptu evening alone. Perking up, the children found the energy to beg her to accept the invitation, which she gratefully did. She headed home, debating what to do with her free evening when Michael called from work.

"I don't know if my mother is trying to set us up tonight, but she's arranged for us both to have a free evening. So, let's humor her and go out."

"That would be wonderful!" she answered happily. He would pick her up after work and she would have just enough time to recover from beach mom to an evening-out mom.

Getting ready, she mused how different this summer had been from the last few. She was finally having fun again and laughing more. It was such a relief to no longer be dominated by the oppressive sadness that had filled her since Leyton's death. With

Chapter 8

a light heart, she studied the rows of teacher-clothes hanging in her closet, searching for something that did not remind her of school or duties. Eventually her eyes settled on a dress, complete with price tags, hidden behind her sparse sampling of winter clothes. She pulled it out, eyeing it critically, as memories flooded of her first attempt at dating again. She couldn't remember the name of the unsuspecting man that had asked her out, but she did remember buying the dress in an attempt to psyche herself into the dating mode. Unable to go through with it, though, she had met her date at the door, eyes red-rimmed, and stammered out an apology that she wouldn't be able to go. He hadn't been very understanding and that had only strengthened her resolve to avoid dating altogether. But, that was then, and now was now, and the dress, having hung for months unworn, would be perfect for an evening with Michael.

After showering and slipping into the dress, she found her anticipation growing, and couldn't help but contrast her feelings with that night months ago, when the same actions had brought an ominous trepidation. Maybe it was Michael, or maybe she was finally ready to be dating, or maybe it was both—the right person for the right time. Whatever it was, her heart leapt as she heard the doorbell, and her happiness increased as she opened the door to Michael's expectant face.

"Hi," his voice was deep with pleasure.

"Hi," she managed back, unable to contain the widening smile that filled her face.

They stood there, caught in the moment, until Katherine finally mumbled something about needing her purse, and leaving the door open, ran to grab it.

"OK," she was breathless, "I'm ready." She turned to pull the door shut and lock it, doing her best not to fumble with the keys, all the while reprimanding herself for her lack of finesse.

"You look beautiful, Katherine." The statement was simple, yet his voice, heavy with emotion, spoke volumes. He wanted to kiss her so badly, she was so close, but being unsure as to her response, reached for her hand instead. Squeezing it, he looked down at their locked fingers, and admitted, "I'm not sure I'll ever feel practiced or suave coming to pick you up for an evening out."

"Good," she laughed with relief, "that makes two of us." Savoring the feel of her hand in his she listened as he abruptly switched gears, explaining that he unfortunately needed to go by St. Mary's Hospital to see a patient. Would she mind? He promised it wouldn't take more than a few minutes and then they could be on their way.

"It isn't an emergency," he said, "but it will be easier to take care of it tonight rather than tomorrow morning."

Katherine acquiesced, but as they exited the interstate towards the hospital, she felt a sickening dread encompass her. Leyton had died at St. Mary's, and she realized now that she had never been to the hospital since that night. To her alarm, Michael pulled in at the ER entrance. Flashbacks of that black night bombarded her mind, and a wave of nausea threatened to overcome her. Her palms were sweating and her hands were shaking.

Oblivious to her turmoil, Michael looked over as he put the car in park, "Fifteen minutes, I promise I'll –" then, as his eyes took in her ashen face and trembling lips, "–Katherine, are you OK?" He reached out and put his hand on her arm as she managed an almost imperceptible nod. His clinically trained mind searched for a medical reason for the abrupt turnaround. Knowing little of her medical history he wondered briefly if she were diabetic, but then, there had never been any indication of any such thing. Surely she couldn't be angry with him for stopping at the hospital? "Will you be OK if I still run in?" he finally asked.

She smiled weakly, "Yes." The sound was scarcely audible and he gave her a long concerned look before hurrying from the car. It was unlike her to act this way, and being Katherine, she probably would not tell him what the matter was. Shaking his head, thoroughly confused by her sudden change in behavior, he entered the hospital.

Katherine, meantime, found herself slipping deeper into the past.

This must be what an anxiety attack is, she thought alarmed. Looking around frantically, she realized that she couldn't stay there by the ER entrance, she had to go somewhere and gain composure. Sliding over to the driver's side, she managed to get the car in drive and direct it toward a different area of the parking lot. She wanted to run, to cry hysterically. Desperately trying to maneuver the car, she could feel her breaths coming in short gasps and the sobs welling from deep within her. She had no control and knowing she could wreck, she simultaneously managed to press both feet onto the brake pedal.

Suddenly, the driver's side door was yanked open. Concerned by her strange behavior, Michael had stopped once inside to look back at the car and had noticed her driving erratically away. Worried, he had run after her. Realizing immediately that she was hyperventilating, he grabbed a leftover McDonald's bag and held it over her mouth. "Here!" he commanded. "Breathe into this!" He squeezed in next to her, easing her feet off the brake pedal and replacing them with his own. Then, reaching past the steering wheel, he jerked the car into park. Next he pulled her sideways onto his lap as he scooted onto the seat, cradling her head with one hand while helping her hold the bag with another. Her breathing began to slow as he whispered soothingly, "It's OK, it's OK. Just cry and let it all out. It's OK." He wiped her tears, and held her tighter against him as the heart wrenching sobs continued. Finally, with her tears spent, her body went limp against him. He cupped her face in his hands and looked down at her, "Can you tell me about it?" he implored.

The tears came fresh again. "I'm so sorry, I'm so embarrassed, I can't believe I—"

"No Katherine, don't apologize, just tell me about it," he said more firmly.

She took a long slow breath. "Maybe…OK… but it's going to take a long time."

"Alright then, let me drive, and we'll go somewhere to talk, I just need to make a phone call first."

He helped her move over to the passenger side, buckling her in, and then called the pediatric wing, explaining he would stop by first thing in the morning instead. Carefully maneuvering the car towards the exit, he reached over and took her hand. Tears had started flowing again but she was calm. They drove in silence until they reached South Ocean Boulevard on Palm Beach Island. Then, parallel parking on the beach side of the street, he reached over and took her hand again. "OK," he said quietly, "we have as long as you need."

Katherine staring unseeingly out the passenger window, took a deep breath, and began.

"Leyton and I had been married for nearly nine years. We were married young, while I was still a sophomore in college. He had worked throughout high school in his father's landscaping business, so after graduation it just seemed natural that he continue doing so. Whenever he felt his knowledge was inadequate, he would take a course at the local community college to fill in the gaps. He must have taken fifteen courses in all, ranging from horticulture to accounting to computer programming. But, he always said he wasn't going to waste four whole years taking English literature and PE when he already knew what he needed, and liked to do. As he got older and his knowledge and experience increased, the business really grew. His father joked that Leyton working full time with him for five years had been more profitable than all his other employees combined over the past twenty years. They had an excellent partnership, and a wonderful relationship. This translated to our marriage. Leyton was a wonderful husband. He paid for my schooling when my father no longer would, supported me emotionally and intellectually. We were so poor at the beginning, but we never cared. I felt like all of my dreams had come true."

"Where did you first meet?" Michael interjected. Then he hastily added, "Sorry to ask, but I just want to get the whole picture."

"Oh, no problem, I'm bound to be disjointed, so feel free to ask what you want." Katherine wiped at her tears, blew her nose and thought for a while, her mind now even further back in the past.

"We were in the same church youth group. My Dad's job forced us to relocate a lot, but when I was a sophomore in high school, my mother put her foot down and told him when he was discussing another move, that if we moved, he had to promise that we would stay put until I graduated from high school. I was an only child, and she promised my Dad that once I graduated, she would move every year if he needed to, but that they owed it to me to have a little stability. My Dad agreed, and was true to his word. We moved here my sophomore year, and we stayed put until I started my freshman year of college. Apparently my Dad turned down two promotions during that time, but has since gone on to make up for it." Katherine stopped and smiled, "I think my parents have indeed moved every year since they left here, but my Mom never seems to mind."

Katherine paused again, collecting her thoughts to draw herself back to Michael's question.

"Anyway," she continued, "as I said, Leyton and I were in the same youth group. Both of our families were Christians, and we were always involved in church. We started attending the same church I attend now, and in a sense, the people in that church became my family. They have been a constant for me all these years. When my parents moved away, I rented a room from an older couple in the church, and commuted to Florida Atlantic University. After moving around all my life, I had no desire to 'go away' to college. My Dad had a hard time with that; he kept pushing me to be more ambitious, to attend what he thought might be a more prestigious school and definitely to pursue a more lucrative profession. But, I longed to be a teacher. Teaching seemed natural to me. I loved my education courses, loved the lesson planning, loved student teaching.

"Leyton and I started dating in high school. However, our parents were very watchful over us, and practically forced us to date other people. My Dad especially did not want me to marry young, and he definitely wanted me to marry someone who had a college degree. He liked Leyton, but he felt that he was not ambitious enough. But to me, Leyton's family was the ideal. They were a happy, loving family, that had all lived in the same place for years and years, who didn't work seven days a week, and I loved being around all of them. I didn't want to live my parents' life. The quest for professional success seemed unimportant to me. Besides, I was already in love with Leyton. We were probably in love before I ever even finished high school. My poor Dad would have been horrified if he had known!

"Anyway, once my parents moved away, we dated exclusively. I think the entire church, along with Leyton's family did their best to keep us so busy that we never had a second to breathe, much less get into trouble. The summer before my sophomore year we were joking that if we ever wanted to get to spend some time alone we were just going to have to get married. So we did!" Katherine was smiling now. She looked sideways at Michael and said, "We sure took a lot of people by surprise." She tilted her head, grinning through her tears, remembering

"You mean you eloped?" Michael asked, surprised himself.

"No, not exactly. We had a really small wedding at the gazebo in his family's backyard. You'll have to see their garden sometime, it's beautiful. There were only a handful of guests, just our pastor and his wife, a few of our closest friends, and Michael's family. My Dad was obviously not too thrilled. It was such a beautiful day, though. Jean's roses were in full bloom and standing before the pastor, with the evening breeze carrying the scent of those roses, I thought my heart would burst with joy. We were so incredibly happy, like we had somehow beat the system: gotten married on a dime with no stressful planning, surrounded by loving supportive people, and a beautiful garden. Best of all, we were finally able to be alone. We rented a small apartment, and furnished it with garage sale items. It was perfect. I had never been so happy in all my life."

Katherine stopped and looked over at Michael. "I'm sorry. This is taking too long, isn't it?"

"No," he rubbed her arm encouragingly, "it's beautiful." There was a wistful note to his voice.

Katherine, catching his tone, hesitated, wondering if she should continue. Her story was so different from his, so full of love, so idyllic.

"Hey, are you going to leave me hanging?" Michael demanded.

"You sure you want me to keep going?" Katherine asked concerned. "I'm fine now, just telling you about Leyton makes me feel better."

"Oh no, I'm not letting you go until I've heard the whole story. But, let's change our venue. The car is getting cramped." Katherine agreed, and they got out, walking along the sea wall quietly, each lost in their own thoughts, until they found a bench.

"Alright, young lady, you have a story to finish," Michael said gently in mock command, once they were settled on the bench.

Katherine smiled and then sighed. If only the ending didn't have to be so sad.

"We lived in the apartment until I graduated from college. Once I started working we took the plunge and bought a duplex in a cheaper section of town. We fixed it up and rented out the side we weren't living in. It was a lot of work and stressful, but we were able to save more money than if we had bought the nicer home that we could have qualified for. My parents, on one of their rare visits, were not happy with our location at all. My Dad, when he found out our combined incomes, was livid that we were living so frugally. He didn't understand us at all. When we had Alyssa, he tried to force us into letting him buy us a house in a better neighborhood. Leyton was way too proud for that. Once Amber came along, though, we were getting crowded, and I was beginning to see that we weren't in a safe enough area to let the girls ride their bikes or play in the front yard. So we started looking. Leyton had just landed a landscaping contract with the development I live in now. He came home all excited about a house, and wanted me to see it immediately. I laughed at him, it was a garden home community and every house only had the smallest of yards in the back. He had always wanted a house with some land, and I didn't understand his sudden change of heart, but I did love the house. Plus, with the anticipated sale of the duplex and the money we had saved we could get into a very comfortable house by our standards with a safe environment for the girls to ride and play.

"Once Leyton had decided on that house he was determined. He wanted it to be perfect. He even let slip once that by the next time my parents visited, there would be no reason for my Dad to turn his nose up at anything. I felt terrible, telling Leyton that was the wrong reason to want something. He laughed and told me not to worry; he would enjoy living in a nice place too! He went over after work every evening, painting, installing new fixtures…new everything. By now, I was staying home with the girls, and we missed him. The days seemed so long. We spent a lot of time with my in-laws. Leyton kept saying that it was temporary, that once the work was complete, he would be done, and we would have a wonderful home to live in.

"Well, he was right, and the house was finally ready. We went out and bought all new furniture. It was so exciting for me. Every few minutes or so on those final moving days he would reach over and hug me tightly and say 'You see! I told you it would be worth it!' He was *so* proud.

"It was a Saturday night, and we had spent the whole day moving our remaining personal belongings over to the house. The girls loved the house and ran around with glee. Amber kept saying over and over again, 'Look Mommy, look Daddy, I can walk!' as she walked in huge circles around her room. There literally hadn't been any space to walk in her old room. Alyssa got caught up in the excitement easily, like two-year-olds do, and she ran around saying something like 'Look Mama, look Da-ee, I jump!' while she did that one-leg-off-the-floor attempt at toddler jumping. Then there was Leyton, hugging me every few minutes with that grin on his face. Until that day, I had actually slightly resented the house because it had seemingly stolen our family togetherness time. But now, viewing the finished product, I was excited too.

"Around nine o'clock, I finally convinced Leyton that we could stop unpacking and just relax, when he realized that we hadn't brought over any of his clothes. We laughed, and I told him that he could sleep in something of mine, but he insisted that it would only take awhile to get a few things and an outfit for church the next day, and then he would be back. He smiled, kissed me quickly, and basically skipped to his car. He was so proud."

Katherine lowered her head, and began twisting the tissues in her hands. She breathed in unsteadily and then continued, her tone low and halting. "A while after he left I remember hearing sirens in the distance and dismissing them, but as ten o'clock approached and he hadn't returned, I was starting to feel unsettled. By ten-thirty, I called his parents. I was hoping, albeit irrationally, that he had stopped by their house for something, and had lost track of the time. Just as I hung up the phone, I got the call. Leyton was in the ER. There had been a severe car accident and Leyton had been flown by Trauma Hawk to St. Mary's. I needed to come down and I needed to hurry. That's all they would tell me. Frantic, I knocked on a neighbor's door, whom I scarcely knew, and asked someone to sit in the house until I could get a babysitter to come. Thankfully, they complied. Before leaving, I called my in-laws back, hysterical. They had farther to drive, but assured me they were on their way. They also said they'd send someone we knew over to stay with the girls. Driving to the ER, I kept saying over and over and over, 'Please, God, don't let him die.' I was having such trouble staying focused enough to drive, when I was stopped by an accident. It turned out to be Leyton's accident—"

"You saw the accident?" Michael was clearly taken aback.

Katherine nodded briefly, "at first I was frozen with horror, but then, something clicked, and I knew that if I wanted to see him again I had to get there, and the fastest way to do that was to pull myself together and drive! I must have run every red light I encountered. I pulled into the ER and ran in. I remember a security guard chasing after me, yelling that I couldn't park in the Ambulance Bay, and I just threw him my keys and ran on. When I finally got to Leyton, he was still alive. He looked like something off a TV show, machines and wires everywhere. There was a team of people around him, and I just barged in. A nurse quietly talked me through what they were doing to him. She said that he had massive internal bleeding. I went to his side, took his hand, and spoke his name above the din. He opened his eyes and looked at me, with all the love and joy that those eyes had always held for me. He had a tube down his throat so he couldn't speak, but his eyes spoke so clearly that to me it seemed audible: 'I love you Katherine, I'll see you in heaven.

Kiss our girls for me and tell them their Daddy loves them.' I squeezed his hand tighter to let him know I had 'heard' him. Our eyes were locked, and I wanted to protest, but no words would come out. Then, with eyes full of tenderness and loving care, I heard him say, 'Goodbye, my sweetheart' and his eyes glassed over. The machines flat lined and they stepped back, I found out later they had already resuscitated him twice. I wanted to scream at them to try something, but in my heart I knew he was gone. Just like that, he was gone. I would never again see him on this earth."

Katherine sat motionless, consumed in the darkness of that memory. Michael waited, staring silently at the moving water in front of them. Finally, Katherine looked up at Michael and said, "This afternoon was the first time I'd ever been back to that ER. I must have been subconsciously avoiding it, because I've visited people at other hospitals but never at St. Mary's. I never knew it would affect me like that. I'm so sorry."

Emotionally spent, she leaned back against the bench. She closed her eyes and sighed deeply. "You know, there I was in this brand new beautiful house without one thing that needed to be done. We were in a safe neighborhood; there was no exterior maintenance, no yard work. The Home Owners Association seemed to cover everything that required any heavy labor. Looking back, I can see how God orchestrated it all. All the work had been done. Plus, being in a new house, I didn't have the constant reminders shouting at me from every angle. Leyton had never lived there. I didn't even have to pack up his things, they were already in boxes. Even so, I kept the boxes for way too long, but finally one day I took them to the low income housing where migrant workers tend to live, and gave them to a man standing on the side of the road waiting to be hired for the day. He was so grateful." Katherine paused, her mind shifting. "You know, it was almost as if we had moved, and Leyton would be joining us at a later date. It helped take the sharp edge off our pain."

"How old was Amber?"

"She was five. She loved her Daddy. It was heart wrenching trying to explain it to her. She has always been such a positive little girl. She kept telling me, 'No Mommy, God will let our Daddy come and visit us because I asked Him to.' One day she woke up and insisted on wearing this little yellow dress that had been her Daddy's favorite. He always used to call her his 'golden buttercup' when she wore it. She told me that was the day he was coming to visit, and we had to get ready and cook his favorite meal. I called his parents, frantic for advice. They suggested that I go ahead and make the meal and play along somewhat, that they would come over at dinner time and bring her something from her Daddy." Katherine started to cry again. "I don't know what I would have done, they were so strong for me, and they were grieving severely too. Besides, Tom had lost his business partner as well as his son. Anyway, they rang the doorbell at dinnertime. I was so anxious, I just kept praying that God would give us all wisdom and help little Amber understand. She ran to the door excitedly, and there was the entire family: Grandma, Grandpa, uncles, aunts and cousins. Everyone had a balloon, a special picture that had Leyton in it, and there was one huge box wrapped in bright pink paper decorated with a hundred streamers. My father-in-law just swooped my little girl into his arms and said, 'Oh boy, your Daddy wanted us to bring you the best present ever so that whenever you play with it you can think of him. He said it was to be a special present for his precious golden buttercup.' I remember the momentary confusion and a flash of disappointment crossing her face as she searched the faces for her Daddy, but what five-year-old can resist a huge present that has a barking, scratching sound coming from the inside? She tore into the gift; it was a cocker spaniel. Her grandpa said she was to call him "Cuddles" so that every time she missed her Daddy, she could give him a cuddle. Then in all her five-year-old wisdom, she looked at us all and said, 'No, I am going to call him "Pwesent" because God told me if Daddy couldn't come, He would send me a pwesent instead.' We were all crying by then, but Amber, completely oblivious, was already skipping and dancing after the excited puppy, all over the house." Katherine stopped again, looking questioningly at Michael. She noticed there were tears in his eyes and wondered if she should continue.

Sensing her hesitation, he squeezed her hand, willing her to continue.

"That night we ate Amber's requested dinner, and everyone got out the pictures they had brought. Tom told Amber to get her favorite picture of her Daddy too. Then we all went around the table and talked about the picture and why we loved him so much. It was truly a beautiful time. Then we all walked outside to the neighborhood lake and we brought one of the balloons. Tom told Amber that she was to kiss it, and then they were going to send it to Daddy in heaven. It was such a poignant moment, watching my little girl kiss all over that balloon and then release it. I was holding little Alyssa and looking at the wonderful loving people I still had all around me, and then I looked up at that speck of a balloon, and it was as if something mentally snapped back into place. The intense pain was still there, but suddenly everything was in focus again. After that night, I began to function again. That was my turning point." She paused, "That's what makes my coming apart back at the ER so embarrassing to me. I thought I was over falling apart."

"Katherine! Please!" Michael exclaimed sitting up straighter, and turning to look her square in the eyes. "You have such a beautiful strength. And, part of what makes you strong is your ability to face what makes you weak. Tonight you faced something huge, albeit by accident, and here you are talking through it, and recalling heartbreaking yet also beautiful memories." He paused and shook her hands willing her to respond, "Katherine?"

She looked up finally and answered simply, "Thank you, Michael." Then she leaned forward and hugged him, "Thank you."

Michael found there was a lump in his throat as he squeezed her closer. "My pleasure," he finally whispered into her hair, "my pleasure."

Chapter 9

SUMMER HAD COME to an abrupt end, seeming endless at the beginning, but then rushing towards its predetermined end much too fast for Katherine and the girls. That all-important first day of school had come and gone, and the Monday-to-Friday rhythm marked by hurried breakfasts, donning school clothes, loading book bags, working on homework, and early bed times had taken over. Katherine once again found herself juggling more tasks then were possible for one person to handle. She would find that she would just get herself into a routine where things were flowing smoothly when something would go wrong, and once again she would be overwhelmed with too many things for one person to manage.

Added to everything, it seemed that Alyssa was constantly getting sick. The sucrose-free diet was no longer working. Katherine had met with Alyssa's teachers and the lunchroom ladies to make sure that she wasn't getting any table sugar, and everyone assured her that she wasn't. Despite these efforts, Alyssa was still having more and more of her episodes.

In addition, between Katherine teaching and Michael working long hours, their time together had been sharply curtailed. The fun events of the summer seemed distant and slightly unreal given the current frenetic pace of life. Thus, she didn't feel at liberty to ask him about Alyssa, especially since she knew he had never supported the no-sugar theory in the first place. She simply felt too tired to try to figure it all out any more.

It was a Tuesday morning, and here she was, missing school again with her sick little girl. She tried to get an appointment with her regular pediatrician, but to no avail. She hesitated for a awhile, not wanting to use Michael's office for fear it would somehow place a strain on their friendship. After her emotional collapse the month before, Katherine had been afraid she had unwittingly moved the relationship to a new level. Thankfully, though, when they did see each other, the same easygoing friendship was present. Since she was determined to have things remain that way, she had been afraid to have Alyssa evaluated at Michael's office. She didn't want to seem as if she were taking advantage of him. Finally, though, out of desperation, she decided to call his office. She could tell that the receptionist did not know of her, and for this she was glad. Besides, the receptionist was accommodating, getting them in that same morning, and Michael was surprised and extremely happy to see them when he walked into the exam room.

"I hope you don't mind that we came here..." Katherine began, gripping the handles of her purse nervously.

"Not at all," he answered her, "I'm happy you gave us a try. We're still new enough that it's actually possible to be seen the same day without a two-hour wait!" Then he turned his attention to Alyssa. "Sore tummy and sore head again? Let's see what we can do for you so that you and Mommy don't have to miss so much school." He sat down on a stool and rolled over to her, taking her little hands and smiling. Katherine could see Alyssa relax as she shrugged and answered Michael's questions in childish monosyllables, and Katherine felt herself relax in turn. How wonderful it was to have someone so competent for a friend. There was a security in it that she hadn't felt in years. She chided herself now for not wanting to bring Alyssa here.

Finally, his questions and examination complete, Michael looked up. "I'm going to send you to the lab for some blood work. Hopefully something will show up that will give us a clue. For now, keep treating the symptoms, and lets both try to figure out if something at school could be bothering her."

"What do you mean?" Where could he possibly be going with this?

Michael shrugged, "Well, many times with children, headaches and upset stomachs are common manifestations of a deeper problem. Maybe she is afraid of her teacher, or maybe she feels threatened by someone or something at school."

"But this happened all summer long —you know that!"

"Yes, it did." His voice was calm and measured. "I'm not saying anxiety is the cause, I'm just saying that we need to be aware that it *could* be the cause. For now, though, keep treating the symptoms, and we'll keep our antennae up for any potential stressors in her little life."

Katherine looked down. She thought that was ludicrous, but she would go along with it temporarily. The lab work would surely show something. At this point, it had to!

Michael leaned back and smiled at them, his eyes crinkling at the corners. "It sure was a nice surprise to see you both today. Let's schedule another appointment for later in the week. By then we'll have the test results and I can go over them with you." He reached over and gave Alyssa a squeeze. "It's sure nice to give you a hug." He handed her some stickers and then turned his full attention toward Katherine. "Hey, not to change the subject but I was wondering if you could find the time to do something for me?"

"Well, that depends…"

He continued, watching Katherine's face carefully. "I have a little patient whose Dad recently passed away. His mother just can't get back on her feet, and I thought you might be able to give her a call to give her some encouragement."

Katherine did not respond. Sensing her hesitation he went on hurriedly, "I could set it up on both ends, if you like. I just think you could give her a little bit of hope. Perhaps, seeing how successful you've become..."

"I wouldn't exactly call myself successful," Katherine cut him short. There was an edge to her voice, and Michael did not know how to interpret it.

"Why sure you are. Look at what you've lived through and how strong you are. If I had a little girl I would want her to grow up to be just like you."

Katherine's features softened a little. "That's very sweet of you, but I don't think I'm the right person for the job right now."

"Could you at least think about it?" he implored.

Katherine stood up flustered. "Sure, I'll think about it, but with all the good solid Christian counselors out there..." she trailed off. She was irritated now. She had come here for help, not to be told her daughter had anxiety, and that she needed to start a counseling service. She took Alyssa's hand and turned to say goodbye. Michael was looking at her puzzled. Instead of shaking her hand, he gave her a quick hug. "I'll call you this evening to check on Alyssa, OK?"

Driving away, Katherine couldn't contain her mounting apprehension. How could she tell him that she went to great lengths to avoid people such as herself? She barely even watched the news. It seemed like any one else's sadness was too much for her, and could somehow upset the equilibrium she so carefully maintained. She knew it would sound selfish to Michael. In fact, she knew it *was* selfish. One day she would be stronger and able to help others, but for now, she wasn't and couldn't.

Chapter 9

Alyssa fell asleep on the way home, and Katherine managed to get her into bed without waking her. She set the coffee pot brewing with her preferred flavored decaf, and after slipping into some comfortable clothes, sat down in her favorite chair—a rocker she had inherited from her mother. Stretching her feet out to the ottoman in front of her, she reached for her Bible, and grateful for the peace and quiet, turned to Genesis. She had restarted a 'read-through-the-Bible-in-a-year' program, and was now reading the story of Joseph. The program required that one read four full pages of scripture per day, but before Katherine had even finished one page, a verse stopped her. It was Genesis 42:21, "*We are verily guilty concerning our brother, in that we saw the anguish of his soul, when he besought us, and we would not hear.*" She knew it was no accident that she had read that verse. It was as if God was telling her that was exactly what she was doing—avoiding reaching out to help others. She knew the anguish of another's soul, but would not help them.

Katherine looked out the window, watching the palms sway against the Florida sky. A row of White Ibis were visible near the community lake, inserting their slender beaks into the grass with precision and finesse, snatching morsels of food buried beneath the surface. Their lives seemed so simple and straightforward next to hers.

But Lord, she argued, *as soon as I start talking about Leyton's death it sends me into a tailspin. I finally feel I have some equilibrium. Please don't ask me to do this.*

For the rest of the day, though, the verse stayed with her. In addition, other verses kept coming to her, counteracting her crumbling arguments, verses like II Corinthians 1:4, "*Who comforteth us in all our tribulation, that we may be able to comfort them which are in any trouble, by the comfort wherewith we ourselves are comforted of God.*" Then there was also Isaiah 58:10, "*And if thou draw out thy soul to the hungry, and satisfy the afflicted soul; then shall thy light rise in obscurity, and thy darkness be as the noon day.*"

Her darkness would *"be as the noon day"*? That was like saying it could be midday in her soul! What a contrast to how she really felt. With that uplifting promise, she knew what she needed to do, and indeed, would do.

That evening, sitting on the back patio, working on make-up work with Alyssa, she called Michael.

"If you set it up, I'll do it," she said without preamble.

"Great!" His relief was unmistakable. They talked awhile longer and then said goodbye. Michael hung up the phone grateful that she had said yes. He knew that it would benefit her greatly. Reaching out and helping others had aided him immensely in the dark days following Morgan's death. Praying silently for her, he turned back toward the hastily thrown-together burgers he was grilling for the boys.

Chapter 10

A FEW DAYS later Katherine found herself back in Michael's office with both the girls in tow. After chatting briefly with Amber and Alyssa about when they could see Jack and Simon again, Michael sent the girls into the well-child waiting room to play under the watchful eye of the receptionist while he talked to Katherine. He knew she wasn't going to like his explanation and didn't want the girls in ear shot.

The tests had shown that nothing was wrong. All Alyssa's lab values were within normal limits, and aside from a slight anemia, which was common in children and easily remedied, there was nothing to suggest that anything was truly the matter.

"I know I've said this before, but I really think she's just a sensitive little girl who lets things affect her. She went back to school, her Mommy is busy as can be, there are no more long days at the beach, and the change has been too much for her. This causes her to get worried and feel stressed and her stomach starts to hurt. Then she throws up, and this gives her a headache and so it goes." He paused, hoping Katherine would accept his perfectly plausible explanation. "Maybe we could refer her to a child counselor..." he added when no reply was forthcoming.

Katherine took a deep breath, shaking her head, "Michael," she said carefully, "I find it difficult to accept that nothing is truly wrong with Alyssa."

Michael looked slightly affronted as he responded. "Katherine, I've done a standard complete blood count and chemistry panel. The *only* thing we found was a slightly below normal red blood cell count. Give her an iron-containing children's chewable multi-vitamin and that will take care of it. Beyond that, I just don't think there is anything seriously wrong with her. Children throw-up. They eat junk, run around on full stomachs, get worried or scared, and then they throw up. It's part of childhood."

Katherine could feel her frustration beginning to build. "But Michael, this was happening while we were on summer vacation! Surely she had less to be worried or scared about than usual. Wouldn't this have occurred less in the summer if that was the reason?"

"But it did occur less in the summer, I remember you telling me that the last few weeks of summer vacation she hadn't had one episode," he countered.

"Yes I did, but that was *after* I put her on the sucrose-free diet. It worked for a good six weeks."

"Until she went back to school..."

"But it was happening a lot before I tried the sugar-free diet." Katherine could see he wasn't really listening, so she raised her voice. "Please hear me out! Alyssa had numerous episodes, I cut sugar out of her diet, and it worked for awhile, and then two weeks ago it stopped working. To me that's an indication that something is wrong with her stomach, not her mind!" Katherine was fully aggravated.

"I don't know," he answered, disliking the challenge, "I'm sure if something was physically wrong, it would have shown up in her lab work. Even the stool samples show nothing. As far as I can tell, I've done the broadest spectrum of tests that I know to do. Saying that your child is stressed and may need to see a counselor is not a bad thing. Her father *did* die. Of all things, that would be enough to make her feel insecure and—"

"She never really knew her father! If we were talking about Amber, I would buy that, but not Alyssa. The way our life is now is what she's always known." Katherine's frustration and aggravation were now full-blown anger. How dare he blame her daughter's health on her husband's death?

"I'm sorry, Katherine," he countered briskly, "her height and weight are normal. She's otherwise healthy and—"

"—and spends many days sleeping off a throw-up session and sore head. That's not normal to me!" Her loud voice seemed to echo in the space between them. She breathed in, and slowly out, forcing herself to calm down and speak more softly. "If you don't think something is wrong could you at least refer us to a pediatric gastroenterologist?" Katherine was fighting tears. She hated herself for that, it made her seem irrational. If she couldn't keep herself in check, he would be blaming Alyssa's illness on her emotional mother.

"No," he said quietly and then thought for a second. "No," he said again, this time more emphatically. "If I referred every child who threw up to a specialist, I would be the laughing stock of my profession. There is just not enough reason to do so." He glanced at his watch as his nurse knocked once and poked her head around the door and whispered something to him. He nodded and turned towards Katherine abruptly, "Listen, I have to go. Why don't you reschedule Alyssa for a follow-up in six weeks?" With that, he turned and walked out of the room.

Katherine sat dumbfounded. Was this the same man they had played "fort" with on the beach? The one who had carried Alyssa to the car after the first time she was ill this summer? Had they really gone out and spent countless hours enjoying one another and each others children? Had she really helped him find a house? And to think she had even briefly entertained the idea of living in that house! He was more concerned about his *reputation* than her daughter's health! She was only asking for a referral. A referral!! Now what was she going to do? She wiped angrily at her tears, relieved that Alyssa and Amber were not in the room with her. She sat there, trying to gain composure so she could walk out the door with her head held high. She managed to collect the girls, thank the receptionist, get to her car, drive home, walk into her house, and put an extra long DVD in the player for the girls. Then, she walked quietly into her bathroom, locked the door, turned on the water for noise, and sat down on the cold tile and sobbed. She had not felt this lonely and abandoned since the first year after Leyton's death. All the helplessness and disbelief seemed to assault her from every angle, until the emotional pain became a deep aching physical pain that rivaled that of the days following Leyton's death.

When her tears were eventually spent, she got up, washed her face, and told herself angrily that it was her fault for letting her guard down with a nice man. If she hadn't, she wouldn't have taken everything so personally today. She would simply shrug it off and go find another doctor. That thought stopped her in her tracks. Yes, that is what she would do: shrug it off and go and find Alyssa another doctor! Better, yet, she would find a gastroenterologist that would see them without a referral. If they thought she was crazy, then so be it. She had nothing to prove to anyone. Besides, she certainly wasn't about to let herself get close to a man again. This was exactly what she got for breaking all her own rules and she vowed it would never happen again.

As the days went by, Katherine did her best to put Michael out of her mind. He hadn't called, and since the children were so busy with school and after school activities, they hadn't asked to get together. Besides, Amber and Jack were in the same grade and saw each other regularly.

Chapter 10

Katherine, it seemed, was spending all the time she could find on the phone to gastroenterologists ranging from Vero Beach all the way to Miami. They either insisted on a referral, were not taking new patients, or had no openings for at least two months. She called Alyssa's original pediatrician and begged them to give her a referral. They wanted her to bring Alyssa in for more tests and Katherine didn't feel like telling them that she had just done that at a different office. She was fearful her insurance would question paying for two separate but similar batteries of tests. Finally, out of desperation, she called the original pediatric gastroenterologist that she had started with. She was met with the same cool, clipped responses to her questions that she had received before. This time, however, she wasn't going to give up.

"If I can't make an appointment, I would like to leave a message for the doctor then," Katherine told the receptionist firmly. A few days of dealing with receptionists had perfected her tone.

"Do you *know* him?" The woman's sarcasm was palpable.

"Why?" Katherine responded, matching sarcasm with sarcasm.

"We just don't take personal messages for the doctor unless you actually know him."

"Well, why not take my message and let him see if he knows me?" Katherine could be catty if she needed to be.

"No, I can't do that."

Katherine thought a while and then tried a new tactic. "May I have your name please?"

"Excuse me?"

"Your name."

"It's Sandra."

"OK Sandra, do you have children?"

"Ye—es. But I don't see how—"

"OK, imagine one of your children was very sick and nobody wanted to help you. Wouldn't you do everything in your power to find someone who could help you?"

"I really need to go...."

"No!" Katherine shouted, "I'm almost done! Just put yourself in my place and then think how nice it would be if just *one* person used some logic and did something as simple for you as leaving a message for a doctor. Now you can do that for me, so why *won't* you?"

"I..." Finally completely irritated herself she said, "Fine! And when the doctor gets angry at me for not following protocol, I'll tell him to yell at *you*. What's your message?"

Katherine was so stumped by her sudden agreement that it took her awhile to readjust her thoughts.

"OK, my name is Katherine Douglas. My daughter Alyssa is five. She throws up every other day, and everybody says there is nothing wrong with her. I want her to see a specialist, but nobody will give me a referral. My cell number is 292-6324. I'm asking the doctor if he will see us without a referral."

She could hear Sandra hastily scrawling on the other end.

"OK, I've written your message. Now if he doesn't call you back, don't blame me." And Katherine heard a click on the other end of the line.

Katherine was trembling as she put down the phone. What was wrong with modern medicine? It seemed as science advanced, people skills and the desire to help declined. Now she would just hope the doctor would call her back.

As the days went by, and the doctor never called her, Katherine found herself praying constantly for wisdom as to what to try next.

The answer came that weekend out of rather unpleasant circumstances. Amber and Alyssa had been at a birthday party all afternoon, and Katherine had been enjoying the free time to get caught up at home. She had just sat down in front of the computer to continue researching Alyssa's symptoms when the telephone rang. It was her friend telling her that Alyssa was sick and probably needed to go home. When Katherine arrived, Alyssa was in the bathroom hovered over the toilet. Another parent was in there with her. She turned out to be a nurse, and after giving Katherine the play by play of the last hour added, "If this were my child I would probably take her to an urgent care."

"Do you think so? I just had her at the doctor this week, and they said nothing was wrong with her."

"Just tell them you're afraid that she's dehydrating. The amount of fluid she's lost in the last hour is definitely a cause for concern. Plus, there's more." The woman, who said her name was Janet, gently plied the sobbing Alyssa away from Katherine's arms. "See here, she probed gently at Alyssa's neck. Her glands are swollen, and look at her stomach." She lifted Alyssa's shirt and pushed gently on her abdomen. "Her stomach is definitely swollen. It's hard to tell in children because they often have round bellies, but you can see how hers is blown up almost like a balloon."

Katherine shook her head in dismay. "I must look like a horrible mother to you! I've spent the last three days trying to get her into a pediatric gastroenterologist, but to no avail."

Janet nodded in understanding. "Yes, we're few and far between."

"Did you say 'we'?"

She nodded her head, "I'm a nurse at Dr. Cantrell's office—he's a gastroenterologist. I think I can figure out a way to get you guys in sometime next week."

"You *could*?" Katherine was incredulous. "So, we could forgo visiting an urgent care?"

"Yes, provided you can get her to keep fluids down over the next few hours. I'll give you my number, and if you can't hydrate her, call me, and we'll go from there."

"Thank you!" Katherine replied in disbelief. "You're the answer to my prayers. Thank you, thank you!"

Janet straightened up, and patted Alyssa's head that was once again buried against her mother. She washed her hands and kept talking, assuring them both that children and sore tummies were their specialty, and that she was sure the doctor would be able to find something.

She purposefully did not elaborate, wanting her doctor to see Alyssa first, but she secretly suspected she knew what was wrong.

Katherine got the now sleeping Alyssa home, leaving Amber at the party to get a ride with one of her friend's parents. She still couldn't believe the sudden and definite answer to her prayer. *Thank you, Lord. You had a solution all along.*

Sunday morning Katherine decided to keep Alyssa at home. It was already past nine o'clock, and she was still asleep. She had managed to get her to take some fluids the night before and had checked on her multiple times to make sure she continued to sleep peacefully. Amber had gone home with a friend after the birthday party, so Katherine, feeling relieved that she had an excuse to avoid Michael at church that day, was happy to stay home. She and Michael had not talked since the encounter at his office earlier that week, and she wasn't sure how she would respond to him when she finally did see him.

Michael, for his part, was surprised when he realized Katherine was not at church that Sunday morning. He kept trying to look around, wondering if she had perhaps chosen to sit somewhere else, but never saw her. Finally he gave up, vowing he would call her when he got home. He had been lonely that week, and also regretful that he had been so harsh. Yet, he felt like he had made the right decision in both the diagnosis and his refusal to give her a referral. On that point he wouldn't back down. He did feel he owed her an apology, just as long as she knew that he wasn't apologizing because he thought he was wrong, he was apologizing for being so abrupt. He managed to get out of church without talking to very many people. He didn't feel like fielding any questions regarding Katherine's whereabouts, which would be followed by the inevitable raised eyebrows when he admitted ignorance.

Breathing a sigh of relief, he got himself and the boys into the car and headed home. The boys didn't waste any time before they began badgering him about finding out where Amber and Alyssa were.

"I'll call them later and find out," he said carefully.

"Call them now, Dad!" Jack insisted.

"Yeah, we haven't seen them forever!" Simon chimed in.

"Well, you see them at school don't you?"

"I only get to sometimes, in the lunchroom or maybe on the playground if we play before lunch instead of after lunch," Simon whined.

"Call them now, Dad!" Jack repeated.

Michael sighed. What difference would it make if he called from the car? Katherine was probably still angry with him. He dialed their number and managed a somewhat strained, "We missed you this morning," after Katherine answered the phone.

"Amber was at a friend's so we decided to play hooky," Katherine said cautiously. She wasn't in the mood to tell him how sick Alyssa had been the night before. To her, a lame excuse was better than hearing him minimize Alyssa's symptoms again.

Michael wanted to respond that he knew her well enough to know she wouldn't miss church simply on a whim. Surely she hadn't missed because of him?

"Oh, well, the boys were begging me to call and find out if you were all OK," he continued awkwardly.

"We're fine. Tell them hello and that we'll see them at school tomorrow," she answered in a tone that showed the conversation was over.

"Katherine, wait!"

"Yes?" Her voice was cool and distant.

"I'm sorry for being so harsh the other day." Michael turned to see Jack listening. Great, now he was going to be given the third degree from his son.

There was silence on the other end of the phone. Now what should he say? "I mean, I meant what I said, and I stand by that, but I could have said it less harshly, and for that, I'm sorry."

"Oh," the response was still cool and distant.

Michael waited. Was that all she could say in response to his apology? He decided to attack the question head on. "So why did you really miss church today?"

"I really don't want to get into it."

"Is Alyssa sick again?"

"Maybe…"

"And you won't tell me about it?"

"There's no point."

Michael sighed; this was going nowhere. Besides, he should not have called while Jack could listen in.

"Well, the boys want to see Amber and Alyssa, so I hope you'll call sometime so that they can all get together."

"We'll see."

"Come on, Katherine. Let's not punish our children because we disagree about one thing." He could feel the anger creeping into his voice.

"The health of my child is more than just 'one thing' to me."

"OK, OK. You're right. For a parent it's huge. Just please call us when Amber is home and Alyssa's better so that our children can play."

"Alright," she answered distantly. "Goodbye."

The click on the other end of the line felt like a punch in the jaw. Michael rubbed his hand through his hair and grimaced.

Chapter 10

"Dad, why were you mean to Amber's mom, and why—?" Jack obviously wasn't going to waste any time.

"Not now, Jack. I'll explain to you later." Seeing a Wendy's ahead, he pulled into the drive thru, promising himself that when he got home he would let them watch the longest DVD they owned. He needed some time to himself in order to collect his scrambled thoughts.

Chapter 11

KATHERINE WAS THRILLED. True to Janet's word, they had gotten an appointment to see the pediatric gastroenterologist that week. It was Wednesday morning, and she was once again missing school, but she was so relieved to have an appointment for Alyssa that she didn't go through her usual mind games about how far behind her students would get and the chaos that would greet her on the day that she got back to her classes.

Janet was the nurse that escorted them back to an examination room and took Alyssa's vitals and weight. Katherine was surprised to see that Alyssa had actually lost weight since the visit to Michael's office just two weeks before. All her clothes were too tight in the waist. How had she lost weight? She mentioned this to Janet who reminded her that a swollen stomach did not necessarily mean weight gain.

When the doctor finally rushed into the room, he briskly introduced himself and then began with a barrage of questions. Katherine, surprised at his abruptness, tried to match his questions with short concise answers.

"How would you describe her appetite?"

"She gets hungry, but seems to fill up so fast. Sometimes she barely eats more than three bites off her plate and then complains that she's full." Dr. Cantrell nodded vigorously, as his pen scratched loudly across the page he was taking notes on. He was tall and awkward, a middle-aged man who had seemingly never grown accustomed to his own height.

"Dental cavities?"

"Yes," Katherine answered surprised. She wished he would sit down; her neck was getting sore from looking up at him.

"Swollen stomach?"

"Your nurse said so…Yes."

"Headaches?"

"Numerous."

"Dairy intolerance?"

"Yes, only just recently."

"When are her worst episodes?"

"After birthday parties, I tried her on a sugar-free diet because of that and it seemed to work for a few weeks…at least the throwing up stopped."

"Hmmm." He actually paused, and sat down, as if this case warranted such a luxury. "What about diarrhea?"

"Never, just the opposite, she's been constipated her whole life."

He cocked his head again quizzically, "Hmmm." He thought a while and then asked Alyssa to sit up on the table so he could examine her.

"Do you know if her glands are always swollen like this?" he said, probing the sides of her neck.

"No, I don't." Why hadn't Michael noticed Alyssa's swollen glands? Katherine started to make an excuse for herself, but then realized that it was probably unnecessary. She wasn't on trial, she was helping a doctor get an exact picture of Alyssa's symptoms.

Chapter 11

Dr. Cantrell probed Alyssa's now obviously distended stomach and kept peppering Katherine with questions.

Finally, he told Alyssa she could get down and then sat down himself. "Have you ever heard of celiac disease?"

"No-o?" Katherine's mind immediately filled with questions, but she kept herself in check.

"Celiac disease is a condition whereby the body is unable to tolerate foods that contain gluten. Gluten is a protein in wheat, barley, rye, and possibly oats. Instead of recognizing that protein as food, the body treats it as a foreign invader and mounts an attack against it, causing an inflammatory response in the gut. Over time the intestinal villi get worn down from all the inflammation, and the body loses digestive enzymes and thus the ability to effectively digest food. At the tip of the villi is the enzyme that digests table sugar, which is the first enzyme to be lost. That would explain why Alyssa can't tolerate sugar right now."

Katherine sat there dazed, she had no science background and words like 'villi', 'gluten', 'enzyme', and 'inflammatory' were leaving her lost.

"So you are saying she's allergic to wheat and…"

"No, not allergic, her body is intolerant to it. However, before we waste any more time talking about this disease, I'm going to order some blood work that will let me know if I'm headed in the right direction, OK? For now, do *not* change her diet, because if it is celiac disease we need to have her consuming gluten for the tests to be positive."

Before Katherine could respond, he jumped up – as if in response to an internal alarm clock – and shook her hand. Telling her the nurse would be in shortly, he disappeared with the door slamming behind him.

Katherine, feeling like she had just dodged hundreds of golf balls thrown her direction managed only to nod mutely.

After another lengthy wait, Janet came in with a lab sheet and instructions on where to go next.

"Could you please explain to me what the lab sheet says?" Katherine asked, desperate for some understanding.

"Let's see," Janet smiled, "ahh, the celiac antibody panel. These are a set of antibodies that the body produces in response to gluten-containing foods. If Alyssa has celiac disease, one or more of them will come back with a high value, indicating that her body is truly fighting the gluten that she eats." Then seeing Katherine's confused face, she smiled more widely and patted her arm. "You know, I wouldn't even try to understand all of this until we get the test results. Why waste your precious time learning about something that Alyssa may not have? If the tests do come back with a high positive, though, then we'll be ready to answer questions and give you the resources you need. We even have a nutritionist here on staff that will be able to get you started on the diet Alyssa would have to follow."

"How long would she have to follow it?"

Janet looked directly at her, knowing that Katherine would flinch at her answer: "For the rest of her life."

That wasn't a golf ball, Katherine thought, her heart sinking, *it was a bomb exploding in my face.*

She drove towards the lab, her mind in a whirl. On the one hand, she felt relieved that the doctor wasn't blaming emotional distress as the root cause of Alyssa's symptoms. On the other hand, she was petrified that this celiac disease was going to be a monster to learn about. It was a paradox—she wanted a diagnosis, but not a bad one!

"Mommy?"

"Yes honey?"

"I don't like that doctor, I want to go and see Dr. Michael again."

"Well this doctor knows all about children's tummies, and he might be able to make yours feel better."

Chapter 11

"So let's tell Dr. Michael to do that."

Katherine sighed. "We're going to use this doctor for awhile because he's an expert about tummies. Now he wants us to go to a lab, and they're going to find out if something in your blood will tell them what's wrong with you."

In response to that Alyssa began to cry. "I don't want them to wrap that thing around my arm again. That other nurse made it so tight for so long—"

—*you didn't even feel the stick,* Katherine completed mentally. "Well, when we get there Mommy will pray with you, and we'll ask God that they won't need to take as long this time, OK?"

"OK," came the resigned response.

"Then, after we leave there, you and I are going to go straight to the toy store. You have been so brave and Amber has been so patient that we're going to pick out a special new toy for both of you. So, what I want you to do is think really hard what you would like and also what would be a great surprise for Amber too. Do you think you can do that?"

"Oh sure! I know all about what Amber's favorite toys are, and plus since she's my sister I can figure out really fast what she would like to play with."

"Good! It will be so much fun when we get home, and you have a new toy, and Amber has a new toy too. She loves surprises, doesn't she?"

"Yes! And I do too. Maybe I need to get more train tracks, or that dolly that cries when you do the wrong thing to it, or those Lego blocks that you can make into cars, or a dress-up set, or maybe, if it's not too much money, we can just buy one of those Barbie Jeeps...."

And so it continued as they walked into the lab and waited their turn. Katherine prayed silently for a good nurse and was relieved when she noticed that the nurse that had called them back seemed friendly and efficient. She kept Alyssa in a steady conversation about the best toys at Toys R Us and nodded in understanding when Katherine whispered to her that Alyssa was unaware that a "stick" was involved. Katherine, feigning calm despite the perspiration sticking to her shirt, sat Alyssa on her lap and told her to look out the window at the storm clouds while the nurse put the 'tight thing' on Alyssa's arm and then the toy discussion continued. The nurse finished, winked at Katherine and then gave Alyssa a sticker for sitting so still. Alyssa turned around wide eyed at the vials of blood in a stand on the counter top.

"Is that my blood?" she asked incredulously.

"It sure is!" the nurse answered cheerfully.

"Did you take all of it?"

"Oh no! You have much much more left in your body, I just took enough for the tests the doctor needs us to do."

"Oh," came the uncertain reply.

Katherine thanked the nurse and then ushered Alyssa out of the cubicle, breathing a prayer of thanks as they set off for the toy store.

Chapter 12

IT WAS LATE Friday afternoon when Dr. Cantrell called with the results from Alyssa's blood work. He asked Katherine to sit down with a pen and paper so she could write down what he had to say.

"We tested the levels of three antibodies, EMA, IgA, and IgG. Now, write those three down for me, OK?" He paused and Katherine thought how nice it was that he wasn't going at ninety miles an hour like he had at his office the previous Monday. Maybe Alyssa's case now ranked high enough in his mind for him to take his time.

"High levels of EMA, IgA, and IgG are a pretty solid indication that a person has celiac disease," he continued. "Alyssa had high levels for two of them—EMA and IgG. Her IgA level was relatively low, but the problem is that IgA is sometimes low, even when a person has celiac disease, if that person is IgA deficient. Therefore, I need to do a total serum IgA level and if that also comes out low, it would mean she is indeed IgA deficient." He paused, "are you following me?"

"I think so," Katherine answered slowly. "Are you saying that then the 'E' and 'G' antibody would be enough evidence to say she had celiac disease?"

"Well, we could then be 99 percent certain."

"Isn't that enough?"

"Not really. If the next test shows Alyssa is indeed IgA deficient we can proceed along our celiac disease pathway. If she is not IgA deficient then we will start testing her for other diseases."

"Like what?" Katherine managed.

"Oh, diseases that involve high gut permeability....but we don't have to think about that yet, not until this next test comes back."

"And if the 'A' ser...sera..."

"...serum antibody..."

"And if *that* is low then you will say she has celiac disease?

"No, we'll—"

"But you said we would be 99 percent certain!"

"I know, but there's no need to put her on a highly specific diet for life before we're 100 percent sure that she actually has the disease. The next step would be to decide whether an intestinal biopsy is necessary."

"A *biopsy*? I thought they did biopsies for people with cancer!"

"No, a biopsy can be done for more reasons than just cancer. In my practice, I like to couple a patient's antibody results with biopsy results before I give a definitive diagnosis...But don't even think about that right now, let's just get the next test done. We need to take this one step at a time to avoid jumping to conclusions too early. I'll call in the lab order for you. Just make sure, for now, that you keep her on a regular diet, even if some foods she eats seem to make her sick."

With that, he hung up. Katherine sat still looking down at her paper. She had written down 'EMA', 'A', and 'G' and had

Chapter 12

circled the 'A' and had written 'low' beneath that with a big question mark. She would have loved to call Michael to have him clarify what she had just heard but since they hadn't spoken since that brief and uncomfortable phone call that Sunday, she knew it was an unwise idea. She stood up and rubbed the back of her neck. It was Friday afternoon, the next blood test would have to wait until Monday after school and there were mountains of work piled up around her house all clamoring for her attention. What should it be, she thought wearily, the laundry, the test papers, the dirty dishes or—

"Mommy, Mommy! Jack is here, Jack is here!" Amber came screaming into the kitchen. Alyssa was not far behind cheering along, "Open the door! Open the door!" Before Katherine could blink, all four children were laughing and hugging excitedly in the entryway. Katherine couldn't help smiling at Michael as he walked belatedly up to the front door. He shrugged helplessly and smiled back.

"They held me at gun point and ordered me to stop."

Katherine forced a laugh, "Well, it looks like it was a worthwhile stop, come on in."

"Can we go over to the park, Mommy?" begged Amber.

"Yeah, let's go to the park!" chimed in Alyssa.

"Put your shoes on and don't forget your hats."

"But we're on our way to eat!" protested Michael.

"I'm not hungry anymore." stated Simon.

"Please say we can go to the park," pleaded Jack.

"OK, but set your watch timer for thirty minutes and come back when it rings," Michael relented.

"Oh, sure Dad...I'll do it right now."

Jack stopped importantly to set his watch while the other children looked on impressed.

"Done!" he exclaimed. "Let's go, everybody!"

"Stay on the sidewalk!"

"Hold Alyssa's hand, Amber!"

And then, silence. Katherine looked at Michael, bemused. "I'm in charge here, really I am!" she managed wryly.

Michael laughed in response, and then they got quiet. An uncomfortable air settled over them as they both remembered their argument and the lack of resolution.

"How are you?" Michael said, noting how worn out Katherine looked.

"I'm fine," she answered with forced cheerfulness. She didn't want any sympathy from him right now, because she knew that if he gave her any, she would probably become an emotional wreck. Just seeing him had made her want to step into his arms and tell him that she had missed him terribly. "Here, I'll get you something to drink, and we can sit and relax while they're gone," she said, exiting hurriedly.

Michael sat down and noticing Katherine's hastily scrawled notes, picked them up and tried to make sense of it. "What's this?" he asked, trying to be casual as Katherine came in with their drinks.

"Oh, I just got off the phone with the doctor we saw this week." Katherine attempted nonchalance.

"Oh yeah? Who did you see?"

"Dr. Cantrell."

Michael thought for a while, trying to place the name and then realizing that it rang a bell because he was the only pediatric gastroenterologist in town, he responded. "Oh, so your usual pediatrician referred you?"

"No."

"He just saw you without a referral?"

"Basically."

And what did you have to say to get an appointment without a referral, Michael thought, *that your current pediatricians were quacks who didn't care a whit about your daughter?*

"I met his nurse at a birthday party last week and she got us in," Katherine decided to clarify.

"Oh, well that worked out then. So, it looks like he did some antibody tests. What's this here?" Michael asked pointing to where Katherine had written 'EMA'.

"To be honest I don't know, other than it's elevated, I haven't had time to process it all or even to look up what everything means."

"Oh. So what is he testing for?"

"Something called celiac disease." Katherine, avoiding eye contact, looked out the window toward the park where she could see the children playing.

Michael thought for awhile. "That's pretty rare." He didn't like how he felt. Not only had she rejected his diagnosis, she had managed to find a doctor who had actually found something definitive.

Katherine shrugged. "He says that Alyssa tests positive for two of the three antibodies involved in celiac disease and that the other one, the 'A' may be showing low since some people don't make enough of it anyway."

Michael, listening to her rendition of what the doctor had probably said, tried not to smirk. He knew he was acting in the way he had warned his boys against – 'don't make fun of someone simply out of the need to feel better about yourself.' Yet, here he was doing the same thing.

"Don't laugh at me," Katherine said self-protectively, "I'm new at all of this jargon, and I haven't had time to learn more about it yet."

"I'm not laughing, Katherine. I just hope you know or that he explains to you that positive antibody tests can mean more than one thing." There! Now at least he sounded reasonable.

"He just said that exact thing to me," she jumped in defensively.

"For instance, have you ever heard of—"

"Michael," she cut him off, "he seems very methodical. He hasn't concluded anything yet. We're going next week to test for the 'A' antibody again, I think he said it was to check for total 'A' levels or something."

"Total serum antibody?"

"Yes, that's it! Then, if that's also low the next step will probably be a biopsy."

"A *biopsy*?" Reasonable or not, Michael couldn't hide his incredulity. "Why on earth would you put Alyssa through such a thing?"

Katherine stood up and shrugged. Tears were pricking the back of her eyes.

"Michael, I can't even begin to argue with you on a medical level. At least this doctor is actually viewing Alyssa's symptoms as if something is truly wrong."

"Well, good for him." Michael answered shortly, standing up. He hated how he sounded, but being put down was not something he handled well. "I need to go and get the boys...maybe I can hurry that thirty minutes up...we haven't had dinner yet. Have a good evening," he added as an after thought. And with that he was gone.

Katherine sat stunned for a moment. Staring at the empty space that Michael had occupied just a short few moments before, she felt as if she had just been kicked in the stomach. Why wouldn't he just listen to what Dr. Cantrell had said? Was he embarrassed that it looked as if his diagnosis regarding Alyssa was wrong? Or, did it hurt his pride that another doctor was actually making headway? Katherine sighed, she was no expert on the inner workings of a man, especially one so obviously brilliant. Maybe it was the high IQ that did it. Leyton had been a hands-on kind of guy. He used to joke with her that the higher the IQ a person had, the less nuts-and-bolts logic they possessed. Maybe he had been wrong. Maybe the higher the IQ, the greater the pride, and the harder it was to admit error.

Her thoughts turned to her girls. Now they were going to come in any minute, upset that Jack and Simon had left, and that made her feel even worse. She sighed and stood up. She had best go to the park with a fun dinner plan in mind in order to counteract the inevitable disappointment. It was unfair to expect them to be reasonable when the fault rested on her and Michael.

Arriving at the park, Katherine was surprised when the children seemed almost happy about their play time being cut short. They were whispering and winking at each other as Michael loaded the boys into the car. Katherine, grateful for their compliance, didn't give their strange behavior a second thought.

"Would you girls like to go out for dinner tonight?" Katherine asked after the boys left, still surprised that there had been no complaining.

"Ummm, how about Pizza Hut?" Amber suggested hopefully.

"What do you think, Alyssa?" Katherine said looking down at her youngest.

"Yes, yes!" she responded as both girls nudged each other and giggled conspiratorially.

"OK, then, Pizza Hut it is, and I'll race you both to the house," and with that Katherine took off while the girls scrambled after her.

Driving to the restaurant that night, Katherine kept replaying her conversation with Michael. Was she in the wrong in any way? Maybe she shouldn't have added that bit about at least one doctor was trying to help Alyssa. That had definitely been a jab. But what did he want her to do? Nothing? How could he be so bullheaded over Alyssa's condition?

Still deep in thought, she walked the girls into the restaurant only to realize that she and Michael had been had. There sat Jack, Simon, and Michael—Michael with a look of surprise and Jack and Simon high-fiving each other and saying, "It worked, it worked!"

The girls rushed over to join them, and Katherine dragged behind. She couldn't believe the girls had been so transparent, and she had failed to see through their scheme. She was surprised that Alyssa especially hadn't let on. *Fooled even by a 5-year-old*, she thought ruefully.

"Well, Michael," Katherine said quietly, "I apologize, it looks like we've fallen for their ploy."

"I should have known something was up when they seemed excited about leaving the park early. Of course you'll join us too? Your girls already have." His voice held a forced politeness as he indicated a place for her to sit.

Awkward, but compliant, she sat, her heart thudding with dismay. Quarrelling with someone she had feelings for was bad enough, but having to sit right across from him and feign normalcy after an argument was simply appalling.

The conversation among the children was so animated that the dead silence between Michael and Katherine wasn't quite as pronounced. Katherine, however, was extremely uncomfortable, and finally with an attempt at some sort of resolution looked over at him and said, "I'm sorry for what I said at the end before you left."

Michael shrugged. "I can understand why you said that. I just get irritated when doctors do test after unnecessary test and—" He paused, no sense in getting worked up all over again. "Never mind," he shrugged, "I'm sorry that on the matter of Alyssa's health we don't seem to agree."

And you should be sorry for being bullheaded and mean and unwilling to accept you might be wrong, Katherine wanted to say.

"I know it seems that I'm not willing to consider other angles," Michael continued, once again seeming to read her mind, "but I just—" He shrugged again. "Never mind, I don't want to argue. How about we declare a truce for the sake of the children and quit being mad with each other?"

Chapter 12

"Sure," Katherine shrugged taking his offered handshake, enjoying, in spite of the situation, the feel of his hand around hers. Then, that brief sense of pleasure quickly vanished as she realized all the fun had gone out of their relationship. It was as if they were on an acquaintance-only level now. He obviously wasn't going to ever admit that he might be wrong. Just another egotistical, narrow-minded—

"Watch out!" Jack yelled. Simon had knocked over his Coke and everyone was scrambling to get out of the way. Michael and Katherine jumped up for napkins, and the children started giggling uncontrollably.

"Yet another fine dining experience—" Michael began.

"—with serenity, ambiance, and relaxing conversation." Katherine continued.

"Pizza Hut, the place to be." Michael completed. They looked at each other, and managed weak smiles.

That's what makes this so difficult, Katherine lamented. *We are on the same wavelength on so many things, we even have a similar sense of humor, yet now we have this huge Alyssa disagreement between us. I wouldn't mind so much if he wasn't so adamant that he's the one who is right and that I'm the idiot.*

Soon the pizza arrived, and everyone began to eat. Katherine found herself tensing up, waiting for the inevitable from Alyssa. Lately it seemed that within just a few minutes of eating she would stop, double over, and start crying that her stomach hurt. She looked over anxiously at her daughter and noted that she had only taken a few bites. Michael, taking it all in reached over and squeezed her hand. "Hey, are you going to eat your food or not?"

"Maybe I'll just sit here and let you hold my hand," she lamely tried to quip back, looking anxiously over at Alyssa again who had stopped eating completely and was biting her lip to keep from crying.

Katherine moved over and pulled her onto her lap. "Come here, honey, it's OK."

"It already hurts, Mommy, and I thought I was so hungry this time!" came the muffled wail against Katherine's shoulder.

Katherine looked up at Michael, unsure what to do.

"If you need to take her home, I can drop Amber off later," he offered.

"OK, that's a good idea," she said, gathering up Alyssa.

She's getting so thin I can carry her easily now, Katherine thought sadly. She left, leaving their food behind. Her worry over Alyssa had affected her own appetite of late too.

Michael sat there with the remaining children who had grown quiet. He felt like a heel. The child was definitely in pain, and he had done nothing to truly help. He wiped his hand across his face and looked up at the three pairs of eyes waiting for him to say something.

"Hey, is it up to me to eat all of this pizza or not?" He forced himself to joke, grabbing at four pieces at once.

The children took the bait and finished the meal happily, spending the time trading stories about the so-called worst teachers at their school as Michael nodded and appeared to listen all the while picturing a sad, burdened mother carrying her sick little girl out into the darkness.

Chapter 13

ON MONDAY AFTER school, Katherine stopped by the lab for Alyssa's blood draw. The nurse, surprised to see them again, gave both girls lollipops to occupy their minds, and once again did a stellar job of keeping Alyssa distracted enough so that she never actually felt the needle. Amber, however, looked up in time to see it pierce her sister's skin, and watched wide-eyed as the vial filled with blood. For the rest of that day Alyssa was Amber's hero. She catered to her, told her she could sit in her coveted seat on the drive home, let her play with her own favorite toys, and kept asking her repeatedly if her arm hurt even the tiniest bit. Alyssa enjoyed all the attention from her older sister, and Katherine thanked God that once again things had gone well.

When the doctor called a few days later, he communicated that celiac disease was highly probable. The latest blood test had shown that Alyssa was indeed IgA deficient, which explained how her EMA and IgG could be elevated without the IgA being elevated. He went on to say that a biopsy would be the final step needed before he could make a definitive diagnosis.

"A biopsy?! Why can't we just treat her for celiac disease based on what we already know?" Katherine asked.

"You could. However, the treatment for celiac disease is a lifelong adherence to a very limited diet—no bread, no birthday cake, no doughnuts, no pizza, absolutely nothing with gluten! A biopsy can give us a certain diagnosis, which will give you and Alyssa the resolve necessary to fully implement the diet for life."

"What if we try the diet to see if she improves, and then decide to do the biopsy later?"

"Well, you could start the diet based on our probable diagnosis and skip the biopsy altogether. If Alyssa gets better and stays better, then we would all be happy. However, if a question arises later and we want to do the biopsy, we're going to have to make her ingest gluten once again for an indeterminate period of time in order for the biopsy to show anything. In other words, we'd have to make her sick again in order for the test to be meaningful."

"Oh, I see." Katherine's words hung in the air as the doctor allowed this new information to sink in.

Once again, he wasn't as rushed as he had been at their first appointment, but finally he cut back into her thoughts. "My advice is to do the biopsy, get a definitive diagnosis, and then you can have a clear cut plan. Why don't you think about it and call the office in the morning with your decision?"

"But how long will it take to schedule it? I mean, I would like to start this diet you are talking about tonight. Alyssa is just getting worse and worse. She barely eats three bites of a meal without doubling over in pain and—"

"I understand. Just call the office in the morning with your decision. If you decide to do the biopsy they will schedule the procedure as soon as possible."

Katherine's mind was in a whirl when she hung up the phone. What was the right thing to do? Without thinking of the ramifications, she dialed Michael's number. He could at least explain to her what a biopsy involved. He had seemed concerned the other night at the Pizza Hut, maybe he would be more understanding. Unfortunately that was not the case.

Michael was incredulous. "You would really put your daughter through a surgical procedure in order to decide if she needs a special *diet*? Just try the diet, if Alyssa gets better then you have your answer."

"But Michael, you said yourself that a positive antibody test can mean more than one thing. Dr. Cantrell says that if the biopsy is positive, it would rule out a host of other illnesses and—"

"Then do the biopsy, Katherine. Why are you calling me if you already know what you want to do?"

"I was just hoping for some clarification, that's all."

"Clarification that you were going too far, or clarification as to what the procedure entails?"

"Never mind, I'm sorry I bothered you." Her quiet voice wavered with emotion. "'Bye," and she slowly set down the phone.

To Katherine, it almost seemed, in regards to Alyssa's health, that Michael had a Jekyll and Hyde personality. She couldn't believe she had been dumb enough to call him and ask for more advice. That had to be the last time. She rubbed her temples, lost in thought, and then with resolve, decided to schedule the biopsy and let Dr. Cantrell guide her through the procedure. After all, he was the specialist.

The biopsy was scheduled as an outpatient procedure at a local surgery center. A nurse at the center answered all of Katherine's questions before the procedure. She said that Alyssa was to be anesthetized, and the doctor would insert a tube through her throat into the small intestine. The tube held a capsule with a tip containing a tiny knife which was used to take the tissue sample.

To Katherine, the most frightening aspect of the whole procedure was knowing that her daughter would be under anesthetic. She kept her fears to herself, and tried to remain upbeat and casual on the outside so that Alyssa would feel comfortable about everything. Despite her fears, Katherine was surprised at how relatively smoothly everything went. The most difficult part for her was being separated from her daughter during the brief procedure. When she was finally allowed to go to her in the recovery room, an immeasurable relief filled her. She couldn't imagine what parents went through when they had to sit and wait through lengthy, potentially life-threatening surgeries.

Alyssa woke up fairly easily, surprised by her surroundings and glad to see her mother.

Dr. Cantrell called them back a few days later with the results. Three out of four sections that he took showed flattened villi on Alyssa's intestinal wall.

"In addition," he continued, "there are indications of mucosal fissures and a reduction of duodenal folds. Her Marsh score, the way we place a number on the damage, is between a two or a three." Katherine wrote down the terms hurriedly.

"What this means," he went on, "is that we can now be 100 percent confident that she has celiac disease. The bad news is that the diet is life long and inconvenient. The good news is that she should make a full recovery and, provided she remains on a gluten-free diet, she will be a regular, healthy little girl in a surprisingly short period of time."

Katherine, doing her best to absorb it all, thanked the doctor profusely and hung up the phone, breathing a prayer of thanks for a certain diagnosis.

That evening, feeling vindicated, she decided to call Michael with the results.

"So you did have the biopsy after all," came the flat response.

"I just thought you would want to know, that's all," she ventured.

"Well, celiac disease is really rare. Alyssa certainly did not present with any of the classic symptoms and her growth is normal. Is the doctor sure he's correct?"

"All the tests indicate he is."

"Well, good for all of you. I know you are probably relieved to have an answer right now but when the euphoria wears off you are going to find yourself hating the diet she will have to follow."

Katherine did not know how to respond. She had called him out of courtesy, and was now anxious to get off of the phone.

"You have a good evening and we'll see you soon," she managed lamely and then hung up the phone when he replied with a stiff goodbye.

There. She had an answer, she'd informed Michael, and now it was time to get on with their lives.

Chapter 14

NOW THAT DR. Cantrell had a definitive diagnosis, he had the secretary schedule them to meet with his on-staff nutritionist. Alyssa was to start a gluten-free diet immediately, and the nutritionist could help Katherine get her started.

Grateful that they finally had a cause and relieved that all it seemed they had to do was follow a diet, Katherine waited blithely in the waiting room. Another woman was waiting across from her, and they struck up a conversation.

"What's wrong with your little girl?"

"Well, we've just found out that she has celiac disease, and we're here to learn about the diet."

"Ahhhh, I'm on a gluten-free diet for celiac disease myself."

"Oh, so you see Dr. Cantrell too? I thought he only saw pediatric patients."

"No, he has a specialty in pediatrics, but he sees adults too. Good thing for me, until I saw him I had been diagnosed with everything but the right thing."

"Like what?"

"Let's see…Ten years ago they told me I probably had AIDS. My white blood cell count was low so an AIDS test seemed to be the next logical step. That was when AIDS tests took two weeks to come back. The people at the lab double gloved and came at me like I was a leper. It was an awful experience, they just didn't know as much about the disease back then. Well, I didn't have AIDS, so the next thing my doctor did was to send me to a rheumatologist."

"But weren't you having stomach problems?"

"Unfortunately not exactly, otherwise I probably would not have wasted years being shuffled from doctor to doctor. Some people don't present with gastrointestinal problems at all, or their other symptoms are so severe that the minor indigestion and gas discomfort that they have dealt with all of their lives just seems inconsequential. That's how it was with me. I constantly had flu-like symptoms, aching joints, swollen glands, no energy, difficulty thinking. None of those symptoms clued me in that the root cause was my stomach.

"Anyway, they next sent me to a rheumatologist, who upon direct physical examination ordered a battery of tests saying that he wanted to test for lupus and multiple sclerosis or MS. I was having extreme sensitivity to sunlight too, and that's a hallmark symptom of lupus. I guess the MS possibility was related to the fact that the symptoms, although always there, would come and go in severity.

"All of the blood tests came back negative, so the doctor, finally exasperated, suggested I see a psychiatrist. He thought I might have a type of bipolar disorder, since sometimes I was energetic and other times I was sick and depressed. I refused to go, because although I knew I was depressed from being sick for so long, I felt like the depression was a result of the illness and not the reverse. Finally, at his limit, he told me I had 'a Chronic Fatigue Syndrome'. Those were his exact words. He told me to go home, rest, take vitamins, and not to get pregnant."

Chapter 14

"What did not getting pregnant have to do with it?" Katherine asked.

"I guess patients he knew who had gotten pregnant were often too sick to take care of their babies, and that complicated matters incredibly for them."

"So did you follow his advice?"

"Well, I didn't get pregnant; I hadn't gotten pregnant my entire marriage, so I didn't really think my body was capable of it anyway. But, I didn't accept the diagnosis of Chronic Fatigue Syndrome either. It seemed like half of the medical establishment didn't even believe that it existed, even though it has been defined by the Centers for Disease Control as a bona fide illness. I went from doctor to doctor, but upon even hearing the CFS diagnosis, many would suggest I go on an antidepressant. Thankfully I refused, because although I believe it would have helped my depression, I still did not believe that depression was my root problem. I knew I was depressed about being sick, but not that I was sick from being depressed. I was anxious to find out the root of the problem.

Anyway, I'm probably boring you...."

"No, not at all, I'm actually very interested," Katherine assured her.

"Anyway, one doctor suggested I take tranquilizers because I would shake when I got hungry. Another gave me migraine pills (that would knock the socks off me for forty-eight hours) to deal with the massive migraines I would get every time I waited more than a few minutes to eat after feeling hunger pangs. Needless to say, I would carry food around with me wherever I went to prevent *that* from happening. Then eventually the stomach pains started. That was my first clue that maybe everything was related to my stomach. I finally came here to see Dr. Cantrell and my blood test results and biopsy results were astounding. He said he didn't know how I was still walking around, much less able to work. Within a week of going on the gluten-free diet, my glands went down to normal. I had dealt with swollen glands for years! It felt so good to not have a tender throat. My migraines disappeared, my energy picked up, and I knew that we had found the root cause. I feel like I lost six years of my life, but I'm so grateful that I now am healthy again. I—"

"Alyssa Douglas?" It was Janet calling them back. Katherine got up and smiled apologetically at the woman who offered her phone number in case they needed advice with the diet. Thinking over what she had just heard, Katherine was grateful that Alyssa's symptoms had seemingly started with her stomach, and thus they had arrived at a diagnosis relatively quickly. Still, there had to be some way to get the word out about this disease, so that other parents wouldn't have to go through the rigmarole that she had experienced.

"I'm sure you just got an earful," Janet said smiling as she walked Katherine and Alyssa back.

"Yes, but it was interesting and enlightening as well," Katherine countered.

"I guess you missed the conspiracy theory part of her story though."

"The 'conspiracy theory'?"

"Yes, although I guess there's a measure of truth in everything. It's just that nutritionally managed diseases are not popular topics in med schools. So much of what is taught is funded by drug companies. I guarantee that if there was a drug for celiac disease, every doctor who came out of med school would know about it and test for it routinely. However, things are looking up for people with celiac disease. The advent of the blood test has definitely helped matters. Also, the media has picked up on it and run stories. I think Dr. Cantrell has a copy of the segment that the Today Show did back in August on the disease. Great Britain has been the leader, though. We are years behind them. If you went to Great Britain now, you could go into any standard grocery store and select from a large variety of gluten-free food."

After introducing them to the nutritionist, Ms. Baddock, Janet left. Unfortunately, 'Ms. Baddock' wasn't overly friendly and Katherine felt a little too intimidated by her manner to ask the dozens of questions that were filling her brain. She did, however, hand Katherine a book called *Kids With Celiac Disease* by Danna Korn.

"Everything you could possibly want to know is in here. The book is written especially for parents whose children have celiac disease, and the author writes from her own personal experience."

Katherine took the book, wondering how it would help her get that evening's meal on the table.

"I'll just give you an overview for now," Ms. Baddock went on. "Gluten is a protein and it's found in wheat, barley, and rye. Oats can also be a culprit sometimes, so to start with we have all of our patients eliminate oats too. Later on, we'll add them back and see how Alyssa does. For now, your best friend will be the health food store. Stop by on the way home and ask them to point you to their gluten-free section. You can buy pasta, bread mixes, cookie mixes, crackers….you name it, and for a price, they'll have it. That will get you started. Learning how to shop at a regular store is a challenge, but it is possible once you learn how to read labels. Plus, some regular stores do have a small gluten-free section of their own."

Katherine nodded.

"Here is a list of ingredients that will sabotage the gluten-free diet," continued Ms. Baddock, handing what looked like a mile-long grocery list to Katherine. "For instance, labels that say 'modified food starch' may or may not contain gluten. It depends if the food starch comes from wheat, oats, barley, or rye or not. Short of calling the company, there's no way of knowing. Sometimes even the company cannot say definitively what their source of starch is. Thankfully some companies are jumping on the gluten-free bandwagon and specifying what the source of their food starch is. Some labels now say 'modified food starch' and then have in parenthesis 'corn'. That would mean that the source of the ingredient is corn and since corn is allowed, Alyssa can eat this product."

Katherine continued to nod, knowing most of it wasn't sinking in. At least Ms. Baddock was handing her resources that Katherine could refer back to.

"How long will Alyssa have to stay on the diet?" Katherine asked.

"For life," came the brisk reply. Her manner was a carbon copy of Dr. Cantrell's. Maybe speediness was a prerequisite for all employees at his practice. Katherine wondered how Janet had managed to remain so calm and helpful.

"What if I mess up or if someone gives her something with gluten?"

"She'll get sick again."

"How long do you think it will take until she starts to feel better?"

"If you follow the diet 100 percent, you will notice a dramatic improvement within just a few days. Sometimes people see improvement even when the diet isn't completely followed, probably because the assault on the body has been dramatically decreased. As time goes on, though, it may seem like a diminishing return: the less gluten in the diet, the less gluten she can tolerate. Eventually you may notice that even the tiniest bit of gluten gives her symptoms. However, symptoms or not, ingesting gluten will damage her intestines. It will probably take a few months for her intestines to regenerate, but once they do, she should be able to consume gluten-free candy and baked goods without any problem." With that, Ms. Baddock looked at her watch and said, "I would suggest you go home and read the book, start on the diet, and write down any questions you might have. We'll schedule a follow-up visit for two weeks from now."

Katherine thanked her and stood up. Ms. Baddock definitely needed to soften up her presentation. As Katherine turned to leave, she gave the nutritionist a slight smile, however, Ms. Baddock had already returned to her paperwork. Katherine hoped Janet would be able to answer any future questions, because Katherine was worn out from having information thrown at her at the speed of light.

Stopping at the same health food store that she had visited weeks before when she had taken Alyssa off of sugar, she went straight to the counter and asked for help with their gluten-free items.

"I think we have to keep her sugar-free for awhile too. The doctor said she will probably have trouble digesting sugar until her intestines heal," Katherine said, sounding doubtful.

The sales person nodded, and showed her where the gluten-free pastas, crackers, and frozen breads were located. Katherine purchased a few of each item, balking at the total price. She would eventually have to learn how to play the game a little more frugally.

Driving home, she tried to explain everything to Alyssa, but after hearing no response, she turned and saw her asleep in her seat. Poor thing, she was in for a big change, but thank goodness they now finally had a game plan that would allow her to be healthy again.

Katherine spent the rest of the drive praying silently, thanking God for an answer and praying for wisdom and understanding as they faced this new challenge.

Chapter 15

KATHERINE NOW FELT that she was working three full-time jobs: teaching, single-motherhood, and keeping her daughter gluten-free. The thought of preparing a meal made her want to cringe. There were no more quick meals at the Wendy's drive-thru or stopping at Pizza Hut on a Friday evening. She supposed that eventually she would learn to be a bit more versatile, but for now, she was having trouble with only the basics of the food purchasing and preparation.

Just making the girls peanut butter and jelly sandwiches had become a major feat. The gluten-free bread she purchased seemed to crumble into nothing the minute she tried to spread something on it. She read that toasting it made it easier to use, so Alyssa had to get used to having her sandwiches toasted. Then, if she made Amber's sandwich on regular bread, she had to remember to avoid putting the knife that had been used on regular bread back into the peanut butter.

No more "double dipping" for us, she thought wryly. That first attempt at peanut butter and jelly sandwiches, she must have used all eight butter knives they possessed. She kept forgetting about the "double dipping" rule and kept having to get a new knife. When she was done, she had one crumbled mass of gluten-free bread, peanut butter, and jelly made for Alyssa, one regular sandwich made for Amber, and eight dirty knives laying in the sink with peanut butter and crumbs stuck to them. When she went to put the sandwiches into a container, out of habit, she put them in the same one only to realize too late that after all that effort, she had just "contaminated" Alyssa's sandwich. Alyssa would just have to eat the top half, Katherine was *not* going to start over!

Then there were the prices. Her grocery budget was no longer in existence. Buying loaves of bread that cost $5.00 and four-serving boxes of pasta for $2.50 didn't fit into her usual spending plan. She gave up trying to save money on the groceries, thinking that she would just have to forget about the prices while she learned the basics.

What made it all easier, though, was watching Alyssa's health improve. She was gaining weight, her energy level had picked up dramatically, and she hadn't vomited or complained of a headache for days. It was a miracle! Even her school work had improved. Her kindergarten teacher was sending home beautiful handwriting samples, and art work that were now proudly displayed all over the house. Katherine wanted to shout it to the world!

A few Saturdays into the diet, Katherine found herself preparing gluten-free food for Alyssa to take to Simon and Jack's combined birthday party. Their birthdays actually fell during Christmas break, and since the entire Manning clan would be traveling during that time, Michael had planned their party in early November. "I do this every year," he had explained, "otherwise their birthdays would get crowded out by all of the holiday events."

Jack was turning nine, and Simon eight. For three days, they were actually both eight, a fact that made Simon very proud. For those three days Simon would drive Jack crazy, walking around reminding him that he wasn't the oldest any more. And, for those same days Jack would grumble and argue that he was still older because he was born first and if Simon wasn't so *young* he would be able to understand that.

Katherine had tried to prep Alyssa before the party. She had explained Alyssa could only eat the food that they had specially brought for her. Trying to make it fun, she had even had Alyssa help her bake a small gluten-free cake. That way Alyssa could bring a piece and eat it when all the other children had their cake. "It's called having your cake and eating it too," Katherine had said with a smile, knowing her daughters were too young to understand the pun.

Despite the mental gyrations of debating how Alyssa could enjoy a party without eating gluten, Katherine found herself looking forward to seeing Michael. In the weeks since Alyssa's diagnosis, they had barely spoken, and if she were honest with herself, she would admit that she missed him. With these thoughts running through her mind, she dressed carefully in her favorite jeans and a flattering blue flutter-sleeved "crushed" blouse. Slipping into some mimic Jack Rogers she had picked up at the flea market, she felt feminine but still casual, and hoped that he would notice and that their disagreement over Alyssa would now be a moot point. Katherine had the diagnosis, they were following the diet, and Alyssa was doing better. Surely, there would be no more reason to argue about it.

When they arrived at the Manning house, the boys greeted the girls so happily that Katharine felt guilty. It wasn't their fault their parents had argued!

Michael, for his part, broke Katherine's apprehension by greeting her warmly. "How have you been?" he asked, taking both her hands and searching her face for any clues.

"We're doing well, Michael, thank you. We've missed you guys," she admitted enjoying the feeling of her hands in his.

"We've missed you too!" He stepped back, satisfied that there seemed to be no anger or animosity between them.

Katherine wished she could just hug him. How had she managed to stay away for so long? Maybe now their summertime camaraderie would return!

As more people arrived, Michael found it impossible to keep Katherine nearby. It felt good, though, just having her at his house, and knowing that they were both happy to see each other. She looked so pretty with her auburn hair against the blue foamy-looking top she was wearing, and he found himself following her with his eyes as she moved among children and parents alike, laughing and talking. However, when the children sat down to eat and Katherine pulled out Alyssa's special food, he couldn't resist raising his eyebrows in mock amusement. Wasn't she taking this special diet just a little too far?

"Can't you just let her enjoy a birthday party?" he asked aloud as he picked up a bag of cheese puffs to add to the children's plates. Moving closer to her, he watched her reaction as he continued to dole out handfuls of cheese puffs. There came her telltale signs of defensiveness that seemed to fuel some hidden desire of his own to highlight how ludicrous her actions really seemed. Then, not bothering to mask the sarcasm he felt, and now directly next to her, cheese puff orange all over his one hand, he added, "It's not like she's going to go into anaphylactic shock or anything. I thought it wasn't an allergy?"

Katherine, felt a wave of disappointment and mortification wash over her—the battle lines were still present. Then anger took hold, and she heard herself snap back, "Why can't you just be happy that something seems to be helping her?" She was acutely aware of the listening-quiet of those around her, but was determined not to back down.

"But what if this is only a temporary fix like the sugar thing was?" Bobby Dunn, the little boy whose plate was still cheese-puff-less, was looking up at Michael expectantly waiting for his serving. Amber and Jack had their eyes fixed on their respective parents, eating slowly as if in robot-motion, their eyes wide and serious, wondering what would come next.

Conscious of everyone around her, Katherine heard herself dive in deeper. "Michael, the doctor said that once her intestines are healthy, she can eat sugar again. It was a temporary fix because for that period of time the villi, or whatever you call them, were only worn down to the point that they couldn't digest sugar anymore. Then they got worn down more, affecting other enzymes and she started having symptoms again." Katherine paused, hoping he would at least nod his head in understanding, but instead he was looking as if he were amused by her unscientific explanation. "Michael," she plead, feeling perspiration dotting her polyester shirt, feeling her face colored in embarrassment at the audience they had attracted, "I can't explain it on your level, but it makes sense to me. My daughter *is* feeling better, so I'm extremely relieved. I wish *you* could just be happy for us."

But Michael, continuing to shake his head, glanced sideways at Alyssa's unique plate of food. "Look Michael," Katherine tried again, this time her voice harsh and angry, "don't stand there and roll your eyes at me like I'm the idiot. Just because you were not exposed to celiac disease in med school doesn't meant it doesn't exist."

Michael raised his eyebrows, this time in surprise. *Wow, now we're getting nasty,* he thought, taken aback as he watched her walk away.

"Hey, Dr. Manning," a nearby father said playfully, "didn't anyone ever teach you to be nice to pretty women, especially *single* pretty women?"

Michael knew he had better not respond, and took a deep breath. His indignation at her comment was being quickly replaced with remorse. He had never heard Katherine speak that angrily to anyone, and it made him feel terrible that he had somehow driven her to it.

"You know, Katherine is under a lot of stress with this whole diet thing, Dr. Manning," put in a nearby mother whose daughter was in the same class as Amber.

Michael looked up at her blankly. Had the entire room been listening to their exchange? And, was everyone here a Katherine fan? He tried to quell his rising embarrassment; the last thing he wanted was to give everyone there something new to gossip about. He mentally shook himself, trying his best to concentrate on helping fill the children's plates, but his mind kept playing her words over and over again. Throughout the remainder of the afternoon, he attempted many times to catch her eye, and every once in awhile she would look up and their eyes would meet, but she would always look away hurriedly.

He felt guilty. Katherine did look stressed and tired. Had he really just rebuilt the wall that seemed down only a few moments before? Had he really been dumb enough to once again alienate the best woman that had ever come into his life?

Katherine, meantime, was fully ashamed she had let him get under her skin so badly, especially at his own sons' birthday party. For the rest of the afternoon, she avoided him completely, deciding it was best to keep things that way. As much as she hated to admit it to herself, she was very much attracted to him, ego and all. Even though she had promised herself that she would avoid relationships and their attached labels, until Alyssa's health problems started, she had come to think of him as her own special friend and confidant. She also knew that others had tried to pin a label on their relationship, and that the audience who had been around the table were probably now chalking up their disagreement as a lovers' spat. She sighed and tried to appear jovial and interested in the activities around her but instead felt uncomfortable under his gaze, self-conscious that others had heard their interchange, and guilty that she had

Chapter 15

let herself get so angry with him. She couldn't help but looking over in Michael's direction and when she did, she would find his eyes on her. That made her more uncomfortable, especially since instead of anger, his eyes held a look of worry and concern and something else she couldn't quite fathom.

Finally, the party ended, and she gratefully gathered the girls. She wished she hadn't come at him with such a derisive comment. It didn't help anything to respond with anger and defensiveness toward his mockery. She could tell when she left, that he felt badly too. He gripped her hand, covering both their hands with his free hand, and thanked her for coming, not wanting to let her go, wishing he could come up with the right words, wishing he wasn't responsible for the sadness on her face. Wanting to make amends, Katherine managed, "I'm sorry for arguing with you today in front of everybody." She found she couldn't quite meet his eyes, and chose instead to focus on the stone column directly behind him.

Michael shifted his feet, clearing his throat, trying his best to get her to make eye contact but to no avail. "I guess it was warranted. I shouldn't have made fun of your efforts. Alyssa does look like she's more energetic," he acknowledged grudgingly.

She turned away slowly, not wanting to respond, "OK then, we'd better go. Say goodbye girls," she added weakly.

He raised his hand in a half-hearted good-bye, letting it drop back to his side when he realized the futility of the gesture. He stood there, unmoving, with the background of childish chatter all around him and the chorus of the girl's good-byes in front of him, watching her walk woodenly towards her car. He knew with a sickening certainty that the wall was still there, solid, impenetrable, and built by his own inability to keep his mouth shut.

That evening, after the last of the party devastation had been cleaned up, and the overtired boys were finally asleep, he sat out on the patio deep in thought. He dug his hands into the pocket of his windbreaker, surprised by the coolness of the evening, as he chastised himself for being overly harsh on Katherine. A "cold front", the weatherman had said. Michael grinned in spite of his somber thoughts—a cold front that merely necessitated a light jacket was almost laughable. His amusement faded, however, as his thoughts returned to Katherine. He knew he had been unreasonable regarding Alyssa, and he felt terrible for it.

Reaching for his Bible, he prayed that somehow God would heal their relationship. He was so attracted to her even when they were embroiled in this huge disagreement, that he felt like he was going crazy. He turned to where he was reading in II Kings 5.

1. " Now Naaman, captain of the host of the king of Syria, was a great man with his master, and honourable, because by him the LORD had given deliverance unto Syria: he was also a mighty man in valour, but he was a leper... "

The passage went on to explain how a captive Israeli servant girl told them that a prophet in Israel could cure him. Following her advice, Naaman went to Israel. After unsuccessfully seeking help from the king of Israel, he was sent to Elijah the prophet. When Elijah ordered him to dip in the Jordan River seven times, Naaman was disappointed and offended. He had hoped for some magnificent event. He did not want to dip into the dirty river, he was too proud for that. When his servants implored him, however, he finally gave in and did as the prophet had said. The outcome was poignantly recorded in verse 14:

14. "Then went he down, and dipped himself seven times in Jordan, according to the saying of the man of God: and his flesh came again like unto the flesh of a little child, and he was clean. "

Michael stopped reading and looked out into the darkness, and a thought came to him with startling realization. When Naaman kept his pride he kept his leprosy, when he relinquished his pride, he was healed of his leprosy. He winced, *Is my problem pride, Lord?*

Chapter 15

Yes. He could clearly recognize God's answer.

He leaned forward and put his head in his hands. Not pride. Dealing with pride was never a comfortable exercise. But he knew in his heart that it was true. He had been too proud all along to consider that something other than his diagnosis was correct. He had been too egotistical to give Alyssa a referral. And now that she had a diagnosis, instead of trying to learn about it, he was mocking her. The accusations continued to come, fast and furious.

Oh God, forgive me. He rubbed his hand across his face, then, taking his Bible again, turned to the classic scripture in Proverbs 16:18 on pride, *"Pride goeth before destruction and a haughty spirit before a fall."*

Has my pride been the destruction of our relationship, Lord?

Yes.

He bowed his head in despair and praying earnestly, asked God to forgive him and to help him know what he could do next. Confessing to God brought relief from the guilt that always came with the forgiveness only God could provide. Yet, he knew he still had the responsibility of somehow making it right with Katherine, but that would involve more than just a simple apology. He needed to research the diagnosis Alyssa had been given so that he could formulate a more informed opinion. That way he could provide some constructive advice to replace the steady stream of criticism he had been supplying. He rubbed his temples, praying that God would give him resources and wisdom. With his mind full, he headed inside to begin packing for a conference in Miami.

Grabbing a suitcase from the otherwise empty hall closet, he walked down to his room and flung it down open onto the rumpled bed. As he added shirts, slacks, and socks in reasonably organized layers, his mind worked continuously on his problem with Katherine. He knew that educating himself was his number one priority, so after closing his suitcase and finishing up the last notes to his mother concerning the boys' school times and daily schedule of activity locations, he padded down the hall to the room he called his office. Although it was past 10 P.M., he was now a man on a mission, so he sat down at his computer and searched Medline for the latest research articles he could find on the disease. He was surprised with the relatively short list his search yielded.

After printing out abstracts from what seemed to be the most relevant articles, he began leafing through them. Titles and statements caught his eye, and instead of placing them in his brief case he found himself reading first one then another and then another. He couldn't believe what he was reading. *Celiac disease affects 1 out of every 133 Americans.*[1] How was that possible? He went back to his computer and printed out the entire paper, reading it fully and shaking his head in disbelief.

He turned to another abstract. *Occipital calcifications occur in patients with celiac disease.*[2] Once again, he turned back to his computer to read the entire article. The paper stated that the calcifications caused symptoms such as epilepsy, migraines, and visual disturbances apparently from a decrease in folate absorption due to damaged intestines.

His mind went back to Alyssa, crying at the beach, complaining that her head hurt, and to all the times that Katherine would have Alyssa laying on the couch sleeping with an ice pack on her head after one of her 'episodes'. The poor child may have been having migraines!

After that, there was no rhyme or reason to his reading; he just wanted to know all he could find out. Sleep was now impossible, and he read into the early morning hours, astounded that something apparently so prevalent was going undetected. He shook his head in disgust, making a list of the variety of symptoms for which celiac disease could be responsible. Next to the list he wrote his standard treatment for each: headaches – children's Tylenol; stomach cramps – possibly Pepto-Bismol;

aching joints – growing pains, they'll go away; diarrhea – remove juice from diet, standard stool culture for parasites; fatigue – let them nap longer, provide an earlier bedtime; persistent swollen glands – rest, treat as a viral illness; lactose intolerance – drink lactaid milk; anemia – take iron supplements. To think that all of these complaints could have a common root cause was astounding to him. What baffled him the most was how one illness could present itself in so many ways.

The thought plagued him as he finally went to bed, and stayed with him as he drove to his conference the next morning. Paging through the itinerary of talks, he was surprised to see that one of the break-out sessions would feature a lecture on celiac disease.

The attendance in the room was sparse, and the speaker commented that there was just no money in a disease that was 100 percent nutritionally managed, and thus it was difficult to get the medical establishment to sit up and take note. He began his talk by listing a set of symptoms that were all seemingly unrelated, and then went on to say that in a disease in which the ability to absorb nutrients was compromised, symptoms would relate to the corresponding malabsorption. These could range from osteoporosis, arthritis, tooth decay, anemia, internal hemorrhaging, diabetes, and infertility to depression and dementia. The symptoms would appear according to which nutrient was not being sufficiently assimilated in the body. He gave the folate example of which Michael had read the night before, how that lack of folate could lead to calcifications in the brain, and from there to headaches and even epilepsy.

"Now, a patient with epilepsy will obviously be directed to see a neurologist, not a gastroenterologist. And, although the neurologist can provide medication to manage the epilepsy, the underlying root cause—celiac disease—will never be found. Serological testing needs to be mandatory at the primary care level, so that all children can be screened. Those with positive antibody tests can then be sent to a gastroenterologist for confirmation of celiac disease. Obviously not all symptoms are because of celiac disease, but if the disease is as prevalent as Fassano *et al* say, then that would make celiac disease the most under treated illness in our country."

Michael, fascinated by what he was learning, waited to speak privately with the speaker at the end of the talk. The two men agreed to meet for coffee later. That quick coffee break turned into an intellectually stimulating conversation that ran well into the next session. The result was that Michael came away with increased knowledge, more references, contacts, and practical ideas he could implement. He felt like he had become a convert of a new faith, and was determined that in his practice celiac disease would be given a consideration for any child that had unexplained symptoms of any nature.

He realized too how wrong he had been with Alyssa. He wanted to call Katherine, to apologize, but was afraid he would sound trite. He decided to bide his time, learn as much as he could, and wait for the right moment.

That moment came in an unsuspected way shortly after the New Year. A local TV station called and asked if one of the doctors at their practice would answer some questions on the Health Segment about celiac disease. Justin laughed when he gave the message to Michael, "Seems like your newfound knowledge is already going to be put to use!" Michael accepted the interview with some trepidation, thinking that if he could get Katherine to watch the TV spot, it would be the perfect opportunity for him to show her how sorry he truly was.

Chapter 16

IT WAS A Monday afternoon. School had been back in session for a week since the Christmas break. Katherine had had a hard time with the holidays. Compared to the sunlit summer, the Christmas season had been full of longing memories of Leyton, and wistful "what-ifs" regarding Michael. If she were completely honest with herself, harder than anything was the knowledge that she and Michael were at odds with each other. Since Simon and Jack's birthday party, she had scarcely seen him. He had attended a medical conference in Miami, and then traveled with the boys over Thanksgiving and Christmas. For Christmas, he had sent her a beautifully framed picture of all their children in front of one of their beach forts. Looking at their sheer joy and uncomplicated happiness had made her feel nostalgic and despondent for what might have been.

That particular Monday was the day of Michael's TV interview, and he had told Jack to go by and see Katherine sometime during the school day in order to tell her to watch the news that night. Not wanting all his effort to be wasted, he wanted to ensure she saw the segment. If Jack forgot to go by,

167

he was going to have to call and tell her to watch it himself, but he didn't want to do that. They hadn't talked except for a curt 'hello' or 'goodbye' in passing since their all too public argument at Jack and Simon's birthday party, and he wanted her to see the TV spot before they spoke again. He was hoping the segment would prove to her how truly sorry he was, and from that would come reconciliation.

Katherine was surprised and pleased to see Jack enter her classroom that afternoon.

"Hi Jack!" she said walking over and hugging him. "Why aren't you getting on the bus?"

"Oh, Grandma is picking us up today," he shrugged. "Where's Amber?"

"She's at the after school play area. Do you want me to take you there so you can wait for your Grandma with her, or do you want to wait here?" Katherine hated that the girls' school day was lengthened by her need as a teacher to arrive early and stay late. There was just so much extra work—it was impossible to fit it all in during regular school hours. She always said that for every lesson she taught, she needed an hour to recover and prep for the next one. Thankfully, the after care workers were sensitive towards the children's needs and allowed them as much outdoor playtime as weather permitted.

"No, I came to talk to you," Jack said, suddenly remembering his mission and straightening up importantly.

"Well, that's nice!" Katherine smiled, and sat down next to him in one of the student desks.

"I came to tell you that my Dad is going to be on TV tonight."

"He is?" Katherine offered him a peppermint from her pocket.

"Yes, he's going to be on the news. Channel five, at six o'clock. We're going to watch it, and we want you guys to see it too."

"Well, I'll write it down right now, and we'll all make sure we watch it, OK?"

"OK."

Then Jack stood up again, unwrapping his candy, "Well, I have to go; my Grandma is waiting in the parking lot. Goodbye!"

"Goodbye Jack," and resisting the urge to hug him again, she squeezed his offered hand. She smiled at him warmly. "Thank you so much for coming by to see me."

"You're welcome," he said seriously, and then hesitating briefly, he stepped forward and hugged her.

"Oh Jack," Katherine said hugging him back, "that's the best hug I've had in ages. Thank you!"

"You're welcome," came the reply as he hurried out the door, suddenly embarrassed.

Katherine looked after him, realizing afresh how badly she missed seeing all of the Manning men. She put the reminder to watch the news on top of her stack of take-home grading, and absentmindedly put her classroom back in order for the next day, wondering all the while what Michael was doing on the evening news.

Fixing dinner, it was after six before Katherine remembered to turn the TV on. Grabbing the remote, she hit 'power' while calling to the girls. When they didn't respond, and she realized that they were in a neighbors' yard still playing, she sat down on her own, hoping that she hadn't missed Michael's appearance.

"And now we have Dr. Michael Manning of Children's Practice," an authoritative voice announced. Well, for once her timing had been perfect.

Katherine caught her breath at how handsome he looked on TV as the cameraman cut directly to Michael.

"Hello Dr. Manning," the correspondent said.

"Hello," he smiled in response. He looked as if were born to be on TV.

"We're here to talk to you today about celiac disease. Could you briefly explain to our viewers exactly what celiac disease is?"

They were interviewing Michael about celiac disease? Katherine was astonished. Didn't they know about Dr. Cantrell? Someone hadn't done their homework.

His practiced answer came quickly. "Celiac disease, also called gluten intolerance, is a genetic disorder whereby the body responds to gluten-containing foods (wheat, barley, rye) as a toxin. Continual ingestion of these foods leads to intestinal damage, decreasing the body's ability to absorb nutrients. People with celiac disease will then not only have the stomach pain associated with the damage, but all the complications that would follow when the body is unable to absorb nutrients."

"So people affected by this disease shouldn't eat any wheat, barley, or rye?"

"Yes, as well as any foods that contain derivatives of wheat, barley, and rye. Even the smallest amount of gluten can make a person with celiac disease sick."

"And what exactly is gluten?"

"Gluten is the protein component of wheat. It's what gives our bread structure. Patients who try to cook with gluten-free flours will attest to that fact."

"And how common is celiac disease?" Katherine realized she was holding her breath.

"Surprisingly, recent research is saying that it affects as many as 1 out of every 133 people."

"Wouldn't that make it an epidemic?" Dumbfounded, Katherine sank back into the couch cushions.

"Not necessarily, but it would make it the most under diagnosed disease of our time."

"Why do you say that?"

"Well, we doctors don't know everything we should about the disease. I was taught, as well as probably many of my colleagues, that celiac disease is a rare disorder that manifests itself with diarrhea, rapid weight loss, and extreme stomach pain. However, I have since learned that this is incorrect. Celiac disease can present itself masked as any number of illnesses."

"Such as…"

"Oh, arthritis, migraine headaches, epilepsy, or just the classic stomach complaints of childhood which we pediatricians usually tend to dismiss." Was she actually hearing this?

"Have you had any such patients in the past?"

"That I've dismissed?"

"Yes."

Then, it was as if Michael looked right through the camera and made eye contact with only her. "I can think of one in particular. Her mother kept asking me for a referral to a specialist, but I was convinced it was a form of childhood anxiety causing her stomach problems."

"So how did you eventually diagnose her?"

"I didn't. Her mother took her to Dr. Cantrell, a local pediatric gastroenterologist. He diagnosed her almost immediately, and she is now thriving on a gluten-free diet."

"Was that surprising to you?"

Michael shifted in his seat. "It surprised me on multiple levels. First, that I had never been taught about the full scope of an illness that is actually quite common; second, that there could be a disease that's managed 100 percent by nutritional intervention; and third that I could have been so completely wrong!" Michael smiled at the camera and Katherine's heart flip-flopped. "We doctors don't like to be wrong, you know, and to that patient and her mother I owe a very large apology!"

The interviewer, obviously not used to real-time confessions, cleared his throat and said, "In our remaining time, could you briefly explain the best course of action parents need to take if they suspect that something like this is wrong with their child?"

While Katherine heard Michael's answer, she was not really listening any more. She just sat there, transfixed, although her mind was racing. He was apologizing to her on local television! She couldn't believe it. When did he suddenly become such an expert on the disease anyway?

All she knew now was that she needed to see Michael. The girls had just come in, and were running around the room screaming about who had the favorite pencil first. Alyssa was crying, the kitchen timer was going off, and the phone was ringing. Absently she stood up, grabbed one of the girls, and took away the offending pencil. Directing Amber to find another pencil with which to do her homework, she turned off the timer, forgetting to remove the lasagna (gluten-free, of course) from the oven, and answered the phone.

"Katherine?" It was Dana from school. "Did you just watch the evening news? Oh my goodness, you're not going to believe it…."

Just then, another call beeped in at the exact time her cell phone started ringing.

Katherine turned off the cell phone, fielded the questions from Dana, hung up, and then unplugged the phone.

"I'm hungry Mommy," whined Alyssa.

Amber looked up from her homework, "I can't do this math, it's too hard. Why does my Mom have to be a math teacher? Everyone expects me to be the best in math, and I don't even *like* it." She waited and when no response was received hollered, "Mom? Mom!"

Katherine finally glanced over. "Just do your best, honey," she said absently. She had to talk to Michael, privately. She couldn't believe to what lengths he had gone in order to prove to her that he truly was sorry. She remembered their conversation in which he had apologized for being rude. Things had not been the same since then. She had despaired that they would never be the same, so long as they disagreed so completely on what was really wrong with Alyssa. Plus, to Katherine, it was his overall attitude toward the whole thing that had kept the barrier up between them. To her, simply apologizing for being rude, but not addressing the root issue hadn't really been an apology.

Well, he had now done everything he possibly could have to prove he was sorry. She was desperate to talk to him. Frantically, she searched through her list of babysitters trying to find someone who could come over and watch the girls. She finally got hold of Madison, a college student that attended their church, who thankfully agreed to come over after the girls were in bed. Breathing a sigh of relief, she went off to find Amber and Alyssa. Amber was sitting staring at her math homework, crying, and Alyssa was wandering around whining that something smelled bad. Katherine smelled it as well, and the realization that it was smoke jarred her into the present. She ran into the kitchen, only to see smoke coming out of the oven – her lasagna! She grabbed an oven mitt and yanked the ruined dinner out of the oven while smoke poured out into the kitchen setting off the smoke alarm. Amber and Alyssa instantly started screaming while covering their ears and hopping madly around Katherine. Katherine banged open the kitchen door and ordered them out while retrieving a stepladder to get to the smoke alarm. She couldn't get it off, so finally in desperation, she yanked the battery out and the alarm came away from the wall. There was silence, except for the muted crying of the girls outside the door. The offensive alarm swung quietly from a cord attached to the ceiling as Katherine surveyed the rest of the damage. Opening all the windows she could, she turned on the ceiling fans, and then went outside to calm her girls down. Good thing she didn't see people she knew on TV more often, the house wouldn't be standing!

Later that evening, after a meal of cold cereal, a partially restored kitchen, and with the girls tucked into bed, Madison arrived. Still smelling like smoke, Katherine mumbled brief instructions and then drove over to Michael's. She hoped his boys would be in bed too. Children were too perceptive and she didn't want Jack or Simon passing unnecessary information onto her girls.

The house was dark as she pulled into the driveway. She knocked softly and nobody answered. Then she remembered that Michael liked to sit out on the back patio once the boys were in bed. Walking carefully around the side of the house, she hoped she wouldn't set off any more alarms. She stopped short when she saw his silhouette on the patio. Swallowing hard, she knocked softly on the screen door. "Michael?" she spoke softly, nervous now that he wouldn't welcome her intrusion.

He looked up sharply, "Who is it?"

She swallowed again. "It's me, Katherine....You didn't answer the front door...I need.....um, could I talk to you?"

"Oh – ah – sure." He got up and fumbled with the latch then held open the screen door to allow her in. The door slammed shut and they stood in the dark, facing each other. She could feel his eyes on her waiting for her to speak, but she couldn't think of where to start. The silence hung between them thicker then the nighttime darkness. A light went on inside the house, and Jack came walking sleepily out onto the patio.

"Dad?" he questioned.

"It's OK, Jack; Katherine came over to see me. You can go back to bed." Jack looked at them quizzically, sighed, and then turned around mumbling about noises in the dark. Michael turned back around to look at Katherine. She had looked away to try and hide the tears that were sliding down her cheeks. His heart contracted, and he wanted to reach out and touch her, but still he waited.

Finally, she looked down and taking a deep breath managed, "I saw you on the news tonight."

"I was hoping you would," he responded.

Chapter 16

"Remember when you apologized for being rude in your office?" she attempted.

"Yes." The answer was brisk. It didn't invite anything further.

Maybe he didn't want there to be an 'us' anyway. She forced herself to continue. "Well, I felt like there was still a wall between us, and it has bothered me profoundly that our friendship could not get back to what it was." She paused again, hoping for some sort of encouragement, but none was forthcoming. "Well," she finally continued, "what you did on TV was more than I could have expected from anyone. I want to tell you thank you." She breathed in deeply and repeated, "Thank you…thank you." She wiped at her tears, "And…would you please forgive me for being so hard on you?"

"No, Katherine, you need to first forgive me for being proud, and unwilling to learn," he countered. "You were right to be hard on me. I was a first class jerk… repeatedly." He reached up and gently wiped a tear from her cheek with his thumb. That motion of kindness only caused them to fall faster. "Please tell me you forgive me?" he pleaded.

"Oh yes, yes, yes," she sobbed. She covered her face with her hands as he gently drew her to him.

"Hey," he said softly. "It's OK." He pulled her hands from her face and rested her head against him. "It's OK," he repeated, gently kissing the top of her head. They stood there together—close, trembling with the relief that reconciliation brings. To Katherine it felt like a fresh rain after days in the desert. "Here, sit here with me," and he pulled her down next to him, keeping his arms around her. They sat in silence until Katherine's tears had subsided.

"I'm sorry for being such an emotional mess," she finally managed.

"Shhhh," he countered, kissing the top of her head again. "It was probably good for both of us. We have a lot to talk about."

And that's what they did, long into the night. He told her about getting convicted about his pride, about his prayer for a chance to show her he meant he was sorry. He told her about the conference, his subsequent study, and then his chance to be interviewed on the Health Segment. "It was clearly the opportunity I needed," he said. "But, when I didn't hear from you after the segment, I figured it had all been in vain, that you hadn't even watched it."

"No, I was home and I saw it all," Katherine said. "It was the most amazing apology that I've ever received."

"Thank you." Then they both fell silent, content to sit there with the night sounds surrounding them. Katherine was growing sleepy now and was about to say that she needed to leave when Michael spoke again: "Could you just tell me one thing, though?" There was a playful note to his voice.

"Mmmm?"

"Why do you smell like smoke?"

"Oh—Oh my goodness!" Katherine sat up and sniffed at her clothes. "I do! In my haste to get over here I completely forgot about needing to change after burning our dinner! What a wreck I must be!"

"Shhhh," he laughed, "you always seem so together and controlled. It's refreshing to see you a little off-kilter!"

"We'll see who's off kilter" she retorted attempting to push him off the chair.

"Hey!" he feigned offense, "I'm stronger than I look!" With that, he pinned both her arms to her sides and hugged her tightly. "There," he said satisfied, "now you're stuck."

"And glad to be that way," came her muffled reply.

Eventually Katherine pulled away. "I must go and rescue my babysitter."

"I'll only let you go if you promise to see me very soon."

"I promise," she smiled into the darkness.

He took her hand and walked her around the house back to her car. Before she could climb in he stopped her.

"Look, Katherine. I know you said before that you don't want black tie and roses, but just for the next few days please don't worry about that, OK?"

"OK, but I don't understand why you want to bring that up tonight."

"I'm bringing it up because I'm going to kiss you goodnight, and I don't want you worrying your sweet self about what it means." Then, before she could respond he lowered his head and kissed her gently, with a sweetness Katherine never dreamed possible.

"There," he said, "I've been wanting to do that since the first day I saw you at the beach."

And with that he opened her car door and helped her in.

Katherine didn't remember much about the drive home. She only knew that she fell into a deep contented sleep that night and woke with the fresh anticipation of a child on Christmas day. Going through her routine at school, she tried to keep her thoughts in check, but it was too difficult to concentrate. The students, sensing that something was different took full advantage of the situation.

It didn't help that over the intercom the secretary announced that she should send someone to the front desk to pick up a delivery of flowers. To the students "Oooos" and "Ahs" a huge basket of food and twenty-four dozen yellow roses were brought into the room. The tag said simply, "no black tie, just roses."

"Let's eat the food," one of the students called out. Katherine went to open the basket but then stopped herself. It was filled with all the expensive gluten-free treats and mixes that she had a hard time splurging on for Alyssa. The attached tag said, "For Alyssa's future birthday parties."

Chapter 17

IN THE DAYS following their reconciliation, Michael and Katherine managed to see each other almost every day. It was a Friday evening, and Michael was on call. They were all swimming at his house, when he had to leave to handle an emergency. When he realized that he would probably be out late, he called Katherine to apologize.

"It's going to be a long night, I'm afraid. Are you doing OK over there?"

"Oh, the children are having a blast, but if you think you are going to be really late, I'm going to go ahead and put them all to bed. They're so tired they're getting wired."

"That's fine with me. You can find extra sleeping stuff for the girls in the spare room closet."

"I know, I helped you unpack, remember?"

Michael smiled, "Really? I thought that was you! Anyway, I'm afraid I have to go."

"OK, 'bye," Katherine answered, and then hung up the phone.

Walking in the 'spare room' as Michael called it, she had to smile. There wasn't one piece of furniture in there. She still wondered why he had insisted that he needed four bedrooms. He had indicated that each of them would have their own room and that would leave one for a study or spare room. But, the boys had been determined to share, so now there were two almost-empty rooms, save for the extra pillows and sleeping bags in the one, and a computer desk, chair, and lamp in the other. Katherine shook her head, bemused, and went about making up pallets on the floor for her girls in the empty room.

When she told the children it was bedtime, little Simon looked as if he was about to cry.

"When's my Daddy coming home?"

"He always cries, even when we stay at Grandma's," Jack put in sarcastically. "Wait 'til we get a nanny to take care of us like in Michigan when my Dad gets super busy again, then—"

"Sometimes when I feel like crying," Katherine cut him off, "I just get a big hug from someone I love." She smiled, reaching out and hugging Simon to her.

"Jack thinks I'm a…a…sissy," Simon said against her shoulder, his voice quavering.

"Tonight he doesn't," Katherine said firmly, hugging Simon's skinny frame a little tighter while looking pointedly at Jack. "Plus, I think that sometimes crying helps us get our sadness out. Why else would God have given us tears?"

No response. The girls were staring at Simon wide-eyed, and Jack was looking a little sheepish.

"Jack, why don't you show me where I can find another pillow? I might just fall asleep on the couch myself."

Jack set off, trailed by Amber, and came back a few minutes later with a rumpled pillow. "Here, just use my Dad's, I don't think we have any more extra ones." He glanced over at Simon who was leaning sleepily against Katherine.

Chapter 17

"Thanks, now you boys go and change into pajamas, and brush your teeth. Amber and Alyssa, you can just sleep in the dry clothes we brought along." She gently stood Simon away from her and he gave her a watery smile before he ran off to do her bidding.

When everyone was ready, Katherine corralled them all into the boys' room and spent the next half hour reading bedtime stories to them.

"You're a cool reader," Jack said, snuggling against Katherine appreciatively.

"Why thanks, Jack! You are all such good listeners that it's fun to read to you."

"Hey Mom, look!" Amber whispered pointing at Simon, who had fallen asleep, leaning against Alyssa.

"Shhh, let's see if we can get him into bed without waking him up!" Katherine whispered conspiratorially. The children shifted and giggled quietly, scrambling to help her out.

"Jack, you pull back the covers and Amber, you turn out the light. Alyssa, help me tuck him in, OK?" she continued to whisper.

Once he was snugly in bed, Katherine kissed him softly, gently stroking his head. Jack looked on solemnly.

"We've never had a Mommy put us to bed before, just a Dad or a Grandma or our old nannies," he stated matter-of-factly.

"Well, I'm sure glad I got to be the one, then," Katherine responded, helping him into bed and trying to hide the catch in her voice. Maybe she should offer to be the next nanny when Michael found himself too busy to rely on his parents alone. She could easily provide far more love than hired help from some babysitting service could. But then again, that might complicate her relationship with Michael. It was probably best to stay on the fringes and let him manage his own life. Tucking the covers around his thin chest, she smiled gently down at him, "You have sweet dreams, OK? I love you, Jack."

"I love you too," he mumbled back.

Turning to hide the tears that had filled her eyes, Katherine ushered the girls out into the hallway toward the spare room.

"Does Jack think you're *his* Mommy too?" Alyssa asked, sounding worried.

"No, silly, he just knows that she *is* a Mommy," Amber answered seriously.

Katherine let it go at that, Jack's statement still echoing in her head. It made her heart ache at the overwhelming losses they had all experienced.

After a long day at school, and an evening of energetic playing in the pool, everyone fell asleep almost instantly, for which Katherine was grateful. She walked around the now silent house, putting things away, and turning off unnecessary lights. The house was so bare it almost seemed uninhabited. The living room, furnished with the prerequisite couch, Lazy Boy and TV, looked stark and uninviting with no pictures, no end tables, and no lamps. The family room was still devoid of any furnishings save the shelf of toys and children's books organized somewhat haphazardly along one wall. There was no dining room table, and the eat-in kitchen had one rickety table and chairs that had long since needed to be thrown out. Katherine walked out onto the patio, and breathed in the evening air. The patio was definitely the best part of the house, with its extended view of the screened in pool and the large yard stretched beyond that. Michael had done well to find a house in South Florida with a real backyard. There was already a fort of sorts built into one of the oak trees, and a rope swing hanging from one of its limbs. Although the yard lacked landscaping, it was definitely a child's paradise.

She walked back into the house, and without realizing it, began imagining how good everything would look with some new furniture, pictures, area rugs, window treatments, and some color on the walls. Thoroughly tired now, she lay down on the couch, shifting the cushions and scrunching Michael's pillow under her head. She breathed in deeply, enjoying his scent and the sense of belonging that filled her. Her mind went back to the house, and she drifted off to sleep, thinking of all the ways she could make this house look like a home.

It was after midnight when Michael finally arrived home. He walked in quietly, setting his keys and wallet gently on the kitchen counter. After working his shoes off his feet, he walked tentatively into the living room while unbuttoning the top buttons of his shirt and stretching his neck from side to side. It had been a long, stressful night, and the welcome silence was a balm to his over-taxed senses. Padding softly into the living room, he stopped short at the sight of Katherine's sleeping form on the couch. With his heart pounding in his throat, he swallowed hard as he moved slowly toward her, savoring the picture of serenity she made. Sitting gingerly down alongside her, he gently touched her hair. Her face was buried in his pillow and her hair lay spread out across it. At that moment, realization hit him like a blow to the gut that took his breath away.

I love this woman! He sat there for minutes, looking at her and letting this new-found knowledge sink in. She looked so peaceful sleeping. The worry that often creased her forehead was gone, and in its place was a restfulness that he had never seen before. He ran his hand down her thick auburn hair that shone even now in the dim lighting.

"Katherine?" he whispered.

She sighed and moved contentedly, snuggling deeper against the cushions she had arranged around herself. His heart contracted at the sight. She was so beautiful and he loved her. What was he going to do?

He would have to keep it to himself, he realized with a sinking heart. She had made it clear multiple times that she had no interest in marrying again. And, with the strong principles he was sure they both shared, even when physical relationships were allowed and expected by the culture they lived in, he knew that torturing themselves with a relationship without marriage was out of the question for them.

"Katherine!" He whispered again, resisting the urge to kiss the smoothness of her cheek.

She isn't making this very easy on me, he thought desperately.

"Hey!" He tried again, gently shaking her shoulder this time.

She opened her eyes sleepily in response to that, and then raised her head and looked at him, perplexed.

"Michael?" Her voice was low and soft, filled with sleep.

"I'm home now." Then seeing the confused look in her eyes, he continued, "Remember, you watched the children for me tonight? You made me promise I would wake you up when I got home."

She closed her eyes again and groaned, "Ohhh, I must have been more exhausted than I realized." With that, she struggled to sit up.

He reached over and steadied her, and then let her lean against him while she regained her equilibrium.

"Wish I could just stay," she mumbled dreamily enjoying the sensation of resting against him.

"You're welcome to, I'll even let you have my room," he offered.

Katherine thought for a while, and then managed, "No, that's not a good idea for me. Plus, it would be a bad example for our children. Here," she said with resolve, "help me up!"

He stood up then, and pulled her up too. They were inches apart, and Katherine, still unsteady, leaned into him. "Oh Michael..." she leaned her head against his chest once more, loving the feel of strength against her face. It had been so long since she had stood this way with a man, gaining strength and support from his presence. Her body seemed to quiver with

Chapter 17

relief, as if to tell her that she had found what she had been missing, that Michael could and would complete her, if only she would allow it.

He slipped his arms around her, and bit his lip to keep from telling her how much he loved her.

Just enjoy the moment, he thought, pulling her closer. *It might not come again...if ever.*

"Will you help me get the girls in the car?" she finally asked, her voice strained with the urgency to break the moment even though her senses were demanding she remain as she was.

"Just let them stay. You can pick them up in the morning. That way you can sleep in. I think you might need it."

"OK." She didn't argue the point, it was just easier on every level.

"Are you sure you'll be fine to drive?"

"In a minute... Standing like this is helping me wake up," she said, a mischievous note entering her voice. Humor always helped to dissolve emotionally charged situations.

"Oh yeah? Well, I can help you out like this anytime you want," he responded.

Katherine smiled into the darkness. "Oh I'm sure you can!" And with that she stepped back, suddenly embarrassed, and looked around for her purse.

"Is this what you want?" he said reaching past her to hand it to her.

"Thanks." They were ill at ease now, so looking down she thanked him quietly and headed for the front door. He followed her, walking her outside, and helping her into her car.

"Be careful, I'm still not so sure that you're fully awake."

"Oh, I'm awake," she mumbled. *But the wrong part of me is awake*, she reprimanded herself. She cranked the car and drove slowly away, angry at her own foolishness. *If I'm going to keep things casual between us, I can't go putting myself into situations that make me forget that!* At the stoplight, she closed her eyes, remembering how good it had felt, being so sleepy, and so close to him. How nice it would be—

A car horn blared behind her, breaking her reverie. The light was green. So, with resolve filling her mind on many fronts she drove home.

Chapter 18

IT HAD BEEN over two months since Michael's TV interview, and Katherine and Michael were still thoroughly enjoying each other's company. They had managed to go out a few times, just the two of them, but mostly they all got together. People at work and church were constantly questioning Katherine about her 'relationship', but she always managed to cut the conversation short, or shrug off their questions before they pinned her down. She savored this friendship, and loved the one-big-happy-family feel that they had achieved without any attached commitments or promises. For her, it was a perfect situation, and although she knew it couldn't last forever, for now she was content. She felt like she had beaten everyone at their label game, and was starting to feel somewhat smug in her success.

Friday-night-game-night at one of their houses had become routine, complete with popcorn, pizza (with a homemade gluten-free version for Alyssa), and yelling over who was cheating at their own variation of Monopoly. Usually the younger children would eventually fall asleep while Amber and Jack sleepily watched one of their favorite movies. Katherine and Michael would then slip out onto the patio to talk and enjoy some solitude.

It was a Friday night in March, and the weather was unusually cool for South Florida. They settled on the swing together, snuggling under a throw Katherine had brought out, seemingly satisfied to listen to the night sounds.

Finally, Michael spoke into the darkness: "Katherine?"

"Mmmmm?"

"Can I ask you something?"

"Sure, just so it doesn't require too much thought."

"Well, actually it might." He paused, debating, and then plunged forward: "I really want to tell you something." Katherine raised her head from the coziness of his shoulder, concern suddenly flooding her heart. "I just want us—" he attempted again "—you know, you and I to have something more than we have now. I mean, I don't want to upset you or anything, but it's hard for me to keep us on a purely friendly basis when—" He stopped once more, searching for the right words. Katherine sat up straight, her heart sinking. "I guess, well…I know…I mean…" He sighed again, aware that she was looking directly at him. "You see, I'm falling in love with you…." The words came faster now, "I want a future with you, I want us to live in the same house, I want to call you my wife."

Deafening silence. Katherine did not know how to respond. She was happy with the way things were. She had promised herself she would never marry again. She didn't want the complications for herself and the girls. She had a great relationship with her in-laws, and it would be hard for them to see her remarry. She loved her house, she wasn't ready to give it up, and it was too small for all of them. She liked her predictable life. True, she was happier now with Michael and the boys in their lives than she had been since Leyton had died. But, she had told herself she would not remarry, and she planned on keeping her resolve.

"Katherine?" His strained voice tore at her heart. How she hated to answer him honestly, the way she knew she must.

"Oh Michael," she finally managed, regret coloring her tone. "Having our families spend time together is wonderful. You're the best thing that's happened to me since my husband died. I just don't want to get married again." She held her breath, hoping he'd understand. She wondered if she was even being fair to him. She wracked her brain for something better to say, something that would dissolve the dreadful tension that now pressed down upon them.

"Maybe we should quit seeing each other then," he finally answered, his voice heavy with disappointment. "It's getting too difficult for me…"

"No!" Katherine interrupted. "Please don't say that! Please? I couldn't stand not to see you again. I know it's unfair of me from your perspective, but could we just *be* for now?" She had turned and grabbed both of his hands, but they were motionless and unresponsive. She shook them impatiently. "Please, Michael? Please just understand. Just give me—" She searched around in her mind frantically for a reasonable solution, "Just give me until the summer. If I still feel the same way, I'll—I'll—I'll help you find someone who wants to get married," she concluded lamely.

"Well, that's about a dumb idea," he said irritated. "Can't you at least tell me some of your objections to getting married so we can work on them?"

"No," she answered, "You'll just come up with a solution for every one of them and then—"

"Then?"

"No. That's all."

He sat staring out in front of him. He was angry with himself for forcing her into this position, angry for his impatience. But, he was also disappointed that she couldn't at least give him some hope, or at a minimum, explain her objections. He wasn't ready to quit seeing her. Besides, the boys would have a fit. Now how was he going to extricate himself from this uncomfortable situation?

Finally he spoke again, "OK. I'm sorry I brought it up. We'll do what you say—apart from the 'you-finding-me-someone-to-marry' part—remain as we are until the summer, and then we'll see." Then he couldn't resist a jab, even though he knew it was underhanded, "I may go ahead and date here and there, though. Just so you know and understand that."

"That's fine," she responded stiffly. If he was already talking about looking for someone else, then his so-called 'falling-in-love-with-her' couldn't be that strong. "You have the right to do whatever you want to."

They sat now in a pained silence, only inches of space between them, but miles apart emotionally. Finally, he stood up. "I need to get the boys home. Thanks for having us over."

"You're welcome," she managed. How had a wonderful evening turned so sour? She helped him get the boys out to the car, said goodnight, put the girls to bed, and went upstairs to her room.

Sleep wouldn't come. She felt selfish, hating to hurt someone she felt so deeply about. Yet she was also angry with him, after all, *he* had ruined it again!

Her mind went around and around... and finally, she fell into a fitful sleep punctuated with irrationally troubled dreams.

She awoke the next morning with a pounding headache, and yet somehow managed to keep the girls occupied while taking care of the myriad of chores that were never completely done.

If we could just take a break from eating and wearing clothes there wouldn't be so much to do, she thought illogically. She jammed the last of the dark clothes into the dryer and slammed the door closed. At least tonight, Jean was cooking for them, so the freshly mopped kitchen would stay clean for one night.

Trying to keep herself distracted, she attacked the remaining chores with a vengeance, scrubbing the bath tubs, wiping the baseboards, and ordering the girls around like a drill sergeant.

"What's wrong with Mom?" Amber whispered to Alyssa as they laboriously attempted to organize their "Littlest Pets".

"She sure is a grump," Alyssa agreed in an extra loud whisper just as Katherine walked by, her arms loaded with freshly folded laundry. Katherine's heart sank as she stopped at the door. Both girls looked up guiltily, their eyes wide with concern.

Setting the folded clothes down next to her, Katherine knelt down on the floor, "Come here girls," she said softly, her voice full of emotion and regret.

Amber came slowly, Alyssa much faster.

Hugging them to her, she whispered softly, "Yes, Mommy has been a big grump today and I'm sorry. Will you forgive me?"

"Sure Mom," Alyssa readily replied, finding hugging her Mommy far preferable to organizing toys.

Amber, though, stepped back unsure. "But why, Mom?"

Katherine took a deep breath, wanting to tell the truth without divulging too much information, "I just let something upset me really badly and I was wrong to let it make me grumpy towards you." She waited, hoping Amber would let her leave it at that.

"Have you prayed yet?" came the next question.

Katherine, taken aback, squelched the defensive answer that came to mind and instead decided to eat humble pie. "No, Amber, I haven't, and that's something I should have done right when I first got upset."

"Well, you always tell *us* to tell God when we are upset. Then, you could—after praying—talk to the person who made you upset," she continued helpfully, clearly enjoying her role as advisor-to-a-grown-up.

"Amber, you are a very smart girl," Katherine pulled her against her, squeezing her tightly and deciding to play along, "I'll be sure to do both of those things, thank you so much."

"—welcome," came the muffled reply. Stepping back again, Amber gave her Mom a goofy grin. "Are we finished cleaning now?" Then, without missing a beat she added, "I really want to go online and play Web Kinz in case Jack is playing too."

Katherine smiled, grateful to comply and relieved that the inquisition with her daughter was over so quickly.

That afternoon they headed over to her in-laws. Katherine was glad to escape the house and hopefully her whirling thoughts. But, the thoughts wouldn't quit, even while working alongside Jean in the kitchen.

I wonder how long I'll consider them my in-laws, she wondered. *I guess no matter what happens, they'll always be my children's grandparents, and Leyton's parents. We'll always have a connection—even if I ever do remarry.*

Remarry? Where were her thoughts taking her? *The plan is never to remarry,* she told herself firmly. *Things are stable, life is predictable, and I am actually happy.*

But was she really happy? Now that Michael had so much as declared his love for her she felt unbalanced, upset, and unsure of herself.

Thanks Michael, she thought despondently, hacking with a vengeance at the potatoes she was peeling.

"Hey, go easy on my potatoes!" Jean protested, eyeing Katherine curiously.

"Oh, sorry, I guess I was just lost in my thoughts, and I wasn't paying attention," Katherine laughed self-consciously.

"Is everything OK?"

"Oh, yes, thank you," Katherine answered, trying to sound nonchalant.

"So how's Michael?" Jean asked, trying a different track.

"Michael?" Katherine looked up guiltily. Why did she have to ask about Michael? "He's, well, um, I guess you could say he's complicated," she attempted, self-consciously.

Jean looked at her steadily, guessing what was probably going on. "You know," she ventured slowly, "you mustn't be afraid to have a relationship with Michael on account of us."

Katherine looked up again, surprised. Then, setting the potato and peeler down, she pulled out a chair and collapsed onto it, resting her chin in her hands. Jean waited, not saying anything. Katherine looked out the window, watching her girls playing with their Grandpa and said, "I just wasn't planning on ever having a relationship with anyone."

"But my dear, you're young. You can't spend the rest of your life alone! Leyton wouldn't have wanted that!" Jean protested, her voice wavering over his name.

"I'm surprised to hear you say that," Katherine answered, her eyes soft and questioning.

"Are you scared that we'll think you're replacing Leyton?" Jean asked gently, sitting down next to her and putting her hand on her arm.

"Of course, but it's even more than that."

"So tell me!"

"I don't know," she sighed in despair. "It's all of us, we're happy again, or as happy as we'll probably ever be able to be. The girls have you, I have the girls, we have a nice family, nice house, and I have a good job. Everything is uncomplicated. It's taken over three years to get to this point, and I don't want to mess it up."

"Don't you think it could be possible that God waited to bring Michael into your life until you were at this point? Any sooner and the relationship would have been in danger of being simply a Leyton-replacer. Now that you're where you are, it can simply be what it is, a relationship with a very nice man."

"Do you *want* me to remarry?" Katherine asked incredulously.

"Well, now don't jump to conclusions! I selfishly would want you to stay as you are too, so that I can be guaranteed to be near you and my grandchildren for the rest of my life. But, what I'm saying is that you mustn't be afraid to open yourself up to Michael. He's a wonderful man, and protecting yourself from him would be doing a disservice to both you and the girls."

"But if we got closer and I ended up marrying him, imagine how confusing it would all be. Four children, two houses, multiple sets of grandparents, I just don't know if I want all of that. I like things the way they are."

"But aren't you thinking too far ahead?"

"No! If I let myself fall in love with him, then the obvious next step is to marry him, and to marry him is to have to make a myriad of complicated decisions."

"Such as…?"

"Would I keep my house? That house is a solid connection to Leyton for me. He spent his last days making it perfect for us, and I feel that living there keeps his memory alive in my heart. Plus, I feel secure there. If I got married, we couldn't stay there, it would be too small for a family of six, yet I don't know if I could stand to leave it. It would seem so final."

"Tell me this, how will that same house feel one day when the girls are grown and gone?"

"That's years away!"

"In the scheme of life, it's really not that far away, you know. The bottom line is that you will be alone. A house, no matter how comfortable, can never be a substitute for companionship. I can't imagine my life without Tom—how lonely it would be. Adjusting to life without children was a shocking transition and to go through that alone…well, I just don't know how I would have handled it."

Chapter 18

Katherine sat, staring out at the girls playing. Their childhood was so time consuming that it was hard to imagine life any other way. But, she knew that what Jean was saying would be true one day. Her mind shifted to another objection:

"OK, then, you win on the house—for now. But, what about being a parent to four children? It's hard enough taking care of two, and I'm having such a hard time just keeping us fed now that I have this gluten-free thing to contend with."

"But there would be two of you," Jean objected. "Besides, Michael has taken care of his two boys their whole lives all by himself. If anything, it may be more of an adjustment for him to allow someone else to do things for them, than for you to have four children to think about. Plus, just think, the girls would have someone who they could eventually call 'Dad'," Jean paused, trying to control the lump that was rising in her throat, "and, those sweet boys would have a Mom."

Katherine sighed, tears pricking at the back of her eyes, leaned over and hugged Jean, knowing how difficult and unselfish it must have been for her to say what she just had.

"You're pretty logical about this whole thing. I appreciate it, but the fact of the matter is, I'm scared to—"

"Hey ladies, we're starving out here!" Tom interrupted, walking in on them, and looking from one to the other. "Uh-oh, have I interrupted something important?"

"No!" Katherine stood up quickly. "We were just about to put these potatoes on to boil, now weren't we?" she said, looking over at Jean as if to say "case closed!" and "don't you say a word!"

Jean winked, and bustled around trying to get the rest of the meal on to cook. Katherine, surprised that Jean wasn't discouraging her from having a relationship with Michael, had a hard time concentrating on anything. Finally, exasperated with herself she looked over and said, "I think I'll just go outside and see how the girls are if you don't mind?"

"No problem, honey. You can even take a walk if you like. Obviously, I have a ways to go on this meal," she said, surveying the chaos.

"OK, I think I will. Thanks!" And giving Jean a quick hug she hurried out of the house.

"What was that all about?" Tom queried, as soon as Katherine was out of earshot.

"Oh nothing, just some 'girl-talk'," Jean winked.

He let out a mock sigh. "I guess I'd better help out with dinner then, otherwise, from the look of things, you're going to let me starve!"

Jean nodded in agreement and handed him the remaining potato and the peeler.

Chapter 19

SPRING BREAK HAD finally arrived. Katherine breathed a sigh of relief as she headed home the Friday afternoon that heralded this much anticipated break. Maybe she would actually get a little ahead over spring break, maybe the girls would actually sleep in a little bit, and maybe she would actually feel rested by the time the break was over. She had told Michael that she would have the boys for at least a couple of the days. Those days would be their beach days. Sometimes taking extra children to the beach was actually less work than just taking her own. Then, tonight was game night with the Manning boys. That was still their routine, although she and Michael never ventured out to the patio to talk anymore. There was a wall between them again, but this time it was probably of her own doing. She sighed again, thinking that at least for now they all got together. And that was her continual dilemma: she loved the time that the two families spent together and loved seeing Michael. She just didn't want to marry him.

To make matters worse, people were really starting to give her a hard time. Just this afternoon in the teacher prep room,

Dana had asked her if Michael was part of Katherine's spring break plans.

"Oh, I'm sure the children will get together," Katherine had responded mildly.

"Yes, but how about the *parents?*"

"We'll see each other, kind of impossible not to when your children play together all the time." Katherine turned her back and began collating papers. What was the point of having a copier/collator/stapler machine if half the time two-thirds of the features didn't work?

"So, you think this is going somewhere?" Dana persisted.

"What?"

"You and Michael."

"And why does it have to go somewhere? Why can't it just be what it is?"

"Oh come on, Katherine. That's not the way the world works, and you know it."

Yeah, and I thought you were my friend, Katherine thought irritated. *If you were, you would quit badgering me about Michael.*

"You know," Dana went on, after seeing that Katherine wasn't responding, "probably every single woman who knows Michael exists, except for you, is dying for a date with him, and you act like...like...nothing."

"Actually he does date other people," Katherine said coolly.

"And you're *fine* with that? Are you *insane?*"

"No, but I am ready to start spring break," *and to get away from people like you,* she added to herself. With that, Katherine bit her lip to keep from saying what she really wanted to say, stacked up her still-not-collated papers, and headed for the door. "Have a good spring break, Dana. Give me a call if you feel like getting together." Then with a forced bright smile she walked out of the room.

Chapter 19

Why did everyone think that her relationship with Michael was open for public comment? She was getting so tired of it. Even at church people were badgering her to label the relationship.

"So are you two an 'item' yet?" she would hear. An *item?* Were they teenagers? What was wrong with people?

"Do you think he's the one?" No! She wanted to scream back. I don't want there to be a 'one', so leave me alone!! She had thought that by avoiding labels, it would have kept the questions at bay, but instead it just seemed to make things worse.

At least no one else would be there tonight, and provided she and Michael avoided being alone, they would all have a good time. She was just about home when her cell phone rang. It was Michael, saying that he had had something come up that evening, and they wouldn't be able to come over.

"Oh," Katherine responded, trying hard not to sound as disappointed as she felt. She wondered what had 'come up' and why he wouldn't just tell her. "We were looking forward to it," she managed to say.

"Yes, the boys will be disappointed too, but..."

"Well, you can drop the boys off if you like on your way to whatever it is that you have to do," Katherine offered awkwardly.

"That just doesn't seem right," he began.

"Why not?" she countered.

Michael hesitated and then blurted out suddenly, "Because I'm taking someone out to dinner."

"Oh...I see."

Yeah, sorry mister, but I'm not babysitting for you so you can go out on the town, Katherine thought angrily.

"Well, we'll see you Tuesday when you drop the boys off, then OK?" She tried to sound casual and normal, feeling anything but.

"Alright then," Michael said, somewhat uncertainly. "We'll see you Tuesday. Goodbye." He hung up the phone, angry and frustrated. She could have at least acted disappointed that she wasn't going to see him, but she acted like she could care less. *Just lets me know I'm doing the right thing by dating other women,* he thought unconvincingly.

When he went to tell the boys that they were going over to his parents instead of Friday night at the Douglas house, they were beside themselves.

"But Dad, why can't we just go over there like we always do? I already saw Amber today at school, and told her I was bringing our new game. Remember, you told me I could!" Jack protested.

Michael just put his head in his hands. Probably Katherine's girls were giving it to her right now too, and it was all his fault for trying to play the silly you'll-want-me-if-I'm-not-available game.

"I'm sorry Jack," he said firmly. "Something has come up, and I can't change it now."

Jack, hearing the tone of finality in his father's voice, walked away dejected to tell Simon the depressing news. Watching him, Michael felt horrible. He should have made the date for Saturday. What had he been thinking? Then in a moment of decision, he picked up the phone and called his prospective date.

"Hey, is it too late to change our plans to tomorrow night?"

Silence on the other end of the line.

"I forgot that I had planned something with the boys, and they're giving me a hard time over here."

"Well, in that case, I guess I can wait until tomorrow," came the sugary reply.

"OK, OK, thanks. I'll call you tomorrow afternoon to make sure, OK?"

Relieved, Michael hung up the phone and dialed Katherine's house. *Come on, Katherine,* he thought desperately, *answer the phone!*

"Hello?"

"Katherine, is it too late to still come over?"

"With your date?" she asked incredulously.

Michael swallowed hard, "No, just us. I....I cancelled it for tonight."

"Oh, I guess that's still fine. The girls will be relieved, they've been wailing over here like a bunch of medieval mourners." Katherine wished she would have had the gumption to say that it wasn't fine, that they weren't some sort of back-up friends waiting around for Michael to free his social calendar, but she was so relieved that he was coming after all, she didn't even care.

"Yeah, same here," Michael laughed back, relieved that she wasn't going to be coquettish over the whole thing.

So, with that, he packed up the boys and headed over to Katherine's. *She must think I'm a jerk,* he thought, *I definitely played that all wrong. Guess I'm not good at this sort of game.*

When they walked into Katherine's, she was attempting to fix a gluten-free pizza and was cursing the crust. "Hi," she said attacking the dough with a rolling pin, "at least it's OK to be angry at inanimate objects." Then she gathered up the dough into a ball and tried afresh to roll it out.

"Why? Am I one of the 'animate' objects you would have liked to be angry with?" Michael asked.

"Oh, sure. You, people at school, students, children that can't handle disappointment, and....I think that's all for now."

"Well, I apologize. I was a jerk to make other arrangements without canceling ours first."

Katherine bit back a retort, and instead pounded the dough again with her fist. "You would think that they could come up with a way to make gluten-free flours a little easier to work with. I think you had better call Pizza Hut for us, and I'll find something else for Alyssa to eat."

"Here, let me try," Michael said edging his way in. He gently tried to flatten the dough with his fingers instead of using the rolling pin. "There, you see, if you just work with it a little and don't rush it, it actually does what it's supposed to!"

"Yeah, just like you've done with me," Katherine responded sarcastically. She was angry with him. He had had the nerve to call and tell her he had a date, to cancel their existing plans, to put her in a major confrontation with her girls, and to make her more jealous than she realized she could possibly be.

"What?"

"I said, just like what you've done with me!"

He stopped and faced her, hands covered in gritty corn flour, while realization dawned on his face. "Katherine, I...."

She raised her own flour-covered hands in protest. It never paid to be angry, what was that verse she always quoted to the girls? Ah, James 1:20, *For the wrath of man worketh not the righteousness of God.*

"Sorry," she mumbled, "now *I'm* being a jerk."

"So we're even?"

She shrugged. What a mess—relationship mess, cooking mess...everything. She sighed, and with an attempt at lightheartedness said, "We will be if you call and order the rest of us some pizza."

"OK, that's what I'll do," he answered, resisting the urge to brush back the hair from her cheek, and the feeling striking him anew how he still loved her, even though he was trying so hard not to.

So, despite the rocky beginning, they all played Jack's new game, got full on ordered-out Pizza (Alyssa even ate her own crumbled-crust pizza concoction and didn't complain), and they enjoyed a fun evening together. Later, as the Mannings were leaving, Michael looked at Katherine meaningfully, "I really enjoyed myself, thank you." *Far more than on a date with anyone else*, he wanted to add.

"You're welcome. I had a good time too," she said, unable to meet his eyes. Then they were gone, and she stood in the doorway

Chapter 19

a long time, looking out into the empty street wondering what was wrong with her. They obviously had something special. She just didn't know how to preserve it without having to meet Michael's demands. Shaking her head sadly, she walked slowly inside and began getting the girls ready for bed. She wondered for the millionth time that night who he had been planning on taking out. Life had definitely become complicated, despite all her efforts to the contrary.

Chapter 20

IT WAS THE middle of April. The short refreshment that spring break had provided had long since worn off. Those picture-perfect beach days with all four children in tow seemed slightly unreal when contrasted with the mounds of work and chores that confronted her now.

Only six more weeks until school was out. Katherine felt like all her energy for the year had been sapped. She sank down gratefully into the pew at church. At least here she could relax, recharge her spiritual batteries, and not have to corral ninety-eight junior high students. Plus, she enjoyed sitting there with Michael. It was a comfortable feeling to be next to him, to know that this man she enjoyed spending time with shared her faith. At least they were still companionable despite the awkwardness that had been between them since March. Thanks to Jack, she knew that Michael had indeed taken a couple of women out, and as time went on it bothered her profoundly. She couldn't help wondering how these dates were, how beautiful the women were, where they went, whether Michael kissed them…she didn't understand how he could date other people if he was in love with her. True, she wasn't ready—and might never be—to reciprocate his feelings, but why couldn't he just give her some time? Was he doing it purely to be vindictive? That didn't seem like him. It just didn't make sense to her. Angrily, she pushed these thoughts from her mind. Trying to redirect them, she glanced down at her bulletin only to see Jack coming to sit down next to Amber.

"Hi Jack," she smiled, "Amber was starting to worry that you weren't coming today."

"Oh," he rolled his eyes dramatically, "we're late because Dad had to stop and pick up that lady. Yuk!" Katherine could hear a ripple of laughter from the people behind her, but before she could look back and feign amusement too, up Michael walked with his realtor, Melissa. Katherine was floored. He was dating *her*? She could not believe it. And why would he bring Melissa to their church? What was he trying to do, parade his dates before everyone? Katherine could feel a prickly heat come over her. She knew she needed to acknowledge them somehow, so as graciously as she could she leaned over and smiled hello.

The realtor, not to be outdone, gushed, "Oh Katie – it is Katie, right? – how *are* you? Michael never mentioned that you attended church here. The way you too were looking at houses together I had figured…" she paused dramatically, allowing everyone to fill in their own blank, and then shrugged, "…oh, never mind!"

Good one, Katherine thought, horrified. It was as if half the church had quietened down to listen to her syrupy voice. Now they would realize she had helped Michael pick out his house. The people around them were getting a real show today. Of course Mrs. Conolley was there, probably taking notes, shaking her head and tut-tutting. Katherine wanted to give one of Jack's eye rolls but instead she smiled and shrugged. There was no point in coming up with an answer to that monologue. She leaned back as the tension in her neck tightened. It felt like someone was turning her neck muscles into a cork screw. How on earth was she going to get through the service? How could he do this to her? There she sat with Amber, Jack, Michael, *and* his realtor.

That was nice of you, she thought. *Rub it in my face and make a spectacle of me in front of all these people who already think everything that happens to me is for public consumption.* She could hear people whispering behind her. Well, she *had* told people over and over that there was nothing serious between her and Michael. Hopefully now they would remember that, and not sit there feeling sorry for her. She managed to get through the service, although she had no idea what the preacher said. She prevented herself from running off as soon as the closing hymn was over by making some forced small talk. Then she collected Alyssa from Junior Church, and got into the car. Amber was already starting to whine about the fact that Jack and Simon couldn't come over. She turned and looked at her and said too sternly, "We're having a quiet afternoon at home, young lady. I don't want to hear any more." Amber started to cry, and then Alyssa decided to join in. Now she was being treated to a duet. Katherine took a deep breath and let out the air slowly, breathing through her mouth like the dentist always told her to do when he was about to start drilling. At that moment, she knew the metaphor was appropriate. Yet, she felt guilty. There was no need to be impatient with the girls just because she was thoroughly frustrated with Michael.

No sooner had they arrived home and the phone was ringing. It was Mrs. Conolley. She needed to know immediately why that nice young man Katherine had been seeing was with somebody else. On and on she went about how if Katherine would just do something a little different with her hair color she could look almost as beautiful as that woman Michael had brought. This was South Florida, where women were expected to never look over thirty, and you just had to keep up. How could Katherine compete with her out-dated clothes and hairstyle when Michael had beautiful dates like that woman to fall back on? Katherine had had enough. She bit back the angry retorts that were on the tip of her tongue, fielded the barrage as best as she could, and then hung up the phone and unplugged it.

Get over it, Katherine, she thought angrily. She should have asked Mrs. Conolley why *she* had obviously done nothing to prevent herself from looking over eighty. However, she knew that the best response to gossip, and empty questions was no response. Responses, no matter how carefully crafted, seemed to fuel the fire, and people had selective memories regarding what you actually *did* say in defense of yourself.

Tiredly, she made lunch for the girls, and then pulled out her school work. Usually she tried to take the day off, but somehow she had gotten behind that week. Probably from too much time wasted worrying about Michael. She opened her lesson plan book, and tried to concentrate on the week ahead. Looking at what she had written for Monday, she realized that she had forgotten all about Alyssa's check-up with the gastroenterologist the following morning and she hadn't even scheduled a substitute. Now what? Frantically she called around, but being Sunday afternoon, nobody was available. What was wrong with her? She couldn't keep anything straight. She would have to call for a sub in the morning and the last minute notice wasn't going to make the middle school secretary very happy. She put her head in her hands dejectedly. So much for her predictable and controlled life, she was a first rate mess.

Thankfully, Michael was at church on his own that night. He still sat next to them, but they didn't talk much. Katherine didn't know what to say to him. She thought of a few things such as, "So, did you enjoy making me look foolish this morning?" Or, "How was your date? She sure is beautiful. She looks like the type who's dying to marry a well-off, eligible, good looking physician." Better still, how about: "It must be convenient for

Chapter 20

Melissa to date you when she already knows so much about your financial status." She kept her thoughts to herself, though, smiling inwardly. She might get some temporary satisfaction from it, but in the end she would just feel bad for trading meanness for meanness. 'Katherine the Saint', that's what she was… She sighed and made sure she listened to the preaching.

The sermon was based on Colossians 2:10: *"And ye are complete in Him…"* She barely even noticed the rest of the verse; the phrase just struck her. She, Katherine, emotional wreck, tired and worn out, was *'complete in Him.'* She drank in the words. It seemed like no matter how many times you read a passage in the Bible, it became fresh and applicable every single time you read it. Sitting there, praying silently, Katherine read the words over and over.

Thank you, Lord, that despite my imperfections I am complete in You, she breathed. *I may be confused and a disaster, but You love me nevertheless. Everyone may think I'm a fool, but You call me your child. You love me no matter how I mess up. Thank you.* Feeling relief, she looked up and over at Michael.

"Hey Katherine," he whispered, "does Alyssa still have her follow-up visit with Dr. Cantrell tomorrow?"

"Oh – ah – yes she does," she responded surprised that he had remembered.

"Would you please call and fill me in on the appointment?" he asked.

Katherine was further surprised, "Oh – OK" was all she managed. She wanted to cry again. Just that simple bit of kindness from him had made her want to cry. She was too tired of thinking to analyze her emotions any more. She fervently hoped that when she made it to summer vacation, some time off would clear her head. Her neck hadn't gotten any better that afternoon and the tension was giving her a pounding headache.

That night she knew sleep wouldn't come so she reached for her Bible and her journal. She had thought by avoiding a relationship, and never remarrying she would avoid all this emotional upheaval, but it seemed to have made it worse. Journaling and reading and applying God's Word had always helped her immensely. Maybe it would help her now.

Dear God, please give me clarity and peace. Everyone seems to think I have been an idiot for messing up the relationship with Michael. Nobody understands my conflicting emotions. Thank You that You understand. Even if my actions have been misguided by confusing emotions, You understand me. Thank you that I can come to You an emotional wreck and You don't condemn me for it, You love me regardless. Thank You that I can be complete in You.

She opened her Bible to Colossians and reread the verse from the evening's sermon.

"And ye are complete in Him, which is the head of all principality and power."

Yes, she thought, *I am 'complete in Him', but I still need direction.* Looking up verses in her subject index that promise direction in life she flipped to Jeremiah 29:11, *"For I know the thoughts that I think toward you, saith the LORD, thoughts of peace, and not of evil, to give you an expected end."* She paused and closed her eyes, allowing the comforting words to wash over her mind. God had thoughts of peace towards her! He had an expected end for her! He knew where she should go, even when she did not! But how was she to find that expected end?

Using her subject index again, she found more verses on direction and turned to Isaiah 30:21, *"And thine ears shall hear a word behind thee, saying, This is the way, walk ye in it, when ye turn to the right hand, and when ye turn to the left."* If she was in tune with God, he would tell her which way to go? But, what if her frantic pace was preventing her from truly listening? Looking back in her subject index she turned to the next verse listed, Genesis 24:27, *"I being in the way, the Lord led me."* She stopped and thought again, putting the pieces together.

Chapter 20

"OK, Katherine," she spoke aloud, "First of all, God has an *expected end* for you; second, He has promised to guide you step by step; third, if you are *in the way*, in other words if you are in His will each and every day, then those steps will lead to that *expected end*! So, your job is NOT to decide whether to marry Michael or not, your job is simply to stay in God's will each and every day." It was approaching midnight, and finally with peace settling in her heart, she fell asleep quoting over and over again the words of Genesis 24:27, "*I being in the way, the LORD led me....*"

Chapter 21

THE NEXT MORNING, Katherine woke up with a fuzzy head and the remains of yesterday's headache—all definitely the result of too much crying, not enough sleep, and too much thinking. She held her head in her hands, surveying her open Bible and journal on the bed next to her, and remembering the promises she had claimed for herself, found the energy she needed to get herself out of bed. She had to hurry. Amber had to ride the bus that morning since she was taking Alyssa to the doctor.

Barely out of the shower, she was scrambling into some clothes when she heard the doorbell ringing. She ran downstairs, and opened the door to a smiling, perfectly dressed Jack.

"Jack!"

"Hi! Dad wants to know if you want Amber to ride to school with us this morning."

"Oh, uh, sure! Let me just see if she's ready, OK?" She walked back inside, calling to Amber.

"Here I am, Mom!" came the frantic response. Amber had seen them pull up from her window, and was doing her best to get ready in record time so that she could indeed ride with them. Katherine, noting how fast her daughter was moving thought ruefully that she should have the Manning taxi arrive at her house every morning. She had to remind Amber to get her school bag and then had to chase her down with her lunch. By the time they were both outside at the car, Katherine was breathless. Michael rolled down his window to say good morning. He had an amused grin on his face, assuming correctly that Katherine must have overslept.

"Hi!" she managed. She caught her breath. Michael looked so handsome, his hair still wet from his morning shower. To think he had thought of them! He knew how she hated to put her girls on the bus.

"You doing OK?" he asked, still grinning.

"Uh, nothing that a little extra sleep couldn't fix…" *In conjunction with some severe relationship counseling*, she added to herself.

Michael nodded, understanding. "Will you call me and let me know how the follow-up goes?"

"Sure."

"'Bye Mom!" Amber yelled excitedly from the back of the car.

"Have a good day sweetie," Katherine said, kissing her daughter through the open window.

"Can I have a kiss too?" Simon piped up.

"Simon!" Jack said in grown-up horror.

"Of course, Simon." Katherine laughed walking around to his side and opening his door to kiss him.

"How about me?" Michael asked, tilting his head to make his cheek available. Katherine, knowing he was teasing her, stepped over and planted a light kiss on his smooth cheek.

"Ha! That's what you get!" she laughed noting his surprise.

"Hmmm," he managed, trying to recover his composure, "I think we'll be by tomorrow morning to pick up both girls, OK?" Then off he drove.

Katherine stood watching them disappear around the corner with a bemused look on her face. *Well, that was certainly a vast improvement to the beginning of the day,* she thought happily. It was hard to believe that just yesterday he had brought a date to church.

A few hours later, sitting in Doctor Cantrell's office, she found herself reading *Curious George goes to the Beach* aloud, for the six millionth time, to Alyssa.

"Mommy?"

"Yes, honey?"

"Will Doctor 'Cartel' say I'm better enough to start eating normal food again?"

"Oh, honey," Katherine said, thinking carefully, "I think he might say you have to eat like you are for a long time."

"But I feel better," Alyssa protested.

Katherine turned and faced her daughter, taking both her hands and looking directly into her eyes. "We're just going to have to think of all that other food that you can't have as poison for your body. It's not poison to many other people, but for you it is. Now, if you start eating that poison again, it's going to hurt your tummy again, and you'll start being sick all over again."

"But I don't like a lot of the different foods you've been making me," Alyssa protested.

"Well then," Katherine tried, "we're just going to have to figure out a better way to make them. Maybe you can help me get them to taste better and better. We can even try and make them together and you can add different ingredients that you think will help, and pretty soon we'll be making the best gluten-free food around!"

"Could I wear one of those cooking hats too?"

"Cooking hats?"

"You know, like the one the Pillsbury Doughboy wears on TV."

"Oh, of course. We'll get you one as soon as we can, OK?" Alyssa nodded, seeming satisfied for awhile, but then started a new line of questioning.

"What about when I'm old?"

"When you're old?"

"Will I still have to eat funny food when I'm old?"

"Oh sure, but by then it won't taste funny. By then you will be such a cooking expert that people will be coming to you for gluten-free meals!"

"But what if I don't have any teeth?"

"What do you mean?"

"You know, some old people don't have teeth and how will I eat my good food if I don't have teeth?"

Nurse Janet saved Katherine from further mental gyrations by calling them back. After the preliminary weight check and brief questions, Janet left them to wait for the doctor who 'would be in shortly'.

Katherine looked at her watch again. The appointment time had long since past and her impatience was building. She had hoped they would be done in time so she could at least make it for half a day of teaching. But, at this rate, that would not be probable. They had already had Alyssa's repeat blood work taken the week before. She wished that Dr. Cantrell had just discussed the results over the phone. That would have saved the office visit. She had long since used up her sick and personal days, so now every day of school she missed was a paycheck deduction.

When they finally did get to see the doctor, he was not very positive. He lectured Katherine that Alyssa's antibody levels were not yet down to baseline. That meant that Katherine was not doing a good enough job at keeping Alyssa's diet 100 percent gluten-free. Then he went on to remind her of the long-term ramifications.

Chapter 21

"Patients with celiac disease who do not follow the diet have a greater risk of developing long term complications such as intestinal lymphoma. Do you know what that is?"

"Yes," Katherine answered meekly, noting Alyssa's expression. Alyssa wasn't used to seeing her mother get into trouble. Katherine wanted to argue that Alyssa *was* doing better, regardless of what the blood tests said but she knew that to argue with the brisk physician was useless.

"Well, I suggest you reschedule a visit with Ms. Baddock, and then go home and go over your kitchen with a fine-tooth comb. My secretary can also give you a form letter that we give to our young celiac patients so that the school, cafeteria workers etc. know how vital it is for Alyssa to stay gluten-free." With that, he turned abruptly and walked out of the door.

Goodbye to you too, Katherine thought despondently, staring at the closed door.

That evening, Katherine called Michael. Maybe he could give her some suggestions or at least make her *feel* better about what had just transpired.

"Hello Michael?" Her voice cracked.

"Hey Katherine, how did it go today?"

"Uh….not too good," she shut her eyes tightly. *Do NOT get emotional, Katherine.* But it was no use. Tears were running down her cheeks.

"What happened?" He sounded abrupt himself, still in his doctor-mode after a day of work.

"Oh," she paused, willing her voice to sound normal, "her antibody levels were not where they should be if she was eating 100 percent gluten-free. Dr. Cantrell kind of got irritated with me, and told me if I wanted to ensure my daughter didn't land up with an intestinal lymphoma I would have to do a better job with the diet."

"What were the levels?"

"I don't know. I was so floored that I couldn't think to ask logical questions." *Yeah,* she thought, *ever since I met you I'm a complete mess.*

"OK, OK. I'll ask him to fax me a copy of the labs."

"You would?"

"Of course! Did he give you any suggestions?"

"No, he just told me to go and see the nutritionist again. Honestly, that woman knows less than I do. I mean, she didn't even know that regular brands of corn flakes have malt in them. Regardless, I'll have to go and see her anyway. I don't want to alienate the only specialist in town that treats celiac disease."

"Are you crying?" his voice was now low and filled with concern.

"Maybe..."

"Oh Katherine, I'm so sorry. No matter what he says, I know how hard you have worked and the level of effort you have put into this. You're a wonderful mother, and Amber and Alyssa are a reflection of that."

There was silence on the other end of the line.

"Katherine? You've got to believe me! Don't allow one doctor to pass judgment on you and negate all of your hard work, OK?"

"OK," she managed.

"Listen, the boys are in bed, otherwise I'd come over. But, if you don't mind we'll come over tomorrow night. I'll bring dinner, and you and I can sit and figure out the source of gluten contamination."

"Thank you," came her feeble reply.

"Now listen, Katherine. Just go to bed and don't worry. Remember, no matter what Dr. Cantrell insinuated, you are a wonderful mother. Take that thought to bed tonight, because it's the truth, alright?"

"Alright."

"I'll see you tomorrow evening?" He closed his eyes, wishing he could just drive over there and simply hold her.

"Yes."

"Goodnight, Katherine."

"Goodnight, Michael…thank you."

Surprisingly, Katherine did sleep well that night. Michael's concern had warmed her heart, and she fell asleep replaying his words in her mind. *Thank you, Lord, I needed that kindness tonight.* It felt so good knowing that someone was going to help her tackle what seemed an impossible task.

The next evening, the Manning men trooped in with a jovial, "Good evening, ladies! Your dinner has arrived!" The boys ran straight back outside when they saw that Alyssa and Amber were playing behind the house. The area was called a "common area" Garden-home lingo, Katherine assumed. It always made her think of the verse in Acts that said, "*they had all things common.*" She smiled at how her brain would jump around. At least garden home communities with all their "common areas" had lawn maintenance and did all the heavy yard work. That was one less thing to worry about.

"Thanks for coming over, Michael," she said. "What's in the bags?"

"Chinese for all of us and this one especially made for Alyssa. I asked the man if there was wheat in the soy sauce so many times that he wanted to kick me out before I had even paid."

"I know," Katherine replied. "Yesterday I ordered her a salad at one of those places where you pick what you want and watch them make it. The guy threw croutons on top. When I told him we couldn't have croutons on the salad because they were made of wheat, he rolled his eyes and took them off. Then he acted like he was going to throw the tongs at me when I told him that he was going to have to start over with a new salad *and* use a new pair of tongs. I think he wanted to throw the whole bin of croutons at me too."

"I guess they get so angry because they think you're just another low-carb dieter who's freaking out about the number of carbs you've already consumed."

"I know, I need to come up with a simple quick way to explain so people are actually helpful."

"Tell them it's a severe allergy," Michael suggested. "People understand peanut allergies and how just the tiniest amount can be deadly."

"But it's not an allergy, it's an intolerance, Doctor," she teased.

"I know, and *you* know, but if you're ordering food at a place where you don't know the people, you're going to have to come up with something that the general public can understand."

"I'll write that down on my 'to-do' list," Katherine grabbed a pen and wrote at the top of the paper as she spoke aloud. "Find a quick easy explanation for gluten-free food that's not a lie."

"Glad to see you can joke about it tonight," Michael smiled at her. "I was concerned for you last night. I fell asleep praying for you."

Katherine warmed at the thought. "So you do that too? Pray while you're going to sleep?"

"Yes, more often than not. I pick a person and just start praying for them. The next thing I know it's morning, I'm rested, and I feel good that I spent my last wakeful moments doing something useful." He didn't add that it was usually Katherine who he most often fell asleep praying for.

"Well, thank you for choosing to pray for me last night. I really needed it."

They called the children in to eat and watched in amusement as they ate as fast as they could so that they could get back outside before it got dark.

"I remember doing that as a kid," Katherine said. "We loved to play hide-'n'-seek tag, and would play until it was too dark to find anyone. My mom had a whistle and would call us back to the house that way." She smiled at the memories.

They continued eating while leisurely recalling childhood memories.

"Well, I guess we had better get down to business," Katherine said, reluctantly standing up.

"Why don't you get me a pen and paper?" Michael concurred.

He started by writing down all the possible events that would involve foods during Alyssa's day. Next to that, he wrote down which people would be responsible for those foods, whether or not Katherine had talked to them and if they had back-up snacks for Alyssa. They went through Alyssa's play dates, the grandparents, and where they most often ate out.

Finally Katherine said, "You know, maybe the problem is right here at home. This is where she eats most often, and her second levels were almost as high as her initial antibody screening. I don't understand whether there's a correlation between the amount of gluten ingested at one time or the frequency that she ingests it that causes the antibody levels to elevate. Does my question make sense?"

"You mean whether it's a one time major mess-up or frequent minor mess-up?" Michael asked. When Katherine nodded the affirmative he went on. "That's a great question, but as far as I can tell from the research there is no answer to it. There are still so many unknowns. For instance, many people will go off gluten before they are tested just because they've discovered it makes them feel so much better. Then, when they finally do see a doctor, their tests for celiac disease comes back negative since they've self diagnosed and treated for so long. Many times, they are not willing to consume gluten again just to prove to themselves and their doctors that they actually have the disease. It's just not worth it to them to get so sick again. Plus, nobody can tell them definitively how long they have to ingest it prior to the test. So they are never officially diagnosed, although they more than likely have the disease."

Katherine nodded, "Sometimes it seems like despite all the medical advancements we are still in the dark ages." She shrugged, "Oh well, for now let's go over my kitchen with a fine-toothed comb."

They went through the refrigerator. Katherine was sure that neither she nor Amber were double-dipping their crumb-covered knives back into the peanut butter or mayonnaise. They reread labels, checked that wheat flour wasn't leaking on to plates or bowls, and checked the cookware. Then Katherine stood up quickly as realization dawned, "What about the toaster! I never thought of the toaster. We use the same toaster for our regular bread as well as Alyssa's gluten-free bread! Could that have been the culprit?"

"Well, it would be a source of gluten," Michael said thoughtfully. "Good for you, for thinking of that. Who's to say if it is the sole culprit, though. You can buy Alyssa her own toaster. That's simple enough. The hard part will be keeping the right bread in the right toaster!"

The label checking continued. Looking through the candy Katherine found "malt" listed as a minor ingredient in one of the mini-chocolate candy bars Alyssa liked. Ironically it was in the one Alyssa loved the most. "Maybe I should just start questioning every food the poor child really likes," she sighed.

"Hey, don't get discouraged. Just pretend you're a forensic scientist."

"And you can be my good-looking partner," Katherine joked back.

"Anytime, Katherine, anytime," he replied, a serious look in his eyes.

Katherine felt her face grow hot so she busied herself with another cabinet.

"Hey Katherine, didn't you just do that cabinet?" Michael asked innocently.

"Oh, ah, yes. I guess I did."

"You're a cute blusher."

"Oh, um, thanks…I guess."

They continued working in companionable silence until it was almost dark and Michael had to call the boys in. Because it was a school night, not long afterwards, they left.

"Hey partner," Michael smiled at the door, "you found two culprits tonight. Unfortunately there may be many more, but for now you've made good progress. I'd say you get a bonus." He leaned forward, kissed her briefly on the cheek, then straightened up, winked and walked out to their car.

Katherine walked into the house a smile playing with the corners of her mouth.

"Why did they have to leave so soon?" Alyssa whined. "I wanted them to stay for at least five or six more hours."

"That would be too late, silly," Amber said with superiority. "It would be two or three in the morning if they did that."

"Good math work, Amber," Katherine said. "Now it's bath time for both of you."

Cleaning up later, Katherine noticed that the boys had left their tennis shoes and socks at the patio entrance. Katherine shook her head and added them to the Manning bag she kept near the front door that already held random items of importance left behind from previous visits. While it was on her mind, she called Michael's cell phone and, getting his voice mail, left a message telling him about the collection of Manning paraphernalia by her front door. One of these days, they would remember and take the whole pile home!

Chapter 22

OVER THE NEXT few weeks, it seemed to Katherine that they were once again seeing less and less of the Manning clan. They would sit together at church, although occasionally Michael would bring a woman with him. Katherine didn't know if he was truly interested, or just doing his best to make her feel terrible. If the latter was his motive, it was working. She hadn't spoken to him alone since the night he had come over and helped her 'de-glutenize' her kitchen. What puzzled her most was the fact that they had shared such an enjoyable and companionable time together that night. So, this seeming avoidance of her and the girls was confusing. That, coupled with his frequent dates with different women was making her feel awful. At times she felt like shaking him, and asking him what on earth he was trying to do to her emotions.

It was a Friday, and the girls were away for the weekend with her in-laws. It had been a discouraging week, beginning on Sunday with Michael bringing yet another 'date' to church. All she wanted was for Michael to come over, take her in his arms and kiss her troubles away…

She stopped folding Alyssa's shirt in midair. Did she really want that? Lately her internal arguments felt empty and selfish. It hurt her deeply each time she saw him with another woman. She wondered if he had kissed anyone else. The night he had kissed her had been such a beautiful night, and the fact that, aside from a few pecks on the cheek, he had never tried to kiss her again, bothered her.

What do I expect? she asked herself angrily. But still it ate at her. Just "friends" or not, she wanted to feel at least a tiny bit desirable.

Putting away the clothes she had just folded, she made a decision to grab her Bible and journal and head to the beach. It was time to address all her conflicting emotions. She needed to reread the verses that had helped her so much a few weeks before, and then read some more. She felt like she had indeed been keeping herself close to God day by day, and she knew in her heart that it was now decision time regarding Michael.

The ocean was beautiful. It always had such a soothing effect on her. Maybe it was the sheer vastness, but the magnitude of beauty before her always seemed to put her problems into perspective. The slanted shadows that indicated 'winter' was upon them were gone, and instead there was the sharp, clear brightness that accompanied the approaching summer.

She had explained to Michael once that that was how you knew it was winter.

"How?" He had laughed, recalling freezing Michigan winters.

"The shadows are slanted."

"That's winter?"

"Yes, that's how you know! Plus, it gets dark earlier."

"Ah, sounds ominous."

"And sometimes, we get to wear sweaters!"

"How exciting."

"The ocean has more waves."

"I thought that meant a hurricane was coming."

She shrugged, "Sure, hurricanes can happen as late as November."

"Is my free lesson on 'Seasons in South Florida' over?"

Katherine nodded, and he had proceeded to give her a lesson on how to skip a rock.

Smiling at the memory, Katherine dumped her beach gear, and struck out on a vigorous walk. It felt so good to be free of responsibility for a while. Whatever had possessed her to take a job with junior high students? They had to be the most difficult age group to teach. Yet, she felt she did have a knack for that age, despite the level at which they continually sapped her energy. Within minutes, however, her thoughts had turned from them back to Michael.

Oh Lord, she prayed, *please help me understand myself, and what it is I want and what it is the girls and I need. I am so confused.*

While she was walking, her mind played out various clips that had happened since she had met Michael. She thought of how he had helped her see the need to reach out and help others. She had met with Sandra, the woman he had introduced her to, who had lost her husband as well. What had ensued was a beautiful prayer partnership. They would get together sporadically, and discuss the difficulties they were facing, share Bible verses that had helped them, and pray together. All because of Michael...

She thought of his humor, how one Sunday shortly after their date during which he had told her about Morgan, he had met her in the lobby of the church and kissed her on the cheek.

"Michael!" she had protested, "We're at church!"

"And I'm just being Biblical," he responded. "I read this morning in I Corinthians that we are to '*greet one another with a holy kiss*.'"

"I think '*holy*' is the key there, don't you?" she had countered.

"Are you calling me unholy?" was his response.

"No, just unscrupulous!"

"Unscrupulous? I think resourceful might be a better word."

"Now, how is kissing me in church resourceful?"

"Why, I can go on the strength of that kiss for the rest of the day!"

Katherine had laughed.

He sure knows how to put a spring in my step, she thought, back in the present again. *And here I am not wanting him in my life permanently?*

She was near the Juno Pier now, so she sat down to rest, and watch the water rise and fall along the pilings as a wave moved in toward shore. She thought how Michael had caused her to step outside of herself, to not be afraid to consider new things.

One evening they had been sitting at his house finishing dinner when Michael had laid a brochure down in front of her. (Funny how she could replay events that involved Michael with minute detail, but couldn't remember what she fed the girls for breakfast that morning…)

"Hey," he had said, "I was wondering if you and the girls would like to go on this overnight canoe trip down the Peace River with us. One of our nurses is promoting it, and she says it's a wonderful parent-child activity, very relaxing and absolutely beautiful."

"Uh, I don't know," Katherine had stalled, "weekends are for me to play catch-up during the school year."

"Well, what do you do on the weekend that can be skipped just once?"

"Everything, absolutely everything – clean the house, finish schoolwork, grocery shop, laundry, pay bills, clean out the car, take some time for myself, get ready for Sunday, plan the next week..." she shrugged.

"Well, why not just 'live on the edge' for one weekend, and let all of that go?"

"Yeah, and the whole next week will be a disaster. No thank you."

There was silence. She looked up to see Michael looking at her seriously, with disappointment but also concern. Finally he spoke quietly: "Katherine, do you realize you're living your life in a bubble?"

"Because I work hard to keep chaos out of my life? What exactly is that supposed to mean?" she answered defensively.

"Look," Michael said, trying to sound reasonable, "don't get angry with me, I was just wondering if you realize that or not."

"You still need to clarify what you mean," she answered shortly.

He sighed. This was not going well. "I just think you've created this little bubble for yourself, and you are too afraid to step outside of it to experience something new."

"A *little* bubble?" her tone was incredulous.

He held his hands up, "Sorry, I guess by 'little' I meant 'safe'."

"And what is safe about raising two girls on my own, teaching nearly 100 junior high students—which is incidentally the most difficult age to teach, participating in church, keeping my children involved in outside activities, keeping Alyssa gluten-free, and making sure that everyone she comes in contact with does the same, besides taking care of the myriad of details that go wrong every day? Oh yes, and in case you've forgotten, I do that ALL ON MY OWN! Thanks for nothing." Angrily she began collecting her things, and walked toward the door to call the girls inside so that they could leave.

"You know," he said stepping in front of her to keep her from walking outside, "Now that we're on the subject and you're already angry with me, I may as well add that I think this is the reason that you're afraid of a serious relationship."

"Oh sure," her voice was dripping with sarcasm now, "and now I can get psychoanalyzed for free."

"No please, just listen to me," he pleaded. He was now directly in front of her, and had taken both of her hands. "It's obvious – you have your schedule and routines as a safety net to keep your life predictable. The most awful thing happened, you lost your husband, and now you have done everything you can to make your life safe and predictable. And, it's working. You are on top of everything, but it has made you afraid to just live a little. You know, one day you may regret that."

The switch in his tone from confrontational to empathetic coupled with his physical closeness was melting her anger. Now she wanted to cry. She wanted to bury her head in his shoulder, and cry like a baby and tell him that he was probably right. Yet, she did not want to cry in front of him again, so trying to sound lighthearted she managed a wry smile and said, "I would also regret being lunch for an alligator. You'll have to go canoeing without us." Then slipping around him, she went outside to collect the girls.

He sighed and followed her out. The girls were already in full complaint mode over the fact that they had to leave already, arguing that *every* time things got super-duper fun, *they* had to leave. Michael looked over at Katherine and said, "Why not let them stay, and you can go and have some time for yourself? I feel like a jerk now, and at least I can do something to make it up to you."

Oh why does he have to be so nice, she thought desperately. Her sudden desire to get away from his probing eyes, and the noise of the children and be alone won out. Nodding her head, she promised to not be gone too long, and then left without a backward look. She could hear the girls whooping for joy as she got into her car. She would head home and get her bicycle. Maybe a long bike ride would clear her head. Pity she couldn't play tennis, hitting something right then would have felt really good.

Driving home, she couldn't help but think that Michael was somewhat correct. Plus, a weekend outdoors, away from all the work that always screamed at her when she walked in her house did sound appealing. She began mentally checking off all of the things that would have to be finished ahead of time to make the trip feasible. Then, in a moment of decision, she picked up her cell phone and called him.

"Hey, aside from all the psychobabble that came with the invitation, I've given the trip some thought, and might be willing to consider it—"

"If—?"

"If the sleeping arrangements are acceptable and you promise to keep all alligators away from me."

Michael let his out own whoop of joy, sounding just like the children. She could hear him rummaging through papers as he located the brochure. "Let's see, here are the details. You could go as my sister and we could all share a tent and—"

"And you're Abraham and my name is Sarah," she retorted.

He laughed and then turned serious as they went over the details. "The organization has cabins at the evening stop off point," he said. "We can just register separately and then it will be obvious that we need separate cabins." They continued talking, and Katherine felt an excitement well up inside of her as they made their plans...

That trip had been cancelled due to a tropical storm, but the lesson she had learned, thanks to Michael, had stuck with her.

Getting up to walk again, she noticed a storm cloud building. Her mind went back to one of their dates when they had been on the beach and a storm had threatened.

"We had better leave. The sky has that, 'if you stay, you're stupid' look about it," Katherine had warned.

"Is that a Katherine original?"

"What?"

"'If you stay, you're stupid,'" Michael quoted.

"Oh, I don't know, but if we stand here and discuss it we're going to get poured on!"

"Then we'll be 'stupid'?" Michael persisted.

"Michael! Let's go!"

"Just wait! What if I wanted to wait and kiss you right here in the middle of the storm? Would I still be stupid?"

"Michael! I don't want to become a lightening rod on my birthday."

"Where's that sense of adventure gone?" he yelled over the increasing wind.

"It's running for the car at the moment," she hollered back, taking off toward his vehicle.

They made it to the car just in time and watched from the cozy interior as sheets of rain drenched the beach and pounded the water.

"Look, there are some 'stupid' people!" Michael said, pointing out some poor souls struggling toward the parking lot.

Katherine just laughed. How could one person be so much pure fun to be around? She was still breathless from their run, and enjoying his companionship thoroughly.

"I heard that kissing in a storm brings good luck," Michael suggested.

"To who?"

"I think it's 'whom'."

"To whom?"

"To us."

"Oh yeah?"

"Do you want to find out?" Then, a complete change of tone: "Oh great."

"What?"

"My work phone is buzzing."

"So, I went from almost being a kissing lightening rod, to a potentially dateless woman, all in the space of three minutes."

"Yeah, this is the occupational hazard of dating a doctor. I'm sorry." Michael was contrite.

"That's fine, you take your call, and I'll sit here and watch for more stupid people, OK?" Katherine said in an attempt to cover her disappointment.

Michael took the call, and Katherine heard him saying that he would meet them at the Jupiter Medical Center.

Oh well, Katherine thought, *we had fun while we could, and that's what counts. It's just as well, the more he kisses me, the more I'm going to forget I don't want to get serious, and that could cause a problem.*

They drove over to her house in silence. She thanked him for a good time and walked inside the too-quiet house, the events of the evening playing out in her mind.

I'm going to have to be very careful, she thought. *I don't want to remarry, but the more I'm with Michael, the less I seem to remember that. I need to watch out, otherwise we're both going to get hurt again.* She meandered around the house, thinking of all the things she could get done with the girls out of the house and an empty evening ahead, but unsure how to transition from the fun she had just been having back to single-mother-never-stop-working mode, she sighed.

So much for a birthday date, she thought, picking up an overfilled clothes hamper and heading into the laundry room. Flinging the washer lid up, she realized she had forgotten to empty it. Sniffing at the clothes, she hoped they hadn't sat wet too long, because she definitely didn't want to rewash them.

Reaching across with her free hand, she swung the dryer door open, only to realize the dryer was jammed full of dry-but-now-wrinkled clothes. She groaned, then in a moment of decision, set the hamper down and left, closing the door firmly behind her. Let the clothes mold, wrinkle, or rot, she was not going to waste a free evening on that mess!

Purposefully she went to her room, dug out a book she had been dying to read for a long time, and went back downstairs. Opening a nearby window so that she could smell the rain, she curled up on the couch settling in for a long good read. *There we go*, she had thought contentedly. *Happy Birthday to me ...*

Yes, she thought, back in the present, *every clear memory I have of this past year involves Michael. He's led me to help others, made me laugh again, coaxed me to step outside of myself, helped me regain my wit, shown me how to relax, supported me immeasurably with Alyssa, and yes, I now know that he's taught me it's OK to love again.*

Reaching her starting point on the beach, she jumped in the water to cool off and then walked to her towel, settled down, and picked up her Bible to read.

God knew the future, He knew her better than she knew herself, and He knew what would be best for all of them. She was currently reading in the book of Psalms. Opening to the chapter she was at that day, she was startled to see Psalms 55:19, "*...because they have no changes, therefore they fear not God.*" The phrase 'it jumped out at me' couldn't have been more applicable at that moment.

In other words, she thought, *I don't want change because I cannot allow myself to have that level of trust again.* Knowing that a significant part of fearing God was having a reverential trust in Him, she wondered if her avoidance of change was due to a lack of true faith in God.

Dear God, she prayed, *forgive me for being afraid to change, for being afraid of a relationship, for being scared to parent four children, for being afraid to complicate my life, for being afraid to trust You. Thank You for bringing Michael into our lives. I realize now he has been the biggest blessing you have brought my way since Leyton died, and I thank You for that. I give all this to You and I trust You for what the outcome will be.*

With that last barrier—her lack of trust—removed, she stood up with purpose and anticipation. Everything was crystal clear, and she knew what she must do.

With determination, she gathered her things, and walked to the car, her mind actively formulating a plan. Taking a deep breath, she dialed Michael's cell phone, her heart racing as she waited for him to answer.

"Hello?" His voice caused her to catch her breath. She swallowed hard.

"Michael?" She could hear her voice crack.

"Yes?"

"I was….ah…wondering if you….would you…..um…." she swallowed again, took a deep breath and said all at once: "I have a kid-free night and would like to have you over for dinner to thank you for your help with Alyssa."

There was silence on the other end of the line. Finally he answered, "Let me call you back, I have to take care of some details."

Wondering what those 'details' could be, she waited nervously until he called back to say that he could. Relief washed over her. They made their plans and Katherine sped up. She stopped at an office supply store, dashed through the checkout with her purchase and went home to get ready.

Rushing around, multiple objections crowded her mind unbidden. What if everything he had said back in March was no longer true? What if he had already fallen for someone else? What if he had decided that he didn't want a permanent relationship after all?

Nervously she wrapped the newly purchased item, carefully filled out the card, and stuck it to the top of the gift. She wrote his name simply across the top of the card and hearing the doorbell, hurriedly placed the gift on the entryway table and went to the door.

Things were a bit uncomfortable at first. They never saw each other alone anymore. So, after some stilted conversation, Katherine declared the meal ready, and they sat down. She wished they had gone to a restaurant instead, because now that she had him here, she couldn't think of how she was going to get around to the real reason she had invited him over. At least at a restaurant there would have been movement around them to help with the small talk.

Finally, searching around vainly for a lead in question, she laid down her fork and said:

"Michael? May I ask you why you have never tried to kiss me again?"

Silence…an embarrassingly heavy silence. She was horrified at herself. What had possessed her to say that? It had plagued her mind repeatedly, but the fact that she had verbalized it mortified her.

By the look on his face, she knew that he was completely taken aback too, and rightly so. In fact, he was dumbfounded.

"*What?* I'm a *man*, Katherine. I can't be kissing someone who never wants a relationship. I can't believe you seriously—Is that really what you wanted to talk about?" He stood up, his indignation turning to confusion and sadness. Had she really brought him over to play with his emotions? He could actually feel tears gathering, burning his eyes. He needed to leave before she saw how upset he was. "I think I'll go," he mumbled, "It's too awkward eating at your house alone without the children anyway."

"No, no wait, please, just wait. I'm an idiot. I guess I was trying to figure out if what you said back in March still held true. I mean, you've been out with a lot of people since then and I—"

His voice was choking up, "I told you I would date other people, remember?" He kept his head turned as he walked toward the front door, looking for his keys, grateful for the diversion of the bag of things near the door that he needed to get.

"Michael, look. I *am* an idiot. I don't know what made me say that, but please don't go yet—"

"No, I...I... need to." And with that, he finished collecting the boy's things that she had accumulated at the front door for him, and was gone, the front door closing firmly behind him. Katherine could not believe it. She had admittedly asked a very dumb question, but she had been nervous and searching for a lead in. Still seated at the table, she just stared down at the half-eaten dinner and then back toward the empty foyer, the memory of his incredulous words bouncing around in the sudden silence.

I won't cry, she told herself. With the sinking realization that something between them was just not meant to be, she left the table and walked out onto the patio. Breathing in the Florida evening, she sank down on the swing. Sitting out there alone, the full implication of what had just happened hit her. Tears came then.

Oh God, I've really messed up now.

Weeping may endure for a night, but joy cometh in the morning, came the quiet response, but she was too distraught to receive the comfort it should have provided.

Mechanically she walked back inside and stacked the plates up, dumping the uneaten dinner into the trash can. Then leaving the dirty dishes in the sink, she walked around slowly turning off lights and locking doors. When she got to the front door, she realized with increasing fear that Michael's gift was gone, along with the bag of boy's stuff she had left there for him to take home.

Oh no, she thought, her heart sinking even lower. *It must have fallen onto the top of the pile. He's going to find it and open it and know I'm a complete fool.*

Walking heavily up to her room and then later, while trying to sleep, all she could think of was that the gift was in the bag. She had to get it out before he ever found it. She would go over the next morning and find a way to sneak it out. Scarcely comforted, she fell into a fitful sleep.

Chapter 23

MICHAEL WAS IN a thoroughly bad mood. After leaving Katherine's house the night before, he had actually allowed himself to cry. Now, appalled by his own lack of emotional control, he was not only angry with himself but also confused as to Katherine's motive for the whole dinner. Regardless, that glimmer of hope he had arrived with had been quickly extinguished by her ludicrous question. He had thought she was above that sort of thing. It was bad enough that he had to deal with the adolescent behavior of the women he had been dating in lieu of Katherine, but he would have never expected *Katherine* to act so juvenile. In addition, he hated the fact that he found himself increasingly uncomfortable in her presence. He loved her so much, that each time he saw her it was a fresh reminder that she might never love him back. The situation left him feeling trapped, hurt, and frustrated. To think that after all those empty years, he finally had found exactly what he had been missing, only to have his love spurned. His mind traveled back around to Katherine's question the night before, and he still could make no sense of why she had asked him over in order to toy with him further. Slamming around in the kitchen, he called irritably to Jack to come and get some of his stuff off the counter and take it to his room. Jack complied hurriedly, as Simon sat on the couch watching anxiously. It was rare for their Dad to be so grumpy and they were unsure how to react to it.

Finally, Jack, feeling wise beyond his years decided to take matters into his own hands and give his grandmother a call. Maybe she would come over, or better yet, let them go to her house again. They had just been over there the night before, but maybe it wasn't too soon to go back.

He dialed the number quietly, looking around to make sure his Dad wasn't anywhere near him.

"Hello?" he heard his grandmother ask.

"Hi Grandma, it's Jack," he whispered into the phone.

"Jack? Why are you whispering?"

"I don't want my Dad to hear me."

"What's wrong with your Dad?"

"I'm not sure, but I think he has PBS."

"PBS?"

"You know that thing that women sometimes get. I think he has it too."

"Ahhhh," she responded knowingly, wondering where on earth he had already heard about PMS. Children these days knew far too much about far too many things. "So, do you think I should come over and get you guys for awhile until your Dad feels better?"

"Yeah, that might be a good idea. But, don't tell my Dad that I called you, OK?"

"OK," his grandmother responded conspiratorially.

Michael had gladly let the boys leave with his Mom when she came. He was not in the state of mind to wonder why she had shown up without preamble. He had barely shut the door behind them when there was a knock.

Chapter 23

What now? he wondered irately, yanking open the door. There stood Katherine looking as miserable as he felt. Yet still the sight of her stabbed at his heart.

"Yes?" his tone was full of irritation in an attempt to mask the hurt and confusion he felt over her behavior.

Katherine pushed in past him, obviously very flustered. "I need to see if something of mine dropped into that bag of the boy's stuff that you took home last night." She was glancing around looking for the bag as she spoke and headed into the kitchen rummaging through a pile of backpacks, jackets, and shoes heaped below the counter. "Is the bag in here?"

"Well, wait a second. I can get it for you!" Michael said rushing after her, actually embarrassed for her to look through the mess. His usual housekeeper had quit on him and he hadn't had the time or inclination to find a new one. But, he was too late, she was already surrounded by their junk, digging through the bag, seemingly oblivious to the disorder all around her.

"What are you missing?" he asked. "It must be pretty important."

She mumbled something that he couldn't decipher, and then purposefully turned her back to him as she retrieved what looked like a present. Fully curious now, he walked up directly behind her and looked over her shoulder.

She was trying to stand up and shove it into her oversized shoulder bag, but Michael, not caring what she thought of him anymore, reached around her and gripped the other side of it.

"Hey, this has my name on it!" he exclaimed, trying to get a better look as Katherine vainly attempted to pull it from his grasp. But, Michael wasn't about to give up now. He was dying to see what all the angst was about.

"Michael, please!" she pleaded exasperated. "Let's not stand here and play tug of war. Please?"

"Oh no!" he responded with a playful yet malicious glint in his eye. "I'm not going to let you out of here until you tell me what's in the package!" Then he twisted it from her grasp and turned his back to her. "Let's just see here, a package with my name on it that you don't want me to have. I wonder what it could be…" His voice held a mixture of amusement and irritation, but in a way, he was enjoying her discomfort. She had put him through plenty, that was for sure.

"Michael, please." She pleaded again desperately. She was openly crying now and didn't care. He couldn't possibly think any less of her than he already did. What had ever made her think that buying something so corny would fix things between them?

Michael ignored her and continued opening the package and then stopped and slowly turned it over, trying to process what it meant. There was a note attached, and he read it once hurriedly and then over again before he turned slowly, reading it a third time, aloud this time.

"*Dear Michael, I know I said I never wanted any labels, but I've come to realize that for you, I'll accept any label you wish to confer upon me. I hope it's not too late. Love, Katherine.*"

Michael stopped reading and looked up at her quizzically. "You bought me a label maker?" He was incredulous and she wasn't sure how to respond.

"I thought it might…." She stopped and looked away, wiping her eyes. "I thought, but then you got so mad at me…. I was so stupid….I was just trying to find a way to…" She gave up and looked down now, grabbing at some paper towels to blow her nose. This had to be the most embarrassing, foolish moment of her entire life: jammed into the corner of a messy kitchen, blubbering like an idiot, while the man she loved was holding the dumbest gift she could have ever possibly bought.

"What does this mean?" his voice was stiff now. He felt too afraid to let any emotion seep into his voice.

"It's a label maker," she answered dully. "I thought it would be a cute way to tell you…"

"Tell me what?" his tone had softened with hope.

"Tell you that I'm ready."

He took a step towards her. "Ready for what?" his voice was now raw with emotion.

"Ready for what you wanted back in March."

He was so close to her she could feel his breath on her face. His eyes were so intense that she had to look away.

"Could you explain?" he implored. But there was only silence. He sat the gift back on the pile and then reached out and took her hands, pulling her against him. "Come on Katherine, I won't be rude or impatient again. I just need to hear it straight."

That gave her confidence and a glimmer of hope. "It means that I'm not afraid of labels anymore. I'm not afraid of black tie and roses. If I'm with you, it doesn't matter, I just need to be with you."

Silence again.

Finally, he said, "What if I wanted to print out 'Michael's wife'?"

She took a deep breath, trying to steady herself, to keep from crying some more.

"I would wear it proudly, with joy."

There was still no response. She couldn't tell what he was feeling. How could he not respond? She had just laid bare her heart. Had his attitude toward her changed that much in just six weeks? Maybe whoever he had cancelled his engagement with the evening before was on his mind. So, she went on: "I've finally realized that you are what I really want, for me, for the girls, for the rest of my life. I may have waited too long; it's just taken me awhile to figure it all out. And lately you have been acting like you're no longer interested in me...."

He smiled wryly, brushing away the fresh tears that were sliding down her cheeks. "That was self-preservation, my dear, pure self-preservation. So," he paused, still trying to make sense of it all, "this is where you were headed last night?"

She nodded, managing a watery smile, "And I botched it, I was so nervous and scared and I…"

"You should have stopped me from leaving…"

"There was no time, you left so fast, that I thought you must actually hate me…"

He cupped the side of her face with his hand wiping the tears with his thumb, "Oh no, no, no, never…I just had all these intense feelings –feelings that I have zero experience with – bottled up inside and the thought that you were taunting me, was too much to bear – I just had to leave."

She buried her face against him then, hugging him as tightly as possible, begging him to forgive her.

"Sh," he admonished, "there's nothing to forgive. I'm the one who has shown you my worst side repeatedly. I'm the one who needs to be forgiven!" He picked up the box then and ripped it open, fumbling with the gadget. "Let's see if we can get this thing to work." Then, after a few moments, he quit – "No batteries," he gave a crooked smile. "You bought me a toy with no batteries."

He set the gift aside and took both her hands again. "So, let me just clarify this…if I could print out…" he took a deep breath, "'*will you marry me?*' you would say 'yes'?"

"Oh Michael," was all she managed looking down.

He reached down and lifted her chin.

"You didn't answer me."

"Oh yes, yes, yes, yes!"

He drew her to him and gently kissed her eyes, her face, and then her lips. There were tears of relief and joy in his eyes too.

"Oh Michael," she whispered, "I'm so sorry. It's been awful. You've been so angry with me."

"No Katherine, just frustrated. Frustrated and hurt that I loved someone who would not love me back. I'll make it up to you, I promise."

"But you kept parading all these women by me, and the whole time I didn't know what to think."

"I know, I know. That was wrong of me. I had my feelings badly hurt—you have to realize that in all these years, you were the only woman I ever wanted—and I thought it would make me feel better to act like I didn't care. But, it only made me feel worse. I was horrible. I know I've had to say this to you before, but please, please forgive me."

"Of course I do. I'm just sorry I didn't realize weeks ago …"

"And I'm sorry I didn't just relax and give you the little bit of time you needed instead of playing a bunch of immature games."

"It's OK. I would have probably been tempted to do the same thing," she said her face once again buried against his chest.

He tightened his arms around her not wanting to let her go. "I should have given you a chance to explain last night too," he ventured.

Her muffled words came back softly, "I don't know if I'll ever be able to think of what I said without complete embarrassment. I was just so anxious and unsure as to how to get to the point…"

"Sh," he admonished once more, "When I remember how I treated you over Alyssa, and when I realize that for lack of patience I put all of us through awkward unnecessary situations, I'm the one who is embarrassed." He paused and took a step back from her, holding her at arms length. "Katherine," his voice was deep and solemn, "I promise from this day forward to do everything in my power to make you feel safe, loved, protected, and completely secure in the love I have for you."

"Oh Michael," she whispered back, her eyes locked on his, "I have every confidence you will. Our mistakes were those of love struck adults who had spent years protecting ourselves from becoming vulnerable again. Now that we're on the same page in every way…" she paused, searching for the right words.

"…we'll be able to be our loving adult selves?" He grinned, attempting to complete her sentence for her.

"Absolutely," she smiled back, flinging her arms around his neck, allowing him to lift her off her feet. Eventually, he looked around and laughed. "How about we go talk in a more appropriate place then this biohazard site I call the kitchen?" He led her into the living room, took a seat on the couch and pulled her down next to him. "You know young lady, I think we've got some planning to do." His voice was low and teasing.

"Can it wait until tomorrow? I didn't exactly sleep much last night."

"Only if you tell me one thing."

"What's that?"

"How soon are you going to marry me?"

"As soon as it's feasible?" she said hopefully.

"Sounds good to me," he said squeezing her tighter. They continued sitting there, close, comfortable, and completely content.

Chapter 24

AFTER THEIR RECONCILIATION, the wedding plans came fast. Katherine felt like they were all caught up in a whirlwind of happiness. She was breathless in anticipation, the children were giddy with excitement, and the grandparents were satisfied that the grown children they loved had found new love out of sorrow.

Despite the excitement, Katherine felt like she had one more personal obstacle to overcome. With it, came a dilemma. The anniversary of Leyton's death was approaching, and for some reason, she had refrained from telling Michael of her annual ritual regarding the date. She didn't want him to feel threatened by the memories she had of Leyton. His relationship with Morgan had obviously been so different, she was afraid he wouldn't understand her need to keep this day sacred for now.

She always took the day off work. Each year, after dropping the girls off at school, or leaving them with a sitter, she would stop and buy a bouquet that included Bird of Paradise. On their honeymoon, he had made her an arrangement with this flower as the focal point, picked from the resort gardens. From then on, the flower had been 'their' flower.

She would go to the gravesite armed with her Bible, journal, and of course the flowers. This anniversary was even more important, because she felt the need to release any guilt she felt over remarrying. It was, of course, illogical, but she still felt disloyal marrying again when at one time Leyton had been the love of her life.

So, that Wednesday morning she sat at the gravesite, fiddling with the engagement ring Michael had given her a few nights earlier, oblivious to the fact nobody knew where she was, and unaware Michael had been trying to call her.

Calling the school, he was told she had taken a personal day. Surprised, he hung up and dialed her home number, and then her cell phone number. He shrugged and went back to work. She was a grown independent woman, and definitely didn't have to tell him of her whereabouts, but it was still very unlike her—especially now that they were in constant contact. He couldn't help wondering why she hadn't mentioned anything, especially since personal days were approved in advance, which meant she would have known about it the last time they talked.

Instead, Katherine sat at the gravesite, reading over her journal. Then, with purpose, she began a new entry, an entry for closure:

Dear Leyton,

We intended to grow old together, and we never had the chance. I thank God daily you left me with two little girls that will remind me of you for the rest of my life. They are beautiful, funny like you, loving, sweet, and already so independent and strong.

The house we bought together has been perfect. You had it all ready for us and never had the chance to enjoy it yourself. Living there has made me feel connected to you since evidence of your labors surrounds me. Now, I'm going to leave our house. I never intended to remarry; I never intended to move. I figured what we had was irreplaceable, and it is. Yet God has sent someone my way 'for such a time as this'.

You will always have the special place in my heart where all first true loves remain, but I will marry again because I'm in love with every ounce of my being. If God had taken me instead of you, I would have wanted you to find someone to love away the loneliness, and I believe you would have wanted the same for me. So please, my dearest, understand I can't live in the past, no matter how beautiful it was. I have 'set my face like a flint', facing the future, full of joy and hope with this new love God has provided for me.

My love always,
Katherine

Katherine read over what she had written, laid the flowers down, wiped her eyes, and with a new lightness, stood up to walk back to her car. She briefly noticed a man sitting over near the parking lot with his head in his hands. Then looking up, she saw her mother-in-law walking towards her. They approached each other silently.

"Oh, Katherine," Jean said with a teary voice, "I knew you would be here." She paused, "He was such a beautiful person, such a son to be proud of. I will never get over losing him." Taking a slow, difficult breath, she continued, "Now, there's a young man over there worried sick about you and of whom Leyton would certainly have approved. Why not go and put his mind at ease?"

Katherine looked over surprised. It was Michael on that bench. He was looking their way, waiting.

Katherine hugged Jean fiercely. "I will never know the strength and understanding it has taken for you to be so wonderful to me, despite your grief. Leyton was a beautiful person because he had a beautiful mother."

"Thank you, dear. You made Leyton very happy, and you deserve all of the happiness God brings your way. Now go, and leave me alone here, please." Then she turned and walked slowly towards the headstone.

Wiping at her tears, Katherine headed towards Michael. He was standing now. Once she was close enough to him, Katherine stopped, trying to gauge his emotions. He looked haggard with worry. She ran and threw herself in his arms. "Oh Michael, I love you."

"Katherine!" was all he could say. "I'm sorry for hunting you down; you have every right to do what you need to do without telling me about it. I just got scared when I couldn't get a hold of you and then I didn't understand why you would have kept this day a secret from me."

"But I didn't mean to keep it from you; I just didn't know how to tell you that I needed to do this."

"I know, I understand now. I called Jean thinking she might know where you were and she put everything in perspective for me. Just please know, I respect your right to mourn and to continue mourning if that's what you need. I just need to know you love me and are not having any regrets."

"No," she hugged him tighter, "no regrets."

"Katherine," he went on, "I never plan on replacing Leyton. I am somebody different. What we have is new. We don't have to live up to each other's pasts. We just have now and we have the future to look forward to, together. It's something new and wonderful and exciting."

"Oh Michael, you couldn't have put it any better."

Chapter 24

They hugged each other then and cried. For Katherine it brought closure, for Michael it brought trust and confidence. Hand in hand they walked toward their cars. Symbolically, it was at this time they truly began to face their future together.

With full hearts and grateful minds, they headed home.

Epilogue

THEY WERE MARRIED on the beach at sunset. Their pastor, their children, and Michael's parents were all there, along with just a few of their closest friends. At the last minute, even Jean and Tom bravely attended. Their photographer captured the poignant event perfectly. The purples of the eastern sky catching the western light from the setting sun created a beautiful backdrop for the glowing couple and giddy children. The framed picture was now a centerpiece on the mantel in their newly decorated living room and alongside it sat the label maker.

Two days after they returned from their honeymoon, Michael insisted the whole family go back to the beach, to the spot where they had first met. The day was reminiscent of that first meeting day. With the sun sparkling off the water, the children looked like whimsical fairies frolicking in the waves. Katherine, watching, wondered how it was possible for one heart to contain so much love and happiness.

Michael, exhausted from beach play, flopped down gratefully onto the sand, leaning against Katherine. He picked up a handful of sand and let it fall onto her upturned palm. "Hi," he said playfully. "Word on the street has it you'll marry the first guy you meet at this spot."

"Oh yeah?" she laughed, "You're too late. I proudly wear this label here," she said outlining an imaginary spot on her chest, "It says, *Michael's wife.*"

End Notes

1. Fasano, A.; I. Berti; T. Gerarduzzi; T. Not; R. Colletti; S. Drago; Y. Elitsur; P. Green; S. Guandalini; I. Hill; M. Pietzak; A. Ventura; M. Thorpe; D. Kryszak; F. Fornaroli; S. Wasserman; J. Murray; K. Horvath. Prevalence of celiac disease in at-risk and not-at-risk groups in the United States. *Archives of Internal Medicine* 2003;163:286-292

2. Crosato, F.; S. Senter. Cerebral occipital calcifications in celiac disease. *Neuropediatrics* 1992; 23: 214-217.

Author's Note

THIS STORY WAS inspired by my own personal health struggles. After years of unexplained health problems and misdiagnoses, I finally learned of celiac disease as a graduate student in nutrition and immunology at Texas A&M University. After discussing my options with my general practitioner, I decided to try a gluten-free diet. The goal was three months, but after dramatic health improvement in only a few days, I knew that I had found the root cause of my problems. Over eight years and two healthy children later, I continue to follow the diet.

I have since learned that diagnosable celiac disease and gluten intolerance are two different conditions. Celiac disease is diagnosed as described in *Trusting for Tomorrow* while gluten intolerance, after all other tests are negative, by symptomatic improvement following a gluten-free dietary trial. Both conditions are treated by following a gluten-free diet for life.

The celiac.com website contains a wealth of information along with summaries of the latest research on the subject. I have tried my best to make sure that everything in my book reflects the current medical literature. However, although I have a graduate degree in nutrition and immunology and live with gluten intolerance, I am not a medical doctor. Any inadvertent errors are my own.

If you, or someone you know, have struggled with the health problems detailed in *Trusting for Tomorrow*, the best advice is always to find a good physician that currently treats others with celiac disease and gluten intolerance. Simply going on the diet isn't always the best route, although in my case, the result was so astounding, I never looked back!

In conclusion, no matter what health trials God may allow in our lives, He is truly our Great Physician. He may choose to heal, or He may choose to allow suffering for a greater good (Romans 8:28). Paul requested three times (2 Cor. 12:7-10) that God remove his personal thorn in the flesh, but the answer was always no. By trials and struggles, we can draw closer to God, who can provide lasting peace and serenity in the midst of the worst possible circumstances. May the hope and trust that Katherine learned in *Trusting for Tomorrow* be yours.

God's richest blessings to you,
Sincerely,
Jennifer Arrington

LaVergne, TN USA
29 September 2009
159260LV00002B/2/P